DESTINATION EARTH

Also by Ali Sparkes:

Frozen in Time

Dark Summer

Wishful Thinking

Out of This World

The Unleashed series:

A Life and Death Job

Mind over Matter

Trick or Truth

Speak Evil

The Burning Beach

The Shapeshifter series:

Finding the Fox

Running the Risk

Going to Ground

Dowsing the Dead

Stirring the Storm

Ali Sparkes

OXFORD
UNIVERSITY PRESS

Great Clarendon Street, Oxford OX2 6DP

Oxford University Press is a department of the University of Oxford.
It furthers the University's objective of excellence in research, scholarship,
and education by publishing worldwide. Oxford is a registered trade mark of
Oxford University Press in the UK and in certain other countries

First published 2014

British Library Cataloguing in Publication Data

Data available

ISBN: 978-0-19-273344-3

1 3 5 7 9 10 8 6 4 2

Printed in Great Britain

Paper used in the production of this book is a natural,
recyclable product made from wood grown in sustainable forests.
The manufacturing process conforms to the environmental
regulations of the country of origin

For Jake

Acknowledgements:

Grateful thanks to Mark King and Level 42 for the soundtrack to this story—and for outrageous liberties taken with the person of Mr King. (I made you taller, though, Mark.)

Thanks also to Arqiva for information on the Rowridge transmitter and to Mark Robson for his useful RAF insights. And to Chris Moxon at Southampton University's Institute of Sound and Vibration Research for giving some advice on alien brain structure (as you do).

And Liz Cross and Claire Westwood—thanks for indulging me. *You know what I mean . . .*

When I was an infant in my mother's arms
I would watch the starlight in her face
'Cause I was reaching out to understand
the cosmic charm
I am just a starchild, born in space.

Level 42, 1981

Chapter 1

'Good morning, Lucy. Time to get up. Cleanse and prepare. You are three hours, twenty-two minutes and fifteen seconds away from your destination. Acclimatization will begin in two hours, forty-three minutes and twenty-nine seconds.'

Lucy lurched awake, her heart hammering, breathing so hard she could hear her excited gasps rattling around the sleep pod.

'Mumgram!' she whispered. 'Is this it?! Is this really *it*?'

Mumgram smiled. 'Yes, Lucy. Time to cleanse and prepare. You are three hours, twenty-two minutes and four sec—'

'Music!' yelled Lucy, undoing the driquilt and flinging it open. 'Earth: England: nineteen-eighties!'

'Specify genre,' said Mumgram, her grainy face showing definite signs of the air ducting that looped down from the low ceiling behind her.

'Genre—Pop. Band—erm—Level 42. Track—your choice,' Lucy grinned. She would be glad to sort Mumgram out. The graininess and see-through-ness had definitely worsened over the past few months as the ship went into powersave protocol in its final stages. It was hard to remember what Mum's proper face looked like. There wasn't much fuel left—but she'd be able to power up *Hessandrea* in seconds, as soon as they docked. Enough power for another circuit of this galaxy—and to sharpen those 'gram features again.

'*Though I live on the edge, time is on my side . . .*' Lucy sang along, skipping into the cleansing booth as the familiar chords and rhythm struck up. She seized a brush and worked through her long dark hair. It was well past her shoulder blades again now. She would *love* to cut it off, but the last time she'd tried that it had been a mess. She hadn't looked anything *like* the girl in the L'Oreal adverts. She eyed the snippers on the shelf. *No.* She would wait. Get it done properly. Someone *else* would cut her hair for her.

Lucy's brush slowed down. Just the thought made her stomach flip. Someone *else.* Imagine.

She took a deep, steadying breath and quickly pulled her hair into a long, thick side plait. She knew this wasn't fashionable. Just above shoulder length, flicky, 'attitude' was what was in, according to *This Morning*. But sometimes girls had hair like hers too. That girl in the woodwind band they'd had on yesterday; the one who played clarinet. She'd had a side plait and nobody had laughed.

'*Oooh, watch her dance . . .*' she sang on, doing a little spin on the floor. Did she have a good voice? Mumgram said she did. But then Mumgram would.

She stripped off her sleep suit and chucked it outside as she hit the steamshower button. Fifteen seconds later she whacked the dry button. It wasn't the most luxurious bath she'd ever taken but she was too excited to waste any time.

'Shall I get into the clothes?' she called out, returning to her sleep pod and eyeing the garments hung up beside her bed. They'd been there for a week now. She'd tried them on three times. Every time felt as exciting as the last. A pair of genes. No . . . not G-E-N-E-S . . . *J-E-A-N-S*. She must remember that. Sounded the same—spelt different. A world of difference in meaning. So—jeans—and a sweatshirt, green. Socks. And trainers. *Trainers*. Why did they call them trainers? She'd never really worked it out. In America they were sneakers. Trainers sounded better than sneakers. Being sneaky wasn't nice.

'You do not need to get into the clothes until five minutes before acclimatization,' said Mumgram.

'But I *want* to!' laughed Lucy. 'I can't wait! I can't!' And she seized the hanger. The sweatshirt was easy—not much different from the travelwear she'd been in for the past ten years. Soft and stretchy. Green, though—after ten years of mostly blue or grey. It slipped easily on over her regulation grey undies. The jeans were trickier, with the tough metal button and the metal zip. They pressed against her lean belly and she couldn't move quite so fluidly in them.

She sprang up and grabbed the exobar beside the pod, pulling herself easily up to chin level and then pumping up and down twenty times. No problem there. But when she curled up her legs into a mid-air crunch, it was definitely harder in jeans. She guessed she'd get used to it. She dropped back down and seized the footwear.

The socks and trainers felt weirdest. She had never needed them before. Her toes and soles were like her fingers and palms. They were used to the feeling of the modular panel flooring around the ship: the exact temperature and texture that they'd always walked upon. With the new footwear on, it was like a part of her was blunted.

But she knew they didn't walk around in bare feet—

not unless they were on the beach or in their houses. She had to get used to it. Should have worn them for a lot longer, really. Should have worn them for the last six months, ever since the blue orb had edged into view. She prodded the black and silver stripes beside the laces and read NIPE. She smiled. It was meant to be NIKE. But the scanner must have misfired and hadn't read it properly, so *Hessandrea*'s assimilator had grown the Earth-style trainers not quite perfectly.

'Please take some breakfast,' said Mumgram, cutting through the music, just as the sleep pod's nutrishute rattled open and delivered a smoothie and four carbisks.

'I'm too excited to eat a thing!' Lucy said, knotting her laces with some difficulty.

'Acclimatization will be suspended until you have eaten,' said Mumgram, with annoying logic. 'Minimal nutritional requirements must be met for safety reasons. Please eat, Lucy.'

Lucy sighed and stood up. She walked awkwardly in the spongy, clingy trainers and picked up the smoothie and the bisks. She took them with her down the walkway to the bridge and settled at the console, so she could sit back and stare through the window at the beautiful blue-white orb which had been growing steadily bigger for weeks.

The automatic navigator had pulled the ship into orbit already, setting off the gyrodines to keep the orbital velocity of exactly thirteen kilometres per second nice and steady. *Hessandrea* was only hours away from the entry point, 367,400 kilometres above the United Kingdom, awaiting the best possible moment to drop through the atmosphere. The on-board forecaster calculated that this would be 11:14:04, British Summer Time.

The landing target was an island off the south coast of the United Kingdom. Lucy had no idea why they had chosen the Isle of Wight. But there had been a logic to everything they did. Their logs, for some reason, hadn't stored this logic, so she could only assume it was because it was a friendly place. She hoped so.

She drained the smoothie and shoved the second bisk into her mouth and then went to stand by the full-length wall mirror beside the sleeping pod and looked at herself. Dark hair. Blue-green eyes. Pale—but not pallid—skin. Regular sessions under the D-Vit lamp had stopped her going see-through. She was of medium height for a fourteen-year-old girl. Medium weight. She was slender but her muscle mass was heavy. Relentless daily exercise for the past ten years had been crucial to stop her bones turning into a brittle mess. The exercise had worked. Bioscans told her she was in the peak of physical fitness and the planes of muscle across her belly confirmed it. If anything, she needed to soften up a bit to look like a normal Earth girl. She might have to say she was a gymnast or something.

Lying. That was going to be strange. Saying things that were not true. When had she last lied? When had there ever been any need? Probably when she was little; up until she was four. She had been a normal Cornelian Eclata child after all . . . hadn't she? Lucy screwed up her face and shut her eyes, trying to remember.

'Nope,' she said, with a shrug, and walked spongily back across to the console to take a seat and scan its collection of lights, dials, and monitors.

'So—how is Earth today?' she said aloud, more to herself than Mumgram, but Mumgram responded.

'Earth is experiencing normal weather patterns and relatively little seismic activity today,' stated Mumgram. 'Other than a three point six scale earth tremor off the north island of New Zealand, epicentre twenty-four point five kilometres south of Wellington.'

'Well, we're heading for another hemisphere,' said Lucy. 'Lucky.'

'Seven point six per cent of the planet's surface is currently affected by hot warfare,' went on Mumgram. 'The closest war zone to your destination is Afghanistan.'

'OK—how far away is Afghanistan?' muttered Lucy, tracing her fingers along the view screen which offered a rotating aerial map of the entire surface of the planet below. Mumgram connected to the screen and a little blob of red blinked within a land mass above the Indian Ocean.

'Distance from London to Kabul is five thousand, seven hundred and eighteen point five kilometres,' said Mumgram. 'From Rowridge, on the Isle of Wight, to Kab—'

'Don't worry, anything over five thousand kilometres is safe enough,' laughed Lucy, kicking back in the chair and feeling excitement course over her again, as powerful as Kwathekki Falls . . . no. No. Like *Niagara* Falls. Kwathekki Falls were long gone. Well . . . they were probably still falling, millions of light years away on Cornelian Eclata, but it was doubtful any mammalian life form was left to see them. The spectacular torrents of three ancient rivers merging into one enormous canyon, under the arcs of seven permanent rainbows, had been one of the biggest tourist attractions on the planet. Nobody visited now, though. Nobody was there. Lucy's young heart had got so used to the clench of sorrow at this fleeting thought that she didn't really notice it any more.

So excitement coursed over her like *Niagara* Falls, which was pretty damn splendid too, judging by the images she'd seen. Maybe she would go there one day as she had been to Kwathekki. She didn't remember Kwathekki, of course. She'd been only three.

'So—how is England?' asked Lucy, trailing her fingers across the screen to spin the globe around to the small, boot-shaped island and then jabbing at the sole of the boot until the scale zoomed up and she could see the southern part, where the Isle of Wight nestled into the instep.

'England's weather is calm and cloudy,' said Mumgram. 'There are no wars taking place today. The economy is depressed, but stable.'

'And the Isle of Wight?' asked Lucy, jabbing again until the diamond-shaped island filled the screen.

'In line with the rest of the UK for weather, but its economy is picking up as the summer months approach,' said Mumgram. 'The island depends upon farming and tourism. Tourism income improves across stretches of good weather.'

'How often does it get stretches of good weather?'

'Not often,' said Mumgram, in a surprisingly vague way. 'The UK is notorious for the unpredictability of its weather. The months of May to July have historically been the warmest, with the least rainfall, but over the past decade, weather patterns have become more erratic. As much on the Isle of Wight and in the South of England as elsewhere.'

'What else do we know about the weather in the south?'

'It's sponsored by PowerOn,' said Mumgram.

Lucy smiled. 'The weather *forecasts* are sponsored by PowerOn' she corrected. 'On the local TV station.' She loved it when Mumgram got something wrong (a very rare occurrence). 'I don't think that has any effect on whether the sun shines, though. Oh—that reminds me.'

She turned in her chair and reached to her left to press a series of blue buttons and pull a lever. Outside, sixteen solar panels moved around eighteen degrees. 'We need a little extra sun today, yes?'

'Correct,' said Mumgram. 'I would have alerted you in ten minutes.'

'I know,' said Lucy. She knew a lot, in fact. Everything that Mumgram had told her since she got up, she really knew already. Hearing it from Mumgram was like asking for a favourite nursery rhyme book to be read to her for the fiftieth time. She had been studying the new home planet all her life—or at least that's what it felt like. She could speak English fluently, because a variation of

English is what all of her people spoke. She had ironed out her Cornelian dialect over the years, listening again and again to Earth's news presenters and talk-show hosts and soap-opera actors, so she could pick up the correct delivery and word usage.

She also spoke fluent French, Italian, German, and Spanish. This had been a precaution, in case the guidance systems which had been set for the UK went adrift during the long journey and she ended up in a neighbouring country.

'Am I going to be OK?' she asked quietly. Mumgram flickered a little over her shoulder and, deep inside the ship's computer brain, some tiny integrated circuit triggered a compassionate expression.

'You will be fine, Lucy,' said Mumgram. 'You have been prepared for this. You have had all your shots against Earth's more dangerous viruses. The gas mix you breathe is now closely comparable to that of Earth's atmosphere. Your language and your clothing match that of females of a similar age. You should not stand out.'

'Will I . . . touch . . . someone?' murmured Lucy, so quietly she didn't think the Mumgram audio pick-up would work.

'Yes,' said Mumgram. 'You will.'

Lucy stared at her fingertips and an old memory in

the very cells of her skin stirred. The last touch. The very last . . . big fingers slipping across little fingers. *'Goodbye, baby. Get home safe.'*

And that was all. Lucy shook her head. The memory wasn't even in it.

She couldn't imagine how it would feel to be touched by another being. She hadn't been touched for ten years. Mumgram was always there for her; helping, teaching, advising, directing. But Mumgram could not touch. Mumgram gave a brilliant impression of love. But Mumgram was a holographic display which would feel nothing if Lucy were to take herself off to the airlock and blow herself out into space. The display would urgently advise against this action, of course, right up to the last second and then, when her body was expanding and blowing into atoms across the nothingness outside, Mumgram would fall silent and all would be peace.

Even so, Lucy loved Mumgram. Because there was nobody and nothing else that she could love.

For now.

Lucy looked at the ever-moving track of glowing numbers along the top of the console. Estimated time of atmospheric entry: three hours, two minutes, thirty-one seconds and counting.

She was nearly home.

Chapter 2

'I CAN'T STOP! I CAN'T STOP! I CAN'T STOP!' screamed Emma. The wind blew her panicked voice back past her ears, along with her streaming brown hair. She was going so fast the hedgerows on either side of her were a blur of green as she gripped the handlebars and stared ahead, the horror of her situation grabbing at her insides like a cold claw.

'HELP! JAY! HELP ME! I CAN'T STOP! I CAN'T STOP!' she screamed again, a sob rippling through her words. Along the narrow track she could see the river winding through the wood, cutting a deep scar through the land. The bank was at least two metres high. When she hit the blind bend she knew she had two choices. Either try to turn at this incredible speed and risk skidding across the road and removing the skin from her left leg and elbow, or go straight on and, if she didn't hit a tree, land in the river.

The part of her brain which should have offered up a more reasonable course of action had cut out, like an emergency overload trip-switch. Fear had blown its fuse.

She could hear Jay shouting, 'BREAK! BREAK! BREAK!' which wasn't much help. She knew she was going to break. She didn't need a prophesy. She needed help.

Jay ran down the road behind his sister, pounding his feet hard against the elderly, eroded tarmac and yelling at the top of his voice, 'BRAKE! BRAKE! EMMA! USE THE BRAKE!' But Emma's brain had seized. He could see that from the way her head was hunched down, preparing for the worst. It was hopeless trying to make her apply the brakes. He stopped shouting and used the spare oxygen to power into a faster sprint, desperate to catch up. A lump in the path slowed her down just slightly.

'CAN'T STOP I CAN'T STOP OH NO I CAN'T STOP!' she screamed. Her terror was awful. Worse than he'd ever heard it. He pitched forward into his best sprint. *IDIOT!* he cursed to himself. *IDIOT! This is YOUR fault!*

He saw the way the road was turning and could calculate what would happen next. Either she would turn with the road and almost certainly end up slewing sideways across it and off the bank, or she would just hold her path and shoot off the bend like a ski jumper. It was hard to work out which one would be more damaging. Oh hell . . . she didn't even have a bike helmet on. *IDIOT!*

Jay called upon one last surge of energy to get to the corner on time. Four seconds later, he grabbed the saddle post just as Emma began to turn and slide on the bend. She was still screaming. The momentum of the bike yanked his arm so hard he thought it might dislocate his shoulder. But the action made Emma glance around at him. 'BRAKE!' he shrieked. 'Use the brake! Em! The brake!'

And somehow, at last, the message got through. Emma's fingers spasmed across the five centimetres from the handle to the brake, and clenched. They both spun up into the air as the hard rubber blocks instantly gripped the front and back wheels and the front tyre drove itself into the road. A whoosh of momentum, the oak leaves, sparkling jewel-green in the sun, the peaty brown bank with its snaky roots, the red flash of a squirrel fleeing the impact zone—all these things Jay saw as if he were turning a kaleidoscope against his eye. Then there was a brutal thud—then another—then . . . pause . . . metallic twang—*thud*—another.

Jay lay with his eyes shut, wondering what was broken. Above him, alarmed wood pigeons flapped clumsily through the trees. 'Em? You OK?' he croaked.

Emma was sitting up, rubbing her elbow, twigs in her hair, her lower lip swelling. A bike wheel spun behind her head. 'I hate you!' she said, tears rolling down her cheeks.

'I'm sorry.' He was. It had been a really stupid idea.

'You s-said I could do it. You s-said,' she gulped. And Emma almost never cried.

'You can,' he said. 'Just . . . not today. I'm sorry. Are you OK?'

'Yes,' she sniffed. They were centimetres from the river. It would have been much nastier if they'd hit the water. There were lumps of rock in it. She stood up awkwardly on the bank, holding the springy branch of a young tree. 'Are you?'

'Yeah,' he said, getting up with a wince. There was a nasty gash on his right knee which was bleeding. But he'd survive.

'I trashed your bike,' she said forlornly, like a little girl.

'No you didn't,' he said. 'It'll be fine. Anyway, it was my fault.'

She sighed and scrubbed at the tears, getting a hold.

'Jay. I'm nearly fourteen. I should be able to ride a bike without stabilizers by now.'

'You *will* be able to,' he said, picking the bike up. Its front wheel was bent around. 'It was just a bit much to go on the slope today. You need to remember to brake as well as steer.'

Emma stared up at him, her grey eyes wet and sad. 'Brake *and* steer. Yeah, right. Oh god. I am so pathetic.'

Jay looked around. There was nobody in sight, so he put an arm around his younger sister's shoulders. 'You're not pathetic. You're dyspraxic. It's a problem the rest of us haven't got.' He sighed. It was very unfair. They were only a year apart in age. They looked alike, they sounded alike, and they had the same sense of humour, the same skinny build, dark grey eyes, and light brown hair. But their brains were different. His was pretty standard. Emma's was different. Not in a bad way, their mum was always saying. Just different.

Emma had dyspraxia and dyslexia and a host of other twiddly little problems related to a part of her brain called her cerebellum. She struggled to read and write and to record anything on paper apart from drawings. And she was clumsy. She found it almost impossible to dance or play ball games or eat a meal without tipping something over. She *looked* graceful enough, and she talked as brightly as anyone twice her age—it was all fine until she started to do anything complicated *and* talk or walk . . . and then it would all fall apart. She took a lot of stick for it at school and he'd got into more than one fight defending her. Not that she couldn't fight for herself. She could certainly do that.

But last week there had been a breakthrough. Emma had managed to keep her balance on Jay's bike. She was finally able to work the pedals without the front wheel curving inexorably round to the right and tipping her over. Usually as soon as she started to pedal she would forget to steer—or the other way around. But for the first time, last week, she had cracked it. She had pedalled *and* steered, along the gravel path around the garden and then up and down the driveway. Jay and Mum were cheering. It was fantastic and Emma had been pink in the face with delight.

Then he had to go and push it, didn't he? He thought she could handle Blackpenny Lane. He'd forgotten about the downhill bit at the end.

'You're bleeding,' sniffed Emma. 'Quite a lot.'

Jay looked down and saw a stream of red running from his knee to his ankle. The wound stung, ached, and itched. He rested his bike on the ground and began to make his way down the slope. The bank was high above the river, but a small stream ran down through it; a dainty fall of water which trickled through sphagnum moss, under cool shady ferns. He knew it was clean. He took a palmful and doused his leg.

'Does it hurt?' asked Emma. She dug in her pocket and brought out a clean tissue. Jay took it and mopped the wound.

'Just stings a bit. Did you break anything?'

'My shoulder hurts,' she said. 'But it's nothing much. Thank you. For stopping me.'

Jay sighed. 'I'm really sorry, Em. I shouldn't have brought you out here. You weren't ready.'

'Meh,' she shrugged. 'I'll probably never be ready.' She sat down next to him. 'I don't hate you really.' She grinned. 'Well—not *every* day.'

'Saw a red squirrel,' said Jay.

'Did you?'

'Yeah—just as we were spinning through the air. It freaked out and ran up that tree.' He pointed up into the boughs of a tall oak.

Emma squinted up. She couldn't see anything. The island was meant to be a red squirrel sanctuary—one of just two islands off southern England where you could hope to see the endangered creatures. She'd only ever seen one twice in her life—and even then she wasn't sure. She sometimes wondered whether it was all a ruse to get more wildlife tourism in the off-season months.

The sky between the branches was darkening and promising rain.

'Come on,' said Jay. 'We'd better get back.' He glanced at his watch, which had a brand new scratch across its glass. 'It's nearly quarter past eleven. We've got beds to do.'

It was then that Emma's eyes went green.

Jay blinked.

'What is *that*?!' said Emma, her eyes wide and still green.

Jay followed her gaze up into the sky and saw the reason for her change in iris colour. There was a weird green light shining through a gap in the grey cloud. It seemed to pulse for a few seconds and then it quickly faded.

'Did you see that?' asked Emma, her eyes back to their normal shade now. 'Did you? That green light?'

'Yeah,' murmured Jay. 'Must be—I dunno—some kind of lightning, maybe?'

Then, as the clouds moved, he saw the familiar outline of the transmitter. The giant TV transmitter that towered over Rowridge. 'Could be something to do with the mast,' he said.

'Should we report it?' said Emma.

'Nah—they've got engineers on-site, haven't they? If there was anything going on, they'd see it.'

Emma shrugged. 'OK,' she said. 'But that wasn't like any lightning I've ever seen.'

'Electrical fault then,' said Jay, returning to his bike and wrestling it back up the slope to the lane.

'*Green?*' said Emma. She looked sceptical. 'Weird,' she added, glancing back. 'Something . . .' She shivered. 'We need to go.' And she picked up speed as if something had snaked down from the green cloud and was following them.

Jay shivered too. Emma may not have a great sense of balance, but her instincts about other things were uncannily accurate. If she said they needed to go—they needed to go.

The brother and sister wove their way up the lane, pushing the bike between them, their light brown heads visible only occasionally through the leafy branches that hung across the track. They were a life form very similar to its last encounter. Very similar indeed. Deep inside, a muscle which had barely registered a beat more than twice in an Earth week for the last nine years began to thud.

The wait would soon be over.

Chapter 3

'You have arrived.'

Lucy still clung to the arms of her landing chair so hard her knuckles were starting to seize. The automatic restraints had unlocked and retracted some minutes ago.

'You have arrived.'

The tumultuous fall to earth had nearly shaken her teeth out. She thought she may have been sick. Her ears were blocked. Her nose ran. She hoped it wasn't with blood. She wasn't ready to open her eyes and find out yet.

'You have arrived.'

She knew that it had gone 'smoothly' in the sense that all the technical data had been correct and the ship's moving parts had done what they were built to do. At 10.45 a.m. *Hessandrea* had begun her descent. She had plummeted to just 35,900 kilometres above the planet, picking her way through the many geostationary satellites that hung at this level, permanently anchored to their bit of land mass, sending satellite TV images and phone calls all around the globe.

The thrusters, swinging into action for the first time in five years, felt every bit as terrifying as they had when she was nine, and the ship had needed to slow its journey to avoid some giant and potentially deadly space debris which had glittered purple and green in the light of a distant sun while it spun past. Lucy had clung to her seat then, too, and believed, in her brain-shaken state, that she seen had seen a tiny spacecraft following the debris. But the thrusters had only needed to work for five minutes. The journey had been so brilliantly planned, glitches like this happened very rarely—so the thrusters had been dormant since then, until today.

It was like someone had grabbed the back of the spacecraft and yanked it to a stop. If she hadn't been strapped in she would have been splatted across the console and the viewing panel. Just a puddle of jam in her new jeans and sweatshirt. The deceleration seemed to last a lifetime, but was only, in fact, nineteen minutes.

'You have arrived.'

'I know! I know!' she whimpered finally. 'Just . . . give me a moment!'

As her ears began to slowly unblock and her galloping heart slowed to a swift trot, Lucy opened her eyes just a crack. The light was blinding. A pearly, white-grey light, brilliant across the monitors and shafting in through the wide, curved viewing panel above. She pulled her fingers away from the armrests and brought her hands up to shield her eyes.

There was a low thrumming sound from the engines and then that subsided and there was silence. And then a button on the console turned green. 'Atmostasis has been achieved,' said Mumgram. 'We are now docked. Final acclimatization stages are now in progress.'

Lucy stood up and stared, blinking, into the light. Soon . . . very soon . . . she was going to see her first tree. Her first tree in ten years, to be precise, but she didn't remember ever seeing a tree, even before they left Cornelian Eclata. She must have done, of course. Trees had been plentiful there.

Before she saw a tree, she saw a bird. A real, living, flying Earth bird. It was grey with a fat body and a small head. 'Wood pigeon,' gasped Lucy, her throat tight with some strange emotion. '*Columba palumbus.* Widespread, year-round. Breeds in woodland and scrub. Feeds in both rural and urban areas.' She put her shaking fingers against her face. 'Makes a monotonous repetitive *coo-coo* sound.'

She was suddenly overwhelmed with the need to *hear*

the monotonous repetitive *coo-coo* of the wood pigeon. The patience trained into her by ten years of careful effort had suddenly evaporated. Lucy turned around and strode off down the walkway, past the sleep pod, bouncing in her Nipe trainers towards the docking bay.

'Lucy—do not attempt to enter the dock!' advised Mumgram, in 'urgent' mode. 'You have not completed acclimatization.'

Lucy ignored Mumgram. She was here. She was here on Earth. Now. Her journey was over. Earth would either welcome her or kill her. She didn't care about getting a headache. She had to get out of *Hessandrea.* She had to get out NOW.

She punched the release buttons on the dock exit panel and they lit up green, with a small hiss. She reached across to the cool metal wheel and spun it round to the right.

'Lucy—do not attempt to enter the dock. You have not completed acclimatization.'

'I'm fine!' yelled Lucy. 'Stop going on at me! I'm going out!'

'You're not going out dressed like *that,* are you?' asked Mumgram. Lucy hooted with laughter as she spun the wheel the last few times. She had programmed *that* phrase and tone of voice into Mumgram herself, after watching several hours of *EastEnders* in succession. How Mumgram had located that phrase right now and opted to use it she would never know.

'Yes—of course like this! This is Earth wear!'

'A bio-adaptive cover-all would be wise.'

'Mumgram! This is home. I will adapt,' said Lucy.

'Take the backpack, just in case,' said Mumgram, looking concerned, standing right there at her shoulder. There were way too many holographic projection points on this ship, thought Lucy.

'OK, OK!' she sighed, and reached through Mumgram's chest to grab the bio-adaptive backpack from its hook. It contained some emergency gadgets in case of atmospheric issues. Like not being able to breathe.

'But I will be able to breathe,' she said. '*Hessandrea* has had nothing but M-class gases pumping through for the last five years—you know that.'

'Wind,' said Mumgram.

'Well, what do you expect after all those carbisks?' Lucy quipped.

'The bulk movement of air between high and low pressure atmospheric—'

'Yes,' sighed Lucy. 'I know. I'm expecting wind.'

'You have not felt wind for ten years, twenty-two days and—'

'I *know*! And I am looking forward to feeling it again!' She shrugged the backpack over both shoulders and then completed the final spin of the wheel. The door clunked and swung open.

'I'll be back soon,' she said. Mumgram didn't respond. She hadn't really been programmed for this. Her job was pretty much over.

Lucy stepped into the docking bay. It was darker here—all grey metal panelling and mesh under foot. Apart, of course, from the shaft of light shining up through the square gap in the floor. A set of metal steps disappeared into the well of light. She gulped. It was now or never.

The force field which held out the Earth's atmosphere offered no resistance as she climbed down through it. Lucy felt like she was in a dream. She had dreamed—awake and asleep—of this moment for as long as she could remember. *Hessandrea docks. Lucy, wearing Earth clothes, walks into the dock bay. Lucy climbs down and reaches for the ladder to earth—the Rowridge transmitter on the Isle of Wight. She climbs down the transmitter. Her feet touch the earth. She is home.*

The transmitter lay below her. The metal rungs sent down by the ship's hydraulics took her to the maintenance ladder which rose up to meet it, through the 149.6-metre-high mast. Why they had chosen this route to Earth she would probably never know. Mumgram had not had an answer for her. Not everything she wanted to know had been programmed into the ship's computer in time.

She had to trust that whoever had made this decision knew she would not be electrocuted the moment she made contact with the mast.

'Oh my god,' she gasped, like the girls on *EastEnders*, as she felt the wind. A steady force 4. Not strong really, but cold and incredibly shocking. It took her breath away—as did the dizzying view of green, green ground, way below her. Her side plait buffeted her chin.

But she *was* still breathing. And her eyes were adjusting all the time. She was no longer blinded by Earth light. She climbed down a few more rungs until the ship's ladder ended in a square metal mesh panel—a footplate. The mast ladder was only half a metre away. She could reach it easily. But she didn't move. In the gap between her footplate and the mast ladder (which was encircled by a wide cage of circular steel struts, easy to climb past) she could see the field below, and some grey stuff too. Buildings. Road. A parked vehicle of some kind. No people, though. She knew this wouldn't be a problem, anyway. *Hessandrea*'s cloakshaft was shining down, like an inverted cone, covering her entire descent and widening out to make sure she was covered for a radius of half a kilometre if she needed it. With the communicator around her wrist she could switch it on or off as and when she needed, anywhere within that radius. As far as any Earth people were concerned, she would be invisible and undetectable—just as long as she didn't bump into any, of course.

So. Time to go. But there was no ignoring it. She was absolutely terrified. She clung to the ladder and thought about going back upstairs to 'acclimatize' after all. But the idea of returning without having heard the wood pigeon made her heart rebel. NO. She was climbing down. Now. Today. This minute. Even if the Earth mast electrocuted her and she died. Now. Today.

Lucy stepped across and grabbed the Rowridge transmitter. And did not die.

Ten minutes later, a young, slight girl emerged out of nowhere on the edge of some woodland. She stood still for a few moments and then bent to take off her trainers and socks, before standing again, her toes pushing into the grass. Nearby, a wood pigeon began its throaty call.

The girl's pale face crumpled and tears ran down her cheeks.

*

'Weird,' said Emma, as they mooched along the lane with the injured bike. Jay had whacked the front wheel round in its shaft until it faced more or less the right direction again. The tyre was a bit flat but it was rolling along OK now that Jay had stopped trying to ride.

'What?' said Jay. 'That green light? Yeah—pretty weird. Cloud's lifting now, though. I reckon it'll be sunny this afternoon.'

'No, not that. *Her.*' She pointed across the field and Jay saw a girl—about their age, he reckoned, screwing up his eyes—standing in the field. Quite still.

'What's she doing?' he wondered. 'Tai chi or something?'

'Not unless they do a "stand still and gawp like you've just been hit with a brick" move,' said Emma.

Jay stopped wheeling the bike and stared across the low hedgerow. The girl was motionless, staring up into the trees. She wasn't gawping, exactly. She was more, kind of, smiling.

'Do you think she's all right?' he asked Emma. 'She's . . . swaying.'

'Hey!' called Emma. 'Hey! Are you OK?'

The girl turned her head to look at them. Her hands flew to her throat and she froze, staring at them as if they were something from another planet. She swayed again, and staggered slightly.

'I think she might be having some kind of fit,' said Emma. 'You know . . . a seizure type thing. I saw a girl at school look like that once. She was an epileptic. They had to cart her off to hospital and pump her with drugs.'

'We should go and check she's all right,' said Jay. He didn't want to. His nerves were shredded by the incident with Emma and the bike—to say nothing of his knee, which was throbbing and still bleeding a bit from time to time. He sighed. Girls. They were nothing but trouble.

'Come on,' said Emma, hoisting herself up on the metal five-bar gate and jumping down the other side. She jogged towards the girl who was still clutching her throat and now staring at them, open-mouthed, a small grey backpack at her feet.

'You all right?' Emma called.

'Wha-what?' said the girl, as Emma got closer. The girl's long dark hair was in a side plait, hanging down across her grass-green sweatshirt. Emma could see that she was a good-looking girl. Beautiful, maybe, when there wasn't blood running out of her nose. There was something else about her though—something odd. Really odd. Emma shivered.

'You OK? You look like you might . . . be . . . having trouble,' said Emma.

The girl continued to stare, her intense blue-green eyes flickering up and down Emma's face, her hands at her throat. 'I—I'm . . . I think . . .' she whispered. A smile began to lift the corners of her pale mouth just slightly.

'She all right, Em?' called Jay, who had stopped to ease his bike down against the hedge, and was now running to catch up.

The girl's eyes switched across to Jay and widened even further. 'Oh . . . my . . .' she breathed. 'A *boy*.'

Emma and Jay looked at each other, and although they both avoided making corkscrew shapes with their fingers at the sides of their heads, their expressions said the same thing. *Cuckoo!*

'Have you hurt yourself?' asked Emma, stepping closer to the girl. 'Your nose is bleeding.'

The girl smiled at her and gulped several times before she breathed: 'A girl. A boy . . . and a girl.'

Emma was getting impatient. 'Look—are you hurt, or what? Because, you know, if you are, we can get help or something, but—' She shut up fast as the girl held out one hand towards her. It was a small, smooth hand with almond-shaped nails, unpolished, and it trembled like a leaf in autumn. Emma stared at the hand. 'Hmmm.

You're a *little bit* weird, aren't you?' she said, not unkindly.

'Oh give her a break, she's just being friendly,' said Jay, and he stepped past his sister and took the girl's hand. 'Hi,' he said, trying to shake it, although the girl didn't seem to have a handshake in mind.

She gasped as their fingers touched, stared up at him with those intense eyes, said, '*Touch!*' and then fainted.

'Well done, Jay,' said Emma, as their new acquaintance tumbled into the grass with a thud, eyes rolling up into her head. 'You always did have a way with the ladies.'

Chapter 4

It was the most peculiar sensation. She was being rolled over . . . onto her side. Quite gently—she knew this—and yet it was the most shocking thing. Their hands were hot through her sleeves, their voices concerned. 'Get her into the recovery position,' the girl was saying. '*Jay!* Come on—help me. She might . . . I dunno . . . choke on her own tongue or something!'

That made Lucy giggle. *As if* she could choke on her own tongue!

'OK—now the laughing! I told you she was nuts,' said the girl.

The boy's face came into view. He was squinting at her in the late morning sun. 'Are you back with us?' he asked.

'Yes,' she said, and even though she was feeling very woozy and there was sticky blood around her nose she couldn't help smiling again. 'A boy!' she marvelled, once more. 'A boy . . . *and* . . . a girl!' A *coo* sounded in the trees above them. 'And a wood pigeon!'

'What's your name?' asked the boy. He had a nice face—open and enquiring, with wide, dark grey eyes, beneath a floppy brown fringe.

'Lucy,' she said. 'I'm very pleased to meet you.'

'We can tell,' said the girl. She looked very like the boy, with the same eyes and the same hair colour, although hers was worn longer. *She must be his sister*, thought Lucy.

'I'm Jay,' said the boy. 'And this is Emma. She's nicer than she sounds. Do you think you can sit up?'

'Yes, I think I can.' Lucy got up carefully, keenly aware that the girl was helping her, with a hand on one shoulder, as much as her brother, who had a hand on her other shoulder. 'Sorry, I must look terrible. I didn't expect a nosebleed. A headache, yes, but not a nosebleed. Mumgr—Mum didn't remind me . . . mind you, I didn't give her much chance after I saw the wood pigeon; I just had to get out and hear it! It sounds so much . . . *happier* . . . than I thought it would. And the grass is tickly and cool . . . like a million shards of water . . .'

She was babbling. She realized this as she watched the brother and sister exchange glances. And worse . . . she was babbling about stuff she must NOT tell anyone.

Mumgram and *Hessandrea* and her ten-year journey were all meant to be a secret. She would have no hope of fitting in here if anyone found out. She snapped her mouth shut and gulped. The lying must start soon. Now.

'Here,' said the girl, handing her something soft, rectangular, and white. 'It's my last tissue. The others are all covered in blood too. Just join in the party!'

The boy grinned and pointed to a gash on his leg. 'Bike accident . . .' he explained.

Lucy mopped under her nose. The bleeding had stopped. It hadn't been that bad, really. She now remembered nosebleeds as one of many symptoms Mumgram had warned her about over the years of preparation for this day. A swimmy head and blocked-up ears were another and she'd had those on the way down the mast.

But by the time she'd hit the grass and begun to experience her new home through all her senses, she'd barely noticed these minor niggles. It was only when the blood started dripping from her nostrils that she was aware she should *probably* have taken Mumgram's advice—but by then she was enraptured, staring at the trees. And then the call from this boy and girl . . . the *touch.* It was overwhelming. She could feel the heat even now, long after they'd withdrawn their hands.

As she came out of these thoughts she realized she was singing the song from *Hessandrea*'s last playlist. '*All the doors to my life . . . are open wide . . .*'

Jay cocked an eyebrow at her. 'Level 42?' he grinned. 'That's a bit retro . . .'

'The Sun Goes Down, brackets—Living It Up—close brackets,' said Lucy. 'Released in nineteen-eighty-three, main vocals by Mike Lindup but backing vocals from Mark King; band frontman and popular exponent of jazz funk slap bass. Resident of the Isle of Wight. Does Mark King still live here . . . on the Isle of Wight?' she asked, with a sudden surge of excitement. 'Could we go and see him?'

'O . . . K,' said Emma. 'I think we may need to get you back to your mental health nurse now.'

Jay gave her a shove. 'Don't be nasty. She's . . . different . . . that's all. And you're different too, so you should be more sympathetic.'

'Different!' said Emma. 'Not *bonkers*! It's not the same . . .' But she leaned in towards Lucy with a kindly expression. 'Seriously—er—Lucy. I think you may have had a bump on the head or something. We should probably get you home. Get you checked over. Where do you live?'

Lucy stared at her. *Engage lie mode now,* Mumgram prompted, in her head.

'Not far from here,' said Lucy, bailing out at the first attempt.

'Really?' queried Jay. 'We've not seen you around here before. Are you new to the area?'

Lucy began to wrestle the socks and the strange, spongy trainers back on to distract herself from the odd heat that was rising through her face, while her heart hammered rapidly inside her ribcage. 'Yes . . . I'm new . . .' she said. 'We've just moved here.'

'Oh—whereabouts?' asked Emma. 'We're just down the road—Woody Bottom; the holiday lets place.'

'Oh . . . not far from here . . .' Lucy said again. 'I'm . . . to be honest, I'm not even sure what the road is called. I only got here today.' She fumbled with the laces on her trainers. She'd taken a little while to tie them on board *Hessandrea*, but now they seemed like an impossible puzzle. She felt herself get hotter. Her first attempt at 'fitting in' was not going too well.

'So where did you live before?' asked Jay.

'Basingstoke,' said Lucy, like a shot. She'd been practising that one for years. Basingstoke, she had learned, was a modern town in north Hampshire, built mostly in the 1960s and 70s. It had been chosen as the location that she must claim to come from purely because it was regarded, in the UK, as boring. In actual fact, it was mentioned in the Domesday Book and its road system noted for an astonishing number of roundabouts . . . but Lucy doubted her new acquaintances would know or care about these interesting details. She was right.

'Oh—Basingstoke—OK,' said Jay. He was actually staring at her feet now, and then across at his sister. Lucy realized why. She still hadn't managed to tie her shoelaces. They must think she was an idiot. She sighed, bit her lip, and let the laces stay undone as she got to her feet. She rubbed her hands across her face and wondered what to say.

'It's OK,' said Emma and suddenly her voice had softened. 'I—I can't do that either.'

Lucy saw that she and her brother were exchanging glances again. 'Well—they are fiddly . . .' mumbled Lucy.

'I'm useless at that kind of thing,' went on Emma, looking a little pink herself. 'I have dyspraxia.'

'Oh!' Lucy's eyebrows shot up as a stream of information abruptly poured into her brain. 'Dyspraxia: a chronic neurological condition which affects balance and coordination, beginning in childhood, related to dyslexia and other specific learning difficulties; sufferers are often clumsy.'

They stared at her, eyes wide, for a few seconds. Then Emma said, 'Yeah . . . that's it. Have you got that too?'

'Oh no!' beamed Lucy. 'I've got great coordination!'

And she performed three backflips across the grass to prove it.

They were speechless for a few seconds and then Jay said. 'O . . . K . . . so you've run away from a circus?'

Lucy chuckled. 'Nooo! Although I'd love to be in a circus—wouldn't you? It would be stupendous! Have you ever been to a circus? Is it amazing?'

Jay laughed and shook his head. 'You are something else, Lucy!'

Lucy turned back to Emma. 'I'm sorry you've got dyspraxia,' she said, furrowing her brow. 'It must be really difficult. But it doesn't affect intelligence at all!'

'Well, thanks,' said Emma, with a tight smile. 'I feel so much better now.'

Jay glanced at his sister, feeling edgy. It took something for her to admit her problems to a complete stranger and he could tell that she was now feeling stupid about it, in front of this incredibly well-coordinated girl who moved like an acrobat and spoke like an encyclopaedia. He waded in fast, to try to make it better. 'So . . . if you're not dyspraxic, what's the problem with the shoelaces?'

'Oh—it's just that I haven't worn anything like this before,' said Lucy.

'What—you've never worn trainers?' said Emma.

'Maybe she means she's always had the Velcro kind before,' said Jay.

'No—I've never worn them before either,' said Lucy. 'I don't normally wear anything on my feet.'

'Aaah . . . a child of nature, then,' snipped Emma. 'You must have soles like tarmac.'

'Um . . . no . . . not really,' said Lucy and Emma remembered that when she'd been lying in the grass her bare feet had looked as soft as a baby's.

Emma drew Jay away to one side as Lucy went back to fiddling with her laces. 'She is seriously weird. I think she may have run away from some kind of . . . you know . . . institution.'

'Emma! Don't be like that!' he hissed back at her. 'Just because she made you feel awkward. I mean . . . yeah . . . she's a bit eccentric, but that doesn't mean . . .'

'I can hear you,' said Lucy. 'I've got really good hearing! But it's OK. You don't have to worry. I haven't run away from anywhere. I'm meant to be here. I'm not dangerous or anything.'

Emma and Jay winced with embarrassment. 'Look—I'm sorry,' said Emma, rubbing her hands up and down her arms, trying to clear some goosebumps. 'That wasn't . . . look, I don't really think you're . . . you know . . . mental. You're just a bit unusual. Where did you say you came from?'

'Basingstoke,' said Lucy and went bright red.

'Yeah, right,' said Emma, raising one eyebrow.

'Look—you don't have to tell us anything you don't want to,' said Jay. 'As long as you're OK and not hurt . . . that's fine. Do you want us to walk you back home . . . make sure you're OK?'

Lucy smiled at him and her greeny-blue eyes glimmered, as if she was fighting back tears. 'You are kind and lovely, Jay,' she said. Jay blinked and grinned, nonplussed. Girls did not usually say that kind of thing to him—especially not girls as good looking as this one.

'But,' sighed Lucy, 'I can't take you back with me. Mumgr—er—Mum wouldn't like it. Not yet, anyway. It's been lovely meeting you both and I hope I see you again. With less blood.'

Jay pulled his mobile phone out of his shorts pocket. 'Can we have your number . . . ? Or your email . . . ?'

'Oh—er—yes!' Lucy remembered, with a little fizz of delight, the mobile number which Mumgram had set up for her, tapping into the networks and finding a stream of figures which she could safely hijack without ever getting a bill from the phone network provider. Lucy recited her number and watched the boy put it into his mobile. She guessed she would have to get one of those for herself.

Emma smirked at him; but she was impressed. Jay would never normally ask a girl for her phone number. Mind you, this Lucy wasn't a normal girl. There was something *very* odd about her. Something which made her skin prickle.

'I'll drop you a text, so you've got my number—so you can, you know, stay in touch,' said Jay. 'You might need someone to show you around and stuff.'

'Will you?' said Lucy, looking absolutely overjoyed.

'Yeah—if you like,' said Jay. 'Or just—you know—call me.'

'I will!' said Lucy. She stared at him, grinning, for a few moments and then shook herself and said, 'Anyway . . . better get back to, er, Mum. And—well—watch *EastEnders*!'

And she picked up the backpack, turned, and walked swiftly away in her unlaced trainers. The ones with NIPE down the side, Emma noted. NIPE . . . almost like NIKE . . . quite believable but not the real thing.

They stood and watched her for a full minute, as she ambled away along the edge of the trees, staring up into them with a look of such rapture she might have been watching a firework display. Jay would have watched her longer but Emma nudged him and said, 'Come on—let's get back. Mum will wonder where we are and we need to see to your leg.'

'Mmmm? Oh—oh yeah,' said Jay, tearing his eyes from the shrinking outline of their new friend as she veered away from the trees and out into the grassy meadow.

Emma smirked at him again. 'Someone's in lo-ove!' she sang, as they clambered back over the gate and he went to get the bike.

'Don't be stupid!' he snorted. He wrestled the bike up into standing position. 'She's just—you know—interesting. Different.'

'No arguments there!' agreed Emma. She glanced back again and saw the girl turning slowly, her arms outstretched like a five year old. 'Are you going to call her—take her off to see the sights?'

Jay huffed and looked a little cross as they wheeled the bike back onto the road. 'You can come too. It won't be like . . . a date!'

'OK, I will.' She grinned at him and clapped his shoulder. 'In case you make her swoon again and I have to help you carry her home.' She turned around to catch a last look at the girl and was surprised to see that the wide expanse of meadow was now completely empty. 'Funny . . .'

'What?' said Jay, also turning.

'She's gone . . . just like that!' Emma furrowed her brow. 'She must be either a *really* fast runner or, I dunno, a ghost!'

'Well, did you see the backflips?' said Jay. 'She probably *can* run a mile a minute.'

'Or maybe she's an alien! And she's just been zapped up by the mothership,' went on Emma.

'Em, you watch too much sci-fi . . .'

Chapter 5

'Aargh! Don't bleed on that, bleed on *this*!'

Jay paused, the white towel clutched in his hand as Mum dashed across the hallway and slapped a dark blue towel into his other hand. 'You *don't* bleed on white towels—bleed on *dark* towels.' She swiped the clean white one away, clutching it to her as if it were a bullied child.

'Thanks for your concern, Mum,' snorted Jay. 'I didn't know about colour-coordinated blood loss until now.'

Sue Hamlyn shook her head, frowned, and crouched down to peer at the deep scrape along her son's calf. 'Eugh!' she said, pushing her untidy blonde fringe out of her eyes. 'How on earth did you do that?'

'It was my fault,' said Emma, trudging in through the front door, behind her brother.

'No it wasn't,' said Jay. 'It was mine.'

Mum stood up, dropped the clean towel on a freshly laundered pile of others, and stepped across to press a warm palm to each of her offspring's foreheads. 'Who are you both, and what have you done with my children?'

'Ha ha!' said Jay, mopping the blood with the old, blue towel. It had started oozing out of the wound again as they came down the drive. It tickled like mad and it was all he could do not to scratch it. 'Where's the first-aid kit? Shouldn't you be rushing for it, whimpering about your poor hurt baby?'

'Oh nonsense,' said Mum. 'It's just a scratch.'

'Remember that time when you said my hurting arm was just growing pains?' queried Emma, inspecting her own wounds which were plentiful across her legs and arms, if not as dramatic as Jay's.

'Yes, yes, I know . . .' sighed Mum, heading into the kitchen to get Savlon and sticking plasters from the bottom drawer. 'You're never going to let me forget that are you?'

'My *broken arm*!? No way!' grinned Emma. 'All those *hours and hours* of pain before you finally took me to A & E for an X-ray. I was emotionally scarred for life! I'm surprised social services didn't come after you.'

'Shut up or you won't get cake,' muttered Mum. The kitchen smelt of recently baked Victoria sponge—and the evidence was sitting on a blue china plate on the woodblock surface next to the hob. High and round, thick jam seeping between its layers and a snowy drift of sifted icing sugar across the top, Jay's mouth watered at the sight of it. Mum was a wonderful baker and her battered but beloved kitchen, all warm wood and ochre quarry tiles, was usually a haven to something warm, sweet, and floury. It was a wonder she wasn't twice her size, but she was small and wiry and still fitted neatly into her size ten jeans. With her hair up in a scrunchy, like today, she looked like a teenager herself at times.

'Come on, Jay—let's get some hot water on that towel and clean you up properly,' she said now, trying and failing to get the squeamish look off her face. 'Then I need your help making up Dovecot and Willow. We've got people coming in less than two hours.'

'I'll sort the wounds out,' said Emma, taking the towel, the Savlon, and the plasters. 'You make some tea, OK? To go with the cake . . . ?'

'Hmmm.' Mum pursed her lips at the order. But she turned to the kettle, happy enough to get away from Jay's leg. 'So—how *did* all this happen?'

'The bike,' said Emma. 'I messed up. Couldn't stop. Jay kind of got in the way. We went down the bank and nearly into the river.'

Mum turned around, a compassionate look on her

face. 'You've still achieved a lot you know, honeybun. You can *ride a bike*!'

'I can hurtle, out of control, for half a mile—and then fall *off* a bike,' corrected Emma with a bitter laugh. She dropped her eyes to the task of unpeeling a plaster and mumbled, 'I couldn't even remember how to *brake*.'

Mum cut the cake, the blade tugging it down for a second before it sliced through and the top layer sprang up with a little puff of icing sugar. 'You know it takes time, Em. You just have to keep at it.' She lay a thick wedge of golden sponge, with a glistening red seam, on a small plate.

'Anyway,' added Jay, 'it was my fault for sending you off down Blackpenny Lane. I should have remembered that it has that steep, sharp bend.'

'Yeah . . .' Emma collected the cake even before Mum had made the tea, and bit a large arc into it. 'None of this is my fault,' she grinned, crumbily. 'It's *you* two.'

'That's the spirit!' said Mum, lifting the steaming kettle. 'Now when you've had tea, can you both crack on with Dovecot and Willow? I've got too much to do on my own today. And, Jay, before that, as soon as you've finished bleeding, could you take some fresh towels down to Mr Dobson in Brook? And don't hang around—just deliver—he's working. Oh—take him a bit of cake too.'

'Cake, eh?' grinned Emma. 'Cake for Mr Dobson. Mother . . . do you *like* Mr Dobson?'

Mum plonked two mugs of tea on the table and gave her a raised eyebrow. 'Any more of that from you, miss, and *I'll* be calling social services myself, and begging them to take you.'

Ten minutes later, patched up and reeking of Savlon, they got on with their tasks. Woody Bottom was their mum's tiny hamlet of five holiday lodges, clustered along a winding stream in a lush green valley, a short distance from their cottage. Despite its hilarious name (people were always saying they should get an ointment for that), Woody Bottom was a serious business. It was their whole family income. It took up all Mum's time—or it *would* if Emma and Jay didn't help. They had grown up with the chores and didn't really think much about them. They could vacuum, scrub baths, make perfect beds, and process laundry like no other kids they knew. OK, so their own bedrooms were a tip, but they knew exactly what paying guests expected. They'd been trained in all of this since they could walk.

As Emma disappeared into Dovecot, a small two-person let with a conical, shingle-tiled roof, much *like* a dovecot, Jay walked on down to the far end of the acre of meadow, wood, and stream the Hamlyn family owned, carrying fresh towels in one hand and a piece of still slightly warm Victoria sponge on a plate in the other. Mr Dobson was a bit of an enigma. He'd first shown up a month ago and was renting Brook, the most remote lodge, for several more weeks yet. They didn't see much of him. Mum said he was working on a book or something, and they were to leave him in peace. Jay stepped across the small wooden bridge which spanned the gurgling stream, and up three stone steps to the lodge. It was, like all the lodges, built of cedar; a mellow reddish-brown colour. Rustic and charming. Through the dappled glass upper half of its front door Jay could make out Mr Dobson, sitting at his desk by the far window. He didn't seem to be doing much writing. He was settled back in his chair, his elbows out and hands clasped behind his head, staring into the middle distance.

Jay knocked and saw the man start slightly. 'It's just me—Jay—Mr Dobson,' he called. 'I've got towels . . . and—er—cake!'

In two strides Mr Dobson was opening the door. He smiled at Jay, rubbing his hand across a slightly stubbly chin and narrowing his pale green eyes at the cake. 'Hmmmm,' he said, in a deep, mellow voice. 'Your mother's on a mission to turn me into a ball of lard.'

Jay grinned. 'Yep. She's good at that.'

'I'm colluding,' sighed the man, shaking his head and stretching his arms over his close-cropped dark hair with a yawn. 'It's been days since I've even had a proper run.' His eyes wandered the high paths across the hills. He certainly looked like he ran every day, thought Jay. In T-shirt and jeans, Mr Dobson was as fit and toned as many men half his age. *He must be . . . what . . . forty?* There was a hint of grey in his hair. But he looked younger in his physique . . . if not his face. Lines around his eyes gave away his years and something else too. A difficult life. In what way, Jay hadn't a clue. And he didn't intend to ask. Mr Dobson was a paying guest. You were friendly—but you didn't pry. That was the deal and it was as ingrained in Jay and Emma as it was in their mother.

He took the cake and Jay followed him inside to deposit the fresh towels on a chair. 'Can I take away the used ones?' he asked.

'I'll drop them up to your mum later,' said Mr Dobson, putting the cake down at his table where an Apple MacBook lay, in powersave mode. Clearly not much writing going on either, noted Jay. The man sat down again and tapped his fingers across a pile of reference books. 'Jay,' he said. 'Was there a power cut or something a bit earlier today? Did the generator have a blip?'

'Um . . . I don't know,' replied Jay. 'Me and Emma have been out with the bike . . . about what time?'

'About eleven-fifteen,' said Mr Dobson, glancing across at the small TV which was relaying some news channel from its corner by the wood burner. 'The picture went completely for two minutes and then came back on again. I thought maybe your mum had had someone round to work on the generator—or maybe the aerial.'

'No—I don't think so,' said Jay, heading for the door.

'Hmmm. That's weird then.'

'Why?'

'Look at the picture,' said Mr Dobson, folding his arms and tilting his head towards the TV screen.

Jay did. 'Wow,' he said, after a few seconds. 'It's never been *that* good before!'

'It hasn't, has it?' said Mr Dobson.

They both stared in silence at the TV. Then Jay said, 'Maybe the guys up at Rowridge have done something . . . you know . . . put a new rubber band in!'

Mr Dobson laughed and at once the worry lines vanished and he looked years younger. 'That'll be it. Yes . . . that'll be it. Nothing weird at all. Not really.'

But as he saw Jay out, there was something in the man's expression which made Jay's skin prickle . . . just a little. He suddenly realized Mr Dobson looked just like

Emma had, earlier that day, after they'd seen the green light in the sky. 'What?' he said, dropping his manners for a moment. 'What is it?'

Mr Dobson gazed at him for a few seconds, as if he was about to tell him something important . . . but then he shook his head and chuckled. 'Nothing! Nothing, Jay. Just writer's imagination! Say thanks to your mum for the cake.'

As the boy wandered away across the little wooden bridge, Nick Dobson found his eyes drawn to the transmitter, thrusting skywards through the distant trees, many small metal dishes, angular outcrops, and wheel-shaped hubs clinging to it like determined parasites, sending out signals for a myriad of communications networks. It must be a kilometre or more away. Most of the time he barely noticed it. Nothing going on there could really have made his hackles rise, could it?

Of course not.

But ever since 11.15 that morning, Nick had been getting a familiar feeling. One he thought he'd left far behind in a different life.

Chapter 6

'Please remain still until the bioscan is complete,' requested Mumgram.

Lucy stopped bouncing. She was incredibly hyper—*wired*, as they'd say on *Hollyoaks*. She had never been so excited in her life as she was today. She could hardly believe everything that had happened. She had trodden in grass! *Real* grass—cool and tickly against her bare feet. She had heard and seen a *real* wood pigeon. And she had met two Earth kids and actually *touched* them! They were living, substantial, actual people. Just like her.

'No significant bacterial change,' intoned Mumgram as the ring of blue light moved up and down Lucy's form in the bioscan chamber. 'No viruses contracted from human contact at present.'

'They looked healthy enough,' said Lucy. 'Well—a bit bleedy maybe, but then so was I. The girl's name is Emma and the boy's name is Jay. They're about my age, I think. They were riding a bike! I could ride a bike, couldn't I?'

'You will be quite able to ride a bike,' agreed Mumgram.

'I just have to get one first,' said Lucy, her heart rate picking up even more at the thought. 'With money. I will need money. What about the money?'

'UK currency has been created,' said Mumgram. 'Ample for your immediate needs, and an investment fund set up for you has reached maturity in a UK-based bank and will be available as soon as you make yourself known to a branch on the Isle of Wight.'

'Right. Yes.' Lucy beamed. She knew all of this, of course. She'd been studying it for years. Not just the planet and the country and the island she was to call home, but the whole elaborate process set up by her people as they fled Cornelian Eclata. Of course, back then, all thirty-one of them had expected to be settling in together on the new planet. Nobody had imagined that only one of them—the youngest—would make it.

But even so, they'd been thorough. For each of them the technology experts had created digital birth certificates, passports, National Insurance numbers, bank accounts with high-interest ten-year savings plans . . . a whole legend for each and every refugee . . .

and placed it right into the core of the UK's online systems. They'd scattered these vital details across the country, planning for the group to disperse from the Isle of Wight soon after they'd docked. Lucy, though, and her mum, had arranged to stay put on the island with two of the others: a small group of sentries to watch over *Hessandrea* and deal with the safe disposal of the ship, should they ever need to.

But with everyone else gone and Lucy all that was left, the whole plan had to be recalibrated. Oddly, it had been easier to plan a brand-new life for thirty-one people than it was for just one. After all, with a mother in tow, Lucy would probably not have raised any eyebrows. With a whole community of people she knew spread across the country she would have instant 'roots'. But alone, at just fourteen, it was going to be much trickier.

Mumgram—who was really the central intelligence of *Hessandrea*—worked out the best plan possible. It was relatively simple. Continue to live on *Hessandrea* until she was eighteen. Keep her secret closely guarded until she was old enough to buy herself a home of her own.

'What about school?' she had asked—years ago. Most children on Earth went to school.

'You must tell anyone you meet that you are home tutored,' Mumgram had advised. 'You must be careful with building friendships. Children on Earth visit each other's homes. This cannot happen. If you visit a child's home you will be expected to invite the child back to *your* home. This cannot happen. Other children's mothers will expect to connect with *your* mother. This cannot happen.'

The exact details of how she was to fit in to Earth society without ever going to anyone's home were not explained. Although Mumgram had a huge amount of information on this planet she could not predict the future, nor the unknowable—human relationships.

But the answer to this problem had seemed to present itself to Lucy only a year ago when she was watching a Channel 4 documentary about people with extraordinary difficulties to overcome. She'd been drawn to it with her own difficulties in mind—although she doubted that it would cover 'how to acclimatize in a new world after ten years alone in space' at any point. The documentary was about a woman who suffered from something called total allergy syndrome. This woman, who was in her late thirties, was allergic to virtually everything; food, drink, clothing, plastics, perfume, animals, pollens, and any household chemical you could think of. Lucy gazed at her in awed pity, this woman who lived in a bubble. She literally spent her life in one room, sealed in by some kind of see-through stuff made from one of the few organic polymers she wasn't allergic to, and her family would poke food and other necessities through a double-sealed hatch. If the woman got even a whiff of ordinary life she broke out in a rash and struggled to breathe.

It was a dreadful thing to watch, especially as there seemed to be no known cure . . . but as the programme moved on to another struggling soul who couldn't stand daylight, Lucy felt a sudden surge of excitement. *This* could be the answer. Her mother was back at home . . . suffering total allergy syndrome! Lucy literally *couldn't* take anyone home with her because they might trigger an allergic reaction.

SORTED! (As they would say on *EastEnders.*)

'You will contract viruses in the coming weeks and months,' Mumgram was now warning her as the bioscan chamber reset to golden light and a glowing column of statistics on her current state of health slid down the small monitor set into the wall at her side. She barely glanced at it. She was fine. She was *home.*

'I know,' grinned Lucy. 'I'll get colds and stomach bugs and flu!'

'It will not be pleasant,' added Mumgram.

'I know! I can't wait!'

'You may feel very ill. Worse than you have felt before.'

'What—worse than chicken pox?' Lucy frowned, remembering the dreadful time she'd gone through when she was five. Even following Mumgram's advice and lying in a bath of cool water and sodium bicarbonate had barely helped the incessant itching. In the early days, while she could still remember how it had felt to have an *actual* mum, the very worst thing had been that lack of physical contact when she was ill or sad. With nobody to catch anything from, she had only suffered the occasional headache or stomach upset but the chicken pox virus, caught from some long dead Cornelian Eclata nursery mate, must have lain dormant in her spine for many months before finally erupting. Although it had itched madly, it hadn't hurt all that much. It had just made her feel lonely. Looking after her unwell self at just five had been tough.

'Yes, worse than chicken pox,' said Mumgram.

'But I'll have friends,' said Lucy, thinking of Emma and Jay and wondering if *they* would be the friends. 'They'll look after me. It won't be so bad to be ill with someone to look after me.'

'That cannot happen,' said Mumgram and Lucy realized, with a dull thud in her insides, that Mumgram was going to use those three words a great deal in the next four years. 'Your friends will expect your mother to be caring for you. You must make them believe that she is.'

Lucy stared at Mumgram's face, just a metre from her own, luminous in the holographic column beside the bioscan chamber. It was fully opaque again now that they'd docked and the ship's power, on save mode for so many years, was fully boosted through the transmitter. Mumgram looked the same as always, a gentle smile on her heart-shaped face, hazel eyes wide and focused eternally on her 'daughter', short brown hair shining in a flop of fringe across her wide, smooth brow. Small gold earrings in each lobe and a chain with a gold B on it glinted around her neck. She wore the regulation *Hessandrea* trouser suit and soft slippers. Of course, had her mother survived, she would now have been thirty-seven. But as Beth Rumier had programmed Mumgram when she was twenty-seven, this was the age she remained, in the last outfit she had worn, for ever. Lucy had toyed with the idea of tweaking the visual programme to allow Mumgram's image to age as Beth would have, or to change the colour of her outfit; she'd learned how to ages ago. But somehow she had never quite got to this.

'Don't worry, Mumgram,' she said, walking through the holographic figure and back towards the bridge. 'It'll all work out OK.'

Mumgram smiled as if she were capable of being reassured.

Lucy sat down in front of the gentle slope of brushed metal with its scores of twinkling buttons and glowing screens. She hadn't started touching them until she was seven. On her seventh birthday, to be exact, when she had at last felt confident enough to experiment with the console and all it had to offer her. The small childish gadgets she had stuck with until then were little more than comfort blankets. Mumgram had pushed her education through their limited screens and chunky, brightly coloured buttons for three years, teaching her enough to wean her off them and on to the console. She had reached it by climbing onto the high stools the adults had used for the five weeks before their time was up. The console, as well as the means to run and pilot the ship, was a complete educational resource, linked to Earth's internet via its satellites. For the first five years this had been all she could receive from the planet; it was only around the age of nine that the first TV feeds started to come through and she could view the channels playing out from Earth only a few days after they had been transmitted. Mumgram steered her towards the educational programmes—history, geography, wildlife—but she had just as often steered herself away, back to dramas and soaps and adventures. She loved the music too—and the comedy and the science programmes, many with lovely ideas about space (most of them a bit wrong). There was *so much* to love. It was overwhelming.

Right now, though, her needs were simple. She pulled up a web browser, and typed 'bike shop, Isle of Wight' into the search bar.

Three options popped up straight away. Two were in Newport, the island's main town, while a third was listed as The Bike Hut, in a more rural area called Maystone. She thought this would probably be a wiser option than going straight into a busy Earth metropolis on day one. On the map it was two hours' walking distance. She could probably run that in half the time. She was a good runner—at least, she was in *Hessandrea*'s gym. She had once run the whole London Marathon in three hours and twenty-two minutes, which was pretty good according to the stats for girls of her age. Of course, it was a virtual run—she wasn't jostling with crowds—but the running belt had adjusted for hills and there had been a breeze manufactured in the gym to compare with the wind conditions on the day. So . . . twelve kilometres, some cross-country . . . she could be there in as little as an hour.

The desire to buy a bike suddenly became a fervent need. She HAD to have a bike. It would be perfect for exploring her new home. She ran to the simulation room and pulled out one of its many drawers to find the currency waiting for her. The notes were in neat, flat packs, a hundred in each. Some twenties, some fifties, some tens. About fifteen thousand pounds in total, she quickly calculated. She shoved nineteen fifties, five twenties and ten tens into her jeans pocket. One thousand pounds should be ample for a good bicycle according to the information on the website.

From another drawer she collected the mobile phone she'd requested, still warm from its creation and already containing a single phone number in its contacts: Jay's. Of course, she *could* ask Mumgram to get a bike created on board *Hessandrea* . . . but she wanted a *real* one. An Earth one.

She pulled the bio-adaptive backpack on once more, mostly to silence Mumgram before she could get going on her warnings again, but also because she really *might* need it this time. She was going to travel much further into this new world. She slung some energy gels into it along with some carbisks and protein nuts, swiftly totting up the likely calorie burn of a sixty to ninety minute run followed by a thirty to forty-five minute return bike ride. Satisfied, she strode back to the exit platform where the world continued to glow up in a blue-white well of light.

'I'm going out, Mum,' she called, over her shoulder. 'Don't worry about me. I'll be back for tea.'

Mumgram smiled and said nothing. Lucy remembered that she would have to programme the words 'see you later' into her memory. For this was the first day in Mumgram's existence when such a phrase had any point at all. Maybe 'take care, love' too . . . or 'mind out for strangers'. Lucy grinned as she stepped down onto the mast. As far as *that* went, nobody was stranger on the island that day than she.

It could not move. But it could see and smell and sense. As the female went past on the high metal rungs its pulse increased. But it could not move.

Yet.

Chapter 7

Jay had finished his work in the lodges and was lying in the grass by the stream, watching a buzzard riding the warm air high above their valley, when his phone went off.

He jumped, shocked. The signal down in this dip was so dodgy he hardly ever got a call. Glancing at the small, cheap Nokia (he'd been pestering for an iPhone for the last three years without success) he noticed that the cell coverage was up to *five bars.* That was new! Like Mr Dobson had said, someone must have been doing something up at the transmitter. Wow!

Bigger wow. The name flashing on the small blue screen wasn't Harry or Ben from school (Ben was in Spain and Harry was probably superglued to his latest computer game)—it was LUCY. Only hours after they'd met. He'd texted her his number on the way back home but hadn't expected to hear from her *this* soon. He grinned, and thumbed ACCEPT CALL. 'Hi, Lucy,' he said, the grin travelling audibly through those three syllables.

'Jay? How did you know it was me?' came a perplexed and slightly stressed voice.

'Caller ID . . . ?'

'Um—oh—oh yes. Of course.' She laughed but only briefly before she cut to the chase. 'Jay—do you think you could come and see me? Only . . . um . . . I think I'm going to be arrested.'

'WHAT?' Jay sat up, wanting to laugh but somehow knowing this was not a joke. 'Why? Where are you?'

'I'm in The Bike Hut.'

This was getting surreal. 'The Bike Hut,' he repeated. Maybe Emma was right and Lucy really was a nutjob.

'Yes—a shop for bikes. In Maystone. I came to buy a bike but the man thinks I'm a criminal.'

'What? Why?' he spluttered, only just stopping himself adding 'how', 'when', and 'who'.

'I don't know. It was when I showed the man the money. I don't understand!'

'Look—put me on to whoever's there!' said Jay, although he had no idea why he was suddenly taking charge. He'd only met this girl this morning. Why should she be *his* concern?

'OK—I'm handing you over now,' said Lucy.

'Hello.' The voice was wary and weary. A man in his forties or fifties, Jay guessed. 'Are you the friend?'

'Erm—yes—I'm Lucy's friend. What's going on?' Jay deepened his voice, wanting to sound calm and authoritative, even though his heart was suddenly thudding. He really had no idea what he was doing.

'Well, your friend's just tried to buy a bike with a grand's worth of brand new notes,' said the man. 'And she doesn't seem too clear about how she got that kind of money.'

'Well . . . what makes you think she stole it?' demanded Jay. He was getting angry now. A pet hate of his was the way older people made assumptions about you just because you were a teenager.

'I'm not saying she did,' said the man. 'But when I asked for a name and address, for her warranty and such like, she didn't seem to know it all of a sudden. Now I think we both know that's a bit odd, don't we, son?'

'Look.' Jay got up and began to walk briskly towards the garage beside the cottage. 'I'm coming over. I'll sort this out. Don't you go upsetting her—she's . . . a bit . . . different, that's all. She's not a criminal!'

'Oh right, if you say so,' said the man. 'I'm not stopping her leaving, son. But I'm not doing business with her either, not until I've got a name and address and an explanation for that kind of money stuffed in her pocket. And I've got it all on CCTV, in case you want to know.'

'Put her back on,' snapped Jay as he pulled open the garage door and made for his bike.

'Jay . . . ?' Lucy sounded scared and puzzled. 'What am I supposed to do?'

'Just—go and wait outside the shop. I'll be there in about half an hour,' said Jay. 'You've got nothing to worry about—I just need to explain a few things to the idiot in charge!'

'Thank you so much, Jay!'

'I'll see you soon. Don't worry,' he said, snapping his phone off and tucking it in his jeans pocket.

'Just going out on the bike for a bit!' he called, three minutes later, through the kitchen window.

'Oh—have you fixed it?' Mum called back from behind the ironing board.

'Yeah—I straightened it all up—it's fine,' he called back, jumping onto the saddle. 'See you later.'

It took him thirty minutes hard pedalling to reach The Bike Hut. Fortunately he knew the shop—had bought stuff there himself. He couldn't recall much about the owner or any of the staff but didn't remember them being unfriendly. On the way he'd tried to work out what he was doing, dashing to the aid of this virtual stranger. He had no idea where she'd got a thousand pounds in unused notes or why she wouldn't give up her address. Maybe she *had* stolen the money. But if so—why hadn't she just done a runner? Why had she phoned *him*?

Outside The Bike Hut, sitting demurely on a small bench beside a swinging sign advertising Shimano gears, was Lucy. The evidence of that morning's nosebleed had dried in an abstract maroon pattern down the front of her green top. He skidded to a stop, panting, and leaned his bike against the end of the bench. Lucy jumped up, beaming, leaving her backpack on the seat. 'Jay! You came! You're my *friend*!' He peered closely at her, glad to note that there was no blood on her face. Did she have some kind of . . . mental impairment? Some kind of syndrome . . . ? He'd seen TV programmes about kids like that who looked normal but didn't really understand stuff.

But as he looked into Lucy's eyes he saw nothing but intelligence—and great delight. 'Yeah—I'm your friend . . . if you like,' he said. He became aware of the man standing in the doorway, arms folded, and he lowered his voice, turning her away from the shop owner's line of sight. 'Look—why didn't you give him an address . . . or your mum or dad's phone number or something?'

Lucy looked down at her feet and her cheeks reddened. 'I . . . I can't.'

Jay suddenly got it. He sighed and shook his head. 'Have you run away from home?' he asked. 'Or—boarding school?' It made sense. She was so polite and pleasant and obviously not used to the harsh realities of . . . er . . . buying a bike. And there were several posh boarding schools on the island. He could easily imagine Lucy at one of these.

'No—I'm home tutored,' said Lucy. She carried on gazing at her feet for a few seconds and then, still looking down, suddenly delivered a torrent of information. 'Mum has total allergy syndrome, sometimes known as twentieth century disease, only it's the twenty-first century now so that doesn't really fit any more, but anyway, she's allergic to more or less anything you can think of and she has to live in a bubble and we have to poke food through to her and not make her ill because she'll come out in blisters and not be able to breathe and so on and that's why I can't take you back for a sleepover or anything.'

She glanced up at Jay to find him open-mouthed.

'You see?' she added, shrugging and giving him a weak smile.

'O . . . K.' Jay blinked and tried to get his head around all this. 'But . . . that still doesn't explain why you can't tell him your address . . . or why you've got a grand in brand-new notes shoved in your pocket.' He stared at her, narrowing his eyes. 'Lucy—just tell me. I'm on your side.'

'I—I really can't,' she said, again. And she looked suddenly small and lost and about five years old, fiddling with her plait and biting her lip.

'Right, well . . . let me see this money.'

She pulled the thick wad of notes out of her jeans pocket. They crackled and their silver strips gleamed in the afternoon sun; Jay could *smell* their newness.

'Just . . . promise me you didn't steal that,' he said.

Her eyes grew round and her voice indignant. 'I didn't! I'm not a thief!'

Jay rubbed his face, turned away from her, and made for the shop doorway. Once again, he had no clue why he was doing this . . . but he *was going* to do this.

'Her name's Lucy and she's a friend of mine,' he said to the grey haired burly man, whose suspicious look seemed as firmly attached as his moustache. Jay motioned into the shop and the man sniffed and went inside with him. The shop had bikes displayed from its concrete floor to its loft ceiling. Assorted colourful accessories—hats, gloves, bike locks, and repair kits—filled two walls. 'She's staying at the holiday place in Rowridge which my mum runs at the moment,' Jay went on. 'She's . . . a little bit . . .' he struggled for the right word, '. . . autistic.'

'Oh. Right.' The man's defensive posture softened. His arms uncrossed and he put his hands into his pockets. 'That explains a lot,' he added. He nodded through a nearby window to the hill that rose gently to the west of the shop. 'She ran all the way over that hill,' he said. 'Like the devil was after her. Non-stop. I was having a break and I first saw her about three miles away—a little dot, running. And she just keeps on running and running and then runs right into my shop, blood all down her front, stops dead, and then starts touching the bikes and grinning from ear to ear. Weird, it was.' He shivered.

'Well . . . she *is* a bit strange,' agreed Jay. 'She can't help it.'

'And the money?' said the man, his brown eyes level with Jay's. 'A thousand pounds in cash . . . ?'

'She got it out of her bank account today,' lied Jay. 'She's been saving for ages. Her mum said she could get a bike today and Lucy couldn't even wait for her to get the car out of the garage. She—just doesn't get that she's a bit full on sometimes. I . . . I can vouch for her, if you like. Check out my name and address on your system. I've bought stuff here before for my bike.'

The man did check and was reassured to find evidence of three modest sales to Jay in the past eighteen months—as well as an address and telephone number. 'Well,' he shuffled some boxes of pump adaptors across his counter, 'if you can vouch for her, I suppose we're all right.' He glanced at the door where Lucy was standing, staring lovingly at a gleaming all-terrain model.

'Good—thanks,' said Jay. 'It'll make her day.'

Now that he was reassured Lucy wasn't lying about being a thief—lying about everything *else*, yes, but not this—Jay was delighted to help her choose a bike. The burly owner, who revealed his name was Bill, suddenly warmed up too and was happy to advise on shock absorbers, hydraulic disc brakes, and Shimano alloy hubs. They chose a ten-speed silver, white, and red Trek mountain bike which cost most of Lucy's budget. Jay got her to spend the rest on a hat, a bike lock, some lights, and a couple of lightweight mudguards. 'Trust me—you don't want mud spattered up your back,' he explained, while Lucy nodded and beamed. 'It's not a good look. Speaking of which . . .' he lowered his voice,

'. . . the blood spattered all down your front is not such a good look, either . . .'

Lucy glanced down and then looked dismayed. 'Oh! I completely forgot all about that!' she murmured. 'It looks awful!'

Jay grinned. 'You're not really the average girl, are you, Lucy?' He'd been noticing other things about her, too. She wore not a scrap of make-up, even though she must be fourteen or fifteen and most girls her age were at least experimenting with a bit of lip gloss. Her body language was really odd, too. Childlike. Unselfconscious. She had made no effort to hide her delight in meeting him. Most girls of her age—and certainly with her looks—would be well practised at playing it cool around boys by now. Not Lucy. He didn't want to give Emma the satisfaction of agreeing with her, but he was beginning to think she may have been right about Lucy coming from some kind of institution—somewhere well away from the ordinary world.

'No—no, I suppose I'm not,' said Lucy, running her fingers along the chunky tread of the brand-new tyres on the Trek. 'Will you help me learn to ride this, Jay?'

Jay and Bill glanced at each other, baffled.

'You mean . . . you don't know how to ride a bike?' asked Jay.

'Not exactly. But I'll pick it up very quickly,' said Lucy, straightening up and getting a grip on the handlebars. 'Then we can ride back together.'

Bill raised an eyebrow and shrugged, moving towards the till to ring up all Lucy's purchases. The body language from *him* was clear enough. *She's all yours, mate!*

Jay was very glad he'd insisted she take the bike helmet. 'Why do I need one if you don't?' she'd asked as they wheeled the Trek outside. Bill had pumped its tyres, set its saddle at the right height, and given it all a quick once over before waving them out of his store with obvious relief.

Jay shrugged. 'I *should* wear one . . . I just . . . don't.'

'But why?'

'Look—I'm well used to the roads. I watch out for myself. I don't really need one.'

'Even if you get hit by an out-of-control truck?' said Lucy.

'Well . . .'

'Because that's what happened to Sharon Biggs on *Casualty*,' went on Lucy. 'She said she didn't need one and she didn't want to mess up her hair and then, just as she was nearly at school, this out-of-control truck ploughed into her and she had to be rushed to casualty and Charlie said it looked like a fractured skull and an intercranial bleed and then she was having convulsions and an MRI scan confirmed all of this. She did survive although she was partially paralysed but happily her parents, who were on the verge of a divorce, were reunited at her bedside.'

Jay found himself gaping at her again. 'What are you . . . a medical drama screenwriter?'

'No—I didn't *write* it,' giggled Lucy. 'I just watched it! On March the twenty-third.' She suddenly seemed to notice Jay's expression and added, 'Sorry—I know I'm a bit strange. I have a photographic memory. For dates and details and so on . . .'

'Right. OK,' said Jay. 'Look—don't worry about me—just put *your* helmet on. You're new to bike riding and you need to take extra care.' He watched, feeling oddly like a parent, as Lucy obediently put the sleek red helmet on and secured the straps under her chin with a click.

'Now . . . first, get on . . .'

She mounted the bike with ease and rested her hands on the black handlebar grips, her back angled from the hips and straight—picture-perfect. Jay was used to helping girls ride bikes—after all he'd spent the best part of the last week finally getting his sister on two wheels . . . with, admittedly, not much success. Was this going to be any easier?

Ten minutes later his jaw was hanging again as Lucy rode up and down the lane, deftly changing gear, braking, turning—and managing the whole business as if she'd just dropped out of an Olympic velodrome.

'Lucy—were you winding me up?' he asked, exasperated. Maybe she *was* as self-aware as other girls and this 'helpless' routine was some kind of elaborate joke.

'What do you mean?' she asked, halting the Trek right by him with only a modest hiss of brake pads and resting one foot, in its odd Nipe trainer, on the tarmac.

'You look like you've been riding a bike for *years*,' said Jay, narrowing his eyes at her.

'Well I kind of have,' she agreed. 'But only in a simulator. It's a very good simulator, I suppose. That must be why I've picked it all up so fast.'

'Where is this simulator?' asked Jay. 'I'd love to have a go.'

'Um . . . it's at home,' said Lucy, looking evasive once again as she leaned over and scooped her bag up from the bench and shrugged it onto her shoulders. 'And you *could* have a go, Jay, but my . . .'

'Mum's allergic to everyone,' continued Jay. He shook his head. 'OK. Whatever. Let's get you back there anyway.'

'Over the hills?' Lucy literally jumped up and down on the saddle with excitement.

'Well . . . I was thinking more of the roads . . .'

'But this is a mountain bike! So is yours! Over the hills!' And she set off up the dirt track on the far side of the lane which led to a sloping field.

'But . . . do you know the way?' he yelled, pumping his pedals and heading after her.

'Yes—I ran across this way earlier,' she called back. She was already tearing up the stony track along one side of the field, her red bike hat bobbing and glinting in the sun. 'Come ON!'

Chapter 8

A sharp rapping on glass made both Emma and her mother jump. Emma had been peering unhappily at her book, wishing the words would just stay in a straight line and Sue had been engrossed in slicking some small apple pies with egg and sugar glaze while Radio 4 burbled quietly in the background.

At the window was an unwelcome face.

'Oh no,' muttered Sue.

'Just tell him to bog off,' said Emma, flicking a dismissive glance towards the figure outside.

Badger was peering in at her. His lank dark hair blew in the breeze and his stubble-framed mouth was stretched into a grin. He was winking and pointing to a grubby box in his hands.

Mum opened the window a crack. 'What do you want, Badger?'

'It's not so much what I want, Mrs Hamlyn, as what

I can offer *you*!' Badger inclined his head and waggled a nicotine-stained finger at her. It was hard to tell what age he was—thirty? Forty? All Emma knew was that he'd been their neighbour for the past three years, ever since he'd inherited the field across the road, and the tumbledown bungalow on it. And he was always on the make.

'What *can* you offer?' sighed Mum. 'Other than impetigo.'

Badger didn't even blink at the insult. 'Fresh eggs! Laid just this morning. Still warm—hen-fresh!' He opened the box to reveal a dozen eggs of varying size, some with feathers still attached.

'Yes, Badger—but *whose* hens?' said Mum. 'You don't have any. Have you pilfered them from Mrs Lamarr's henhouse again?'

Badger held his hand to his heart and adopted the expression of a kicked puppy. 'Now is that a nice thing to say to someone who just wants to share a little bit of nature's bounty with a neighbour?'

'It's other people's bounty you want to share,' snapped Mum. 'But OK—if you want to give me some eggs, fine. Leave them on the windowsill. Very kind of you.'

'Um . . . well . . .' A wheedling smile crept across Badger's face. 'I was after, you know, a little bit of wonga . . . special price and all that.'

Mum shut the window. Badger went on talking, muffled, on the far side. Mum pulled the blind down. 'GO AWAY!' she yelled. But the figure remained there, a dark shadow beyond the pale yellow cotton.

Mum looked at Emma and Emma looked back. They'd always laughed about Badger but he was getting worse. Mum sighed as the dark shadow pressed itself closer against the glass. 'C'mon! Help me out here! I'm broke and Brad needs some dog food!'

'I'm going to hit him with this,' said Mum, seizing the broom from the corner.

But then there was a sudden thud and the shadow abruptly departed from the window. They heard voices. Badger's, whining, trying to be defiant, and another male voice responding curtly. 'Get away from this house. If I catch you back here again I'll make you sorry.'

Emma and Mum stared at the window, then at each other, then at the door as there was a gentle knock and a voice said, 'Sue, Emma—you OK?'

Mum shot across the room, opening the door smartly. 'Hello, Mr Dobson. Yes! We're fine! Did you bump into our annoying neighbour? I am sorry about that. He can be a bit of a pain.'

Nick Dobson stood in the doorway, his head almost touching the top, and regarded her with a flat expression. 'He will be *in* pain if he comes back and bothers you again.'

Mum spun around and walked back to the pies, laughing unconvincingly, thought Emma. 'Really—he's harmless,' she said.

Nick said nothing until she looked around at him again. Then he said: 'Nobody's harmless, Mrs Hamlyn.'

There was an odd moment of tension and Emma felt her heartbeat pick up. Then their guest suddenly changed gear. 'I brought some laundry,' he said, offering a canvas sack with a shrug and a slight smile. 'Sorry!'

'No—not at all,' said Mum, her voice rather high. 'That's kind of you . . . you know . . . to save Jay the bother.'

'And your plate,' he added, holding out the cake plate—washed and dried. 'Thank you for the cake. You are an excellent baker.'

'No problem,' said Mum, taking the plate and returning it to the crockery cupboard. She seemed to be avoiding eye contact; seemed to want him to go. Emma couldn't understand why. There he stood—all six foot whatever of him—nice-looking and, let's face it, pretty fit. You'd think Mum might quite like that . . . but she really did seem to miss the point of being single.

'Thanks for seeing off Badger,' Emma said, to fill in the gap. 'He's gross—and his dog's just as bad. We're used to him, though.'

'Well, hopefully he'll take the hint and not come back,' said Nick, giving her a smile. 'Well . . . I won't keep you.' But as he went to leave he paused and stared at the radio on the shelf, which was still emitting the afternoon play. 'That's a much better signal, isn't it?'

Mum looked up, frowning. 'Sorry?'

'Your radio . . . the signal is . . . much clearer than before,' he explained. 'Mine is too. And my TV reception has never been better. No pixellation or cut-outs all day. Did you get someone in to work on the aerial?'

'No,' said Mum, shrugging. She paused and listened. 'You're right . . . it *is* better. That's odd.' Being so close to the transmitter, most people imagined they would get excellent reception—but Woody Bottom was down in a dip, with a pretty ropey digital aerial and sometimes subject to the 'null' effect which caused their signal to drop out completely from time to time.

'Isn't it?' said Nick. He paused for a moment, as if he was about to add something else, but then shook his head, smiled thinly, and left.

'Mu-um!' Emma protested, as soon as the door closed behind him.

'What?' Mum concentrated hard on something stuck to her apron.

'Why were you so *off* with him? He just came to our aid like a knight on a—'

'Emma—he told Badger to push off. *Badger!* I could have seen him off myself, you know that,' said Mum, stalking back across to her pies. 'I don't need a man, who is virtually a stranger anyway, butting in to do that for me!'

'He's not a stranger. He's nice,' said Emma. 'Why don't you like him?'

'One—he may have lived in Brook for six weeks but we still know next to nothing about him,' said Mum, shoving the pies in the oven and banging the door shut. 'And two—I don't *dis*like him. I just don't know him.'

'Hmmm. And you never will, will you?' grunted Emma.

'What's that supposed to mean?' snapped Mum, glaring at her.

'Well . . .' Emma took a breath. 'Mum—it's been *four years* since Dad went. Don't you think it's time you started going out again? You know . . . with men?'

'Oh great.' Mum leaned against the sink unit. 'Dating advice from my teenage daughter. That's all I need!'

'Ellen's mum has had *three* boyfriends!' said Emma. 'And she only got divorced last year!'

'Well pardon me for not trailing a legion of men through your life!' Mum raised her hands, palms upward. 'There's me thinking that my kids deserved better, but *no*—apparently you want me to take up with anything in trousers with a pulse! Maybe I should just run after Badger and ask him back for a snog!'

Emma snorted with laughter at the thought, and happily, so did Mum after a few beats. 'Stop worrying about my love life, Em,' she said, rubbing her daughter's head as she passed. 'It's just too much fuss, that's all. You and Jay are all I care about.'

'And Johnny Depp,' added Emma, turning back to her book. 'Don't forget Johnny.'

'Yeah,' said Mum, heading upstairs. 'For Johnny I'd make an exception.'

Emma went back to her wayward textbook, sliding a yellow-tinted sheet of plastic across the page in a bid to make the words behave. But her concentration was shattered a minute later when Jay staggered into the kitchen looking like he'd been attacked by evil woodland fairies.

'What happened to *you*?'

He went to the sink and drank several gulps of cold water directly from the tap before turning around, wiping his hair and several bits of twig and leaf off his brow. There was a dark smudge of something on his chin and mud spattered up his legs, vying with the bike crash wounds for attention.

'Lucy happened to me.'

'Lucy?' Emma's eyebrows shot up. 'What—weird nosebleeding, backflipping Lucy from the field?'

'Yup.' He nodded. 'She phoned me.'

'My—she's keen. Must get her to talk to Mum,' muttered Emma.

Jay ignored that. 'She phoned up to tell me she was about to be arrested!'

'What?' Emma shut her book.

Jay told her the story of The Bike Hut rumpus as he made himself a cup of tea. 'And then she goes shooting away, off-road, like she's dirt-trekking for Britain!' he concluded. 'And I had to follow her to make sure she was OK . . .'

Emma laughed, clapping her hands to her cheeks. 'She made you go cross-country? Wow!'

'Not wow!' he grumbled. 'You're right, she's bonkers. And I think she must be on some kind of speed drug. I've *never* seen anyone bike that fast up a muddy bank. She was doing wheelies and leaping streams! I had to keep shouting at her to slow down.'

'So . . . did you get to see her house?' asked Emma. 'Or her circus camp?'

'No.' Jay shook his head. 'She wouldn't let me follow her all the way. Keeps going on about this allergy thing her mum has—apparently she has to live in some kind of bubble and if anyone goes near her she'll erupt in hives and start spewing.'

Emma looked at him, incredulous.

'I know. It's nuts. And she's making it up, I can tell.'

'So . . . if she's lying about that, what makes you think she *wasn't* lying about the money?' asked Emma.

'I just knew. She's a terrible liar. She can't look me in the eye—she blushes, she stammers. But not with the money thing. She was telling the truth about that. I could tell. She's all right. You know she is.'

'Hmmm,' said Emma. 'She didn't seem like a criminal—I'll say that much for her. So . . . are you going to meet up with her again?'

'We both are,' said Jay. 'I told her we'd meet her in Newport tomorrow morning.'

'Oh did you?'

Jay gave her a grin. 'Well, you don't *have* to come. I mean . . . she *might* take my advice instead.'

'On what?' Emma shot him a suspicious look.

'On buying a whole load of clothes and shoes.'

Emma gasped. 'You're not telling me she's got another grand to spend?'

'Yup—and more if she needs it. Of course, if you're not interested—'

'I'm in!' For Emma, who rarely got to spend much on herself, shopping with friends and offering her opinions on their fashion choices was very nearly as good. She guessed shopping with Lucy, though, might be even more entertaining than with Maisy and Tia.

'Right—well, I said we'd meet her outside the museum, after she's had her hair cut.'

Emma stood up. 'She's getting her hair cut?' She looked alarmed.

'Yeah—she thinks it's too long. She wants to look more up to date, she said.' He blew out his lips and shook his head. 'Whatever . . .'

Emma gripped his shoulder. 'WHERE? Where is she getting her hair cut?'

'I could only think of that place on South Street. Um—Millie's? Yeah—Millie's Salon.'

'Oh dear god!' Emma looked horrified. 'You told her to go to Millie's?!'

'Yeah—it's a hairdressers, isn't it?'

'No, Jay,' she said. 'It's a lawnmower shop.'

'What?!'

'Jay—we've got to stop her!'

Chapter 9

'So . . . you going anywhere nice this weekend?'

The girl in the purple outfit vigorously worked shampoo into Lucy's scalp as water hissed and gurgled into the basin. The question was asked in a very friendly voice, but the inquisitor was staring out of the window of Millie's Salon and didn't really seem that interested in the answer.

'Um . . . I was thinking of . . . Alum Bay,' ventured Lucy, still trying to get used to the weird sensation of being leaned over backwards across the unforgiving ridge of a basin while someone she'd just met rummaged through her hair. The unfamiliar angle and unprecedented human contact was alarming. Her heart was beating fast.

'That's nice,' said the girl, whose name badge read KACEY. Her eyes still rested on the outside world. 'Water not too hot for you?' she said in a similarly sweet, cooing voice.

'No—it's fine, thank you.'

'Conditioner?'

'Erm . . . OK.' Lucy wished desperately that someone would just *cut her hair*. She had been unprepared for all this fuss when she had arrived.

'Shiatsu massage?' asked Kacey.

'Um . . . *what*?' Lucy was baffled. She had come in for a *haircut*. They had given her a hair *wash* and a hair *condition*. And now they were offering her a hair *massage*?

'Shiatsu massage,' repeated Kacey. 'For your scalp.' She gave it a couple of exploratory digs with the tips of her fingers as the water hissed and gurgled on.

'Um—not really. Thanks, but I'd just like to get on with the actual . . . cutting,' said Lucy. Pins and needles were running down her arms now. The back of her skull had been pressed against the china rim for so long her blood supply was restricted.

'OK,' said Kacey and whipped the towel from Lucy's shoulders, wrapping it around her soaked head while she shoved her chair forward.

Millie herself took over as Lucy was led back to the seat in front of the mirror. Millie was a plump, middle-aged woman, also dressed in purple—to match the beige and purple colour scheme of the salon. Her hair was purple too. She looked very much like a plum on legs, thought Lucy, and had to stifle a giggle.

'So—going anywhere nice on holiday?' asked Millie, as she drew a thin metal comb through Lucy's waist-length dark hair, leaving cold prickly tracks across her scalp.

'Um . . . not sure yet,' hedged Lucy. 'Maybe Germany.'

'Germany?' Millie looked surprised.

'Well, no,' said Lucy, hurriedly—remembering that Germany wasn't a particularly common holiday destination for British people. 'Spain . . . probably. Yes. Spain.'

'Oooh, lovely. I love Spain,' said Millie, checking her watch and then staring out of the window as she continued to comb. Lucy began to wonder if the staff here were expecting something exciting to happen in the street. A carnival maybe. Or a robbery. 'Loads of sea, sun, sand, and . . . sangria!' went on Millie. 'And sexy men of course. I love a man with a tan.'

'Er . . .' said Lucy, but Millie didn't seem to expect an answer.

'You should get some highlights!' said Millie, abruptly snapping her attention back to Lucy's hair. 'You want some highlights? Everyone has highlights if they go on holiday. It's the holiday look. Streaks . . . I could do blonde streaks on you and leave it brown underneath. That'd look really amazing.'

'It would?' Lucy's photographic memory shuffled assorted pictures of hairstyles she had liked the look of when researching them back at the console on *Hessandrea.* None of them included streaks or two colours of hair on one head.

'Or pink,' went on Millie, smiling enthusiastically. 'KACEY—go and get the pink hair samples!'

Kacey scurried to the back of the small salon and retrieved a cardboard display board containing a dozen teardrop-shaped loops of . . . hair? Was that *hair*? Lucy stared, aghast, as Kacey began waving the display board under her nose.

'Here you go,' said Millie. 'Strawberry, peach, cherry . . .' Lucy thought, for a moment, she was being offered a fruity snack—but then Millie prodded a plump digit at the loops of hair on the card. They were all different fruity shades of pink. 'Of course, we'd need to bleach you first, so we could put the pink on top. Wouldn't work on dark hair like yours.'

Did they not like dark hair? Kacey had blonde hair, scrunched up on top in a little fountain of ringlets which didn't move when she shook her head. Another hairdresser, with ALEEESHA on her name badge was also blonde, with a fringe which looked as if it had been dipped in red ink. It clashed horribly with her orange lipstick as she silently wrapped an old lady's grey wisps into tight curlers.

'See,' said Millie, plonking a *Heat* magazine into her lap. 'It's all the rage!'

On the cover were three famous women, wearing very few clothes, lots of tattoos, and assorted shades of pink hair. 'U-um . . .' said Lucy, a wobble in her voice. How could getting a haircut suddenly turn out to be so complicated? And so hard to control? If she wasn't careful she was going to leave this place looking like a candyfloss on a stick. With tattoos, maybe.

'Let's get your cut done first, though,' said Millie. 'Then you can decide on the right shade while we're bleaching. Now . . .' She lifted a smooth ebony lock, pinching it out about a hand's length from Lucy's scalp. 'Nice and short and flicky, I think!' she muttered, more to herself than Lucy. And she lifted a pair of sharply pointed metal scissors, opened their sleek jaws, and plunged them towards the hair in her grip.

'STOP!'

The voice rang out in chorus with the door crashing open, its bell chiming frantically on a spring above.

Millie, Kacey, Aleeesha, the old lady, and Lucy all

jumped and then turned to stare. In the doorway stood Emma, Jay just behind her. Emma strode across to Lucy and tugged her hair out of Millie's hand.

'What's going on?' squeaked Millie.

'Nothing personal,' said Emma. 'She's just come to the wrong place.'

The stylist stood back, hands on her hips, looking affronted, while Emma whipped the damp towel away and hauled Lucy out of the chair.

'What's that supposed to mean?' snapped Millie, dropping her scissors into some blue anti-nit liquid in a glass container.

'Just that she's after a *real* haircut. Not a comedy one,' replied Emma.

'I beg your pardon!' squawked Millie.

'You should! I haven't forgotten, Millie, even if *you* have,' said Emma, grabbing Lucy's jacket from a hook and getting the phone from its pocket as Jay propelled their wet-haired evacuee towards the door. 'Two years ago,' went on Emma. 'Came in for a bob—went out with a bubble perm. *"Boost your roots, love,"* said you. *"Just let me give it some lift!"* Let me frazzle your hair and turn you into a frizzy fluffy *freak* for the next six months, more like!'

'Well, I never . . .' gasped Millie.

'Cut a decent style since the mid-nineteen-eighties?' clipped in Emma. 'No—you never. Come on, Lucy. Get out while you've still got your looks.'

Out on the pavement, Lucy stood, speechless, her hair hanging in damp clumps across her face.

Emma shook her phone in her face. 'Why didn't you switch this on? We've been trying to call you all night!'

'But . . . why?' asked Lucy, swaying slightly with the shock of it all.

'Because I told you to go to Millie's,' said Jay, looking embarrassed. 'How was I to know it was the worst hairdresser's on the island? I'm a boy. I'm not supposed to remember stuff like that!'

'How you can forget, I will never know!' Emma shook her head as they moved away from the steamed-up window of Millie's Salon, where the plum coloured proprietress was even now mouthing something unlovely at them behind the glass. 'I was traumatized by that woman's perm attack for *months.* At school they called me Puffball!'

'I—I didn't pay—for my hair *wash* and shiatsu massage,' said Lucy, putting her jacket on and looking back anxiously.

'You got a *shiatsu massage*?' asked Jay, looking baffled.

'Well . . . not really,' sighed Lucy. 'And the hair washing

was horrible. And they were trying to make me dye my hair pink.' She shuddered and then started to giggle. 'It was really, really stupid! I just didn't know how to get away. I'm so glad you both came in and rescued me.'

'Do you think we could rescue you from somewhere slightly more interesting next time?' asked Jay. 'I mean, open field, bike shop . . . hairdressers . . . it's not very action-hero, is it? A collapsing cave or a blazing high-rise would be much cooler.'

Lucy laughed. She *loved* Jay and Emma. They were like something off the comedy shows on TV. Then she noticed that Emma was peering closely at her phone; at the wording down its side to be more precise.

'Motokola?' Emma blinked and stared over at Lucy as they came to a stop by a crossing. 'Moto Kola?'

'I think that was a . . . a glitch . . . at the . . . the factory,' said Lucy, feeling her stupid face getting all hot again. *Why* did it keep doing that every time she lied? The assimilator had messed up a letter again, as it had for her Nipe trainers. How could something so incredibly clever make such stupid mistakes?

'It's a knock off,' said Jay, taking the phone from Emma and examining it with a grin. 'Why would a girl who spends a grand on a bike have to buy a cheap copy of a Motorola?'

'I . . . um . . . well . . . Mumgr—*Mum* gave it to me,' Lucy explained, taking the phone back from him and pocketing it in her jacket—which had at least got GAP printed on it, and not PAP or GAK. 'I don't know where she got it.'

'None of our business anyway,' said Emma, taking her arm and leading her across the road and around the corner into the next street. A couple of minutes later she drew to a halt. 'So—do you want a haircut or not?'

Lucy stared at the tall arched windows of HQ. In an instant her brain had registered everything about this place which was right—and compared it to everything about Millie's which had been wrong. This one was not steamed up. It didn't have greeny mould in the corners of the windows. It was beautifully lit inside and its pale cream tiled walls and floors were impeccably clean—no clumps of hair in the corners. There were no cardboard signs offering special wash-and-dry deals on Wednesdays for pensioners either—which was bad luck for the pensioners, because this place was so much better.

'Come on,' said Emma. 'If you must get your hair cut, you're getting it done here. It'll cost twice as much and look ten times better.'

Forty-five minutes later Lucy emerged into the warm, late morning sun feeling floaty and strange and delighted. Her long, long hair was now shorter—but not by much. It was what Paul, the immaculately groomed hair 'designer', called a 'manageable' length—just down to her shoulders. And he'd cut it with great concentration. At no point did he look out of the window or at his watch. He focused on her hair as if he were sculpting it out of marble for an emperor.

The way it hung in soft curves and moved in the breeze was fantastic. She felt like one of the girls on TV. 'I look like . . . a newsreader!' she murmured, staring in awe at her reflection in the HQ window.

Jay and Emma burst out laughing. 'You're nuts,' said Emma, but in a friendly way. 'Come on—let's get you some decent clothes.'

'Don't you like my GAP jacket?' asked Lucy, anxiously peering down at the label to be sure it really *was* spelt right.

'Yeah—it's OK,' said Emma. 'Funny material, though.' She rubbed a bit of the sleeve of the black denim-look jacket.

Lucy stared at the material, feeling her face redden *again.* The jacket was meant to look like thick cotton denim. So were her jeans. And the top was meant to look like cotton or viscose. But none of her clothes were made of anything from this world and when the light hit them at a certain angle, they looked . . . odd. She had hoped nobody would notice.

'Don't look so upset! You look fine!' Emma smiled and gave her a prod, sending yet another of those bizarre jolts though her nervous system that Lucy really hoped weren't obvious. She wondered if she would ever get used to physical contact with other people. It had been, after all, such a long time . . .

The shopping trip was exhausting. As much as she loved finding clothes and getting advice from Emma, as much as she enjoyed Jay's jokes and how embarrassed he got in the underwear department (he sidled off fast to the TV section)—it was all so incredibly new and intense. Much of what she saw was familiar to her because she'd been studying it all for so long, not just on *Hessandrea*'s console but in the recreation room too, where you could programme lots of 360-degree simulations of places on Earth and run through them. But nothing could fully prepare her for the onslaught of sound and smell and touch and taste in this new world—especially in busy shops. The constant babble of words and music and tannoy announcements and the beeps of the tills and the security systems and people's phones pinging and singing and ringing . . . it was all she could do not to turn and run, non-stop, back to Rowridge and its lovely, lonely transmitter, with home just a short vertical climb away. If she had been on her own she definitely would have by now. But Emma and Jay kept her just about calm enough to keep going. It would be rude and ungrateful to suddenly run away, after all the rescuing they'd done (she shuddered again as she recalled the pink loops of hair). So she kept her breathing steady and a smile on her face. She recognized some of the music played in the shops they trailed around—Michael Jackson, Madonna, The Kinks, Madness, The Cure . . . even a Level 42 track. And that made her feel better. Music always did.

'That's your favourite band, isn't it?' asked Emma, remembering Lucy's odd information-packed outburst about Level 42 the day they'd met her. Everyone on the island knew about the band. The musicians in it had grown up here before making it big in the eighties.

'Yes,' smiled Lucy. 'I love loads of bands and musicians. Music makes me so happy. Mark King is brilliant at bass guitar though, and I love bass. I'd like to learn and have my own Status Graphite KingBass one day.'

'If you say so,' chuckled Emma, shaking her head. 'Have you heard any twenty-first-century music recently . . . ?'

At last even Emma decided they'd done enough. They'd spent £789.45 on clothes and shoes and a couple of hats, and all three of them were loaded up with bags.

'We need food!' said Jay.

'Let me buy it for you!' said Lucy, quickly. 'After all your help, I should buy you lunch.'

Jay and Emma glanced at each other and then Jay said, 'Nah—you don't need to do that. We've got money. Let's just get some chips.'

'Really—I'd like to . . .' insisted Lucy.

'No need,' said Emma. 'Some other time maybe. It's been brilliant fun for us, helping you spend your money. You don't have to, like, *reward* us, you know. You don't worry about that with friends.'

Lucy stopped walking, carrier bags swinging to stillness in her hands. She realized, suddenly, and with complete certainty, that Jay and Emma *knew*. They may not know *what* they knew . . . but they knew. That she was an alien in their world. They were trying to *teach* her things. Basic things which any *normal* person would understand.

'What's the matter?' asked Jay, close beside her. Emma stopped next to him and waited, watching Lucy as she lifted her flushed face and glanced from one to the other.

'I know you know,' said Lucy. 'That I'm . . . strange.'

Jay shrugged. 'Define strange! We're pretty weird ourselves.'

'No . . . that's not what I mean. You *know* . . .' Lucy took a deep breath and tried to think clearly. It was all very well for Mumgram to tell her to keep her secret—but Mumgram knew nothing of this world. Not really. She was just a brilliant, highly intelligent machine. She couldn't *feel* anything. '. . . I have secrets,' went on Lucy. 'And I've made things up. But there are reasons. Good reasons.'

They were quiet, waiting for her to go on as shoppers bustled around them and a bus lumbered past. She noticed Jay tilt his head to one side, crinkling his eyes up, trying to work her out.

'Will you give me some time . . . a few days, maybe?' Lucy continued. 'And then I think I might be able to explain it to you—maybe. I just need . . . a bit more time here.'

Emma nodded and a second later Jay did the same. And then Emma said, 'Chips! I want chips *NOW*!'

When at last she climbed back up into *Hessandrea*, shopping bags knotted together and hanging off her shoulders, Lucy was so tired she could barely stand. She dumped her purchases on the lobby floor and staggered into her sleep pod. The feel and smell of her bedding drew her into its old embrace and she drifted into oblivion in less than thirty seconds.

On the bridge of *Hessandrea*, Mumgram suddenly emerged in a shaft of light. Her pleasant features remained untroubled but her words were grave. 'Atmostatis breach alert,' she said. 'Further data will follow.' An amber light on the console began to flash.

On the cloaked outer hull of the ship, four metres away from the slow-burn radiation of southwest England's TV, radio, and mobile phone cell transmitter, the stowaway made another tiny convulsive movement as its lifeblood began to ease back into motion.

Chapter 10

'God, you sound *awful.*' Emma made a sympathetic face at the phone, as if she could be seen through it.

Jay, lolling in the tree next to her, raised his eyebrows and then mouthed '*Lucy?*' His sister nodded and rolled her eyes but her smile was warm. She'd been looking forward to another Lucy episode as much as he had over the past two days since the haircut and the shopping spree. Lucy's arrival in their lives had doubled—no, tripled—the entertainment count. She'd hung out with Tia and Maisy over at Tia's place yesterday and tried to explain what Lucy was like to them, but it was impossible. You had to meet her to understand.

'Yeah—sounds like a cold,' went on Emma. 'What else would it be—malaria?' She paused and bit her lip, trying not to laugh as an alarmed squeak issued from her mobile. 'Lucy—it's a JOKE! Of *course* you haven't got malaria. Where on earth would you have caught malaria from?!'

Jay grinned. 'Tell her to come over. Mum can do her some honey and lemon.'

'Lucy—LUCY! We don't GET that sort of mosquito on the Isle of Wight!' went on Emma. 'Stop freaking out and come over to our place. Mum can make you some honey and lemon. What? No . . . no we don't mind you being infectious. We've probably had it anyway.'

One kilometre away and 153.2 metres up, Lucy caught her breath. She knew she was being ridiculous. She wasn't so stupid that she didn't know about the symptoms of malaria—and where you had to be to catch it. But the cold had filled her head with clog and left her feeling weak and feeble. Her skin was sore. She had been warned all about this by Mumgram but it was still scary. What had made her breath catch, though, was that offer . . . oh so casual . . . to go to Emma and Jay's house.

'I—I don't know if I should come,' she went on.

'Why not?' demanded Emma down the phone. 'You're not *that* ill. Don't be such a wimp!'

'It's not that . . . it's . . .'

'Look—surely your mum will be glad to get rid of you. All those coldy germs will be giving her a panic attack.'

'But . . . I couldn't invite you back here in return,' admitted Lucy.

'Lucy—you're not a guest of honour at a gala dinner!' spluttered Emma. 'We're just saying drop in, you daft tart!'

Lucy giggled, suddenly picturing a semi-human treacle tart in bloomers, blowing a whistle, and insanely dancing about. She felt a swell of longing to see her new best friends again. 'OK. I'm coming over.'

'Great!'

'See you in about twenty minutes.'

'Wait—Lucy!' Emma's voice rang out. 'Don't you think it would help if you knew our address?'

Lucy only just stopped herself saying she already knew it. Emma and Jay's locations were each picked out, thanks to their mobile signals, in yellow dots on the satellite view of *Hessandrea*'s console—a map overlaying the greenery, its fine glowing blue lines marking out the roads and dwellings. Jay was clearly right next to Emma now, as their dots were converging.

'OK—where are you?' asked Lucy and Emma relayed their address. It was just over the hill from the Rowridge station. Lucy could have seen it in *real* view from the bridge if there weren't so many trees in the way.

'I'll be there in twenty minutes,' she repeated and

ended the call with a frisson of excitement which made her claggy, coldy head buzz.

'Mumgram—I'm going out!' called Lucy, as she pulled on her trainers. *Real* ones, this time. Actual Nikes, bought in Newport. Not *Nipes*, synthesized in space. The Nikes went well with her genuine Levi jeans and her authentic Topshop checked shirt. Lucy grinned at herself in the full length mirror beside her sleeping pod. Did she look normal? She thought she did. She slid her phone into her jeans pocket, along with a thin wad of notes (tenners, Jay called them) which she might need, and a thick wad of tissues, which she definitely would.

'Your virus is still active,' stated Mumgram, at her shoulder. 'It would be wise to wait a further twenty-four hours before leaving *Hessandrea*.'

'I'm *fine*,' insisted Lucy. And she did feel much better than she had ten minutes ago when she'd phoned Emma. Perhaps it was just the prospect of seeing them again. It didn't matter. She was going.

'You have an elevated temperature. You need more recovery time,' pointed out Mumgram, but Lucy ignored her. She was singing a song from her favourite band as she ran to the exit bay. Her rendition was a little bunged up and sniffly, true, but it still sounded good to her own ears. '*Can't slow down, got to do what I do . . .*' She sang the next line even louder, adding the percussion and the bass bits so loudly that when Mumgram added, 'Warning. Possible atmostatis breach alert. Further data will follow. Consult bridge console,' she didn't even hear.

The hot honey and lemon seemed to go down well. Jay watched Lucy, fascinated, as she sipped at the steaming concoction in its small china mug and stared, wide-eyed, around their kitchen.

'Here you go,' said Mum, sliding a plate of homemade gingerbread in front of their guest. 'Ginger's also really good for colds. It boosts the immune system.'

'Well, yes . . .' said Lucy, '. . . it's more commonly used for gastrointestinal ailments and is a traditional remedy for morning sickness among pregnant women but it is also recognized for its antibacterial benefits in the upper respiratory tract.'

There was a short silence as everyone digested this information. Lucy suddenly looked around at them all, abashed. 'I'm sorry—I'm doing it again, aren't I?'

'Doing what?' asked Mum, agog. She was fascinated by Lucy too.

'Talking like an encyclopaedia,' said Lucy. 'It's a thing I do . . . I have a sort of . . . photographic memory and I store away information and then, when somebody mentions a bit of that information, all the rest of it just floods out . . . of my mouth.'

'You'd be very useful in a pub quiz,' said Mum, patting Lucy's shoulder.

Not for the first time, Jay noticed the way Lucy stiffened just a little, and then relaxed almost as quickly—as if she were in combat with her own nervous reactions. Now she was staring up at their mum as if she'd just discovered a new species. 'You're a great mum, aren't you?' she said, eyes wide, without a hint of mockery. 'A *real* one.'

Mum laughed, going to the sink to dry some dishes. 'I hope so! I haven't checked my label recently.'

'And you talk just like Jay and Emma do. You're funny,' said Lucy.

'I gather *your* mother's not too well.' Mum's voice sounded kind.

Lucy immediately reddened. She opened her mouth to reply and then sneezed rapidly, three times, burying her face in a tissue. 'Oh dear—I'm so sorry,' she mumbled. 'I really shouldn't have come. I'll infect you all and that would be awful.'

'You're only carrying the cold virus,' pointed out Jay. 'Not a deadly plague. You're not going to wipe out humanity.'

'No,' giggled Lucy. 'Of course not.' She bit into the gingerbread and it tasted so extraordinarily fabulous she was glad she had a cold to disguise the tears in her eyes. She'd bitten into her first apple that morning and nearly passed out with delight. Would she ever get used to being overwhelmed?

A kilometre away, 153.1 metres up, on the cloaked outer hull of the ship, the stowaway unfolded wings of thin, tough skin as its blood warmed and coursed faster through its dilating veins. The movement sent ripples of disruptive energy into the thick soup of radiation around the mast which tethered Hessandrea to the new world. Its senses had been acute for four days, mapping the locality and the suitable hosts it contained. But its physical recovery was much slower. It would need to feed as soon as it could descend.

Feed.

And then breed.

'So—when did you arrive on the island?' Mum asked, whipping up some chocolate cake mixture. 'Quite recently?'

'Yes—just a few days ago,' said Lucy, on her third bit of gingerbread. 'This is fantastic! I *love* real food!'

She held the sticky golden square in her hand

reverently, gazing at it as if it were a lump of moon rock, thought Jay.

'Don't you get any real food at home, then?' asked Emma, pulling some towels out of the drier and folding them onto a nearby chair. Only Jay wasn't busy; he was lazing in a chair opposite Lucy at the table, studying her like she was a zoo exhibit. Lucy didn't seem to mind, Emma noted.

'Oh well—yes,' said Lucy. 'I mean—a very balanced diet. Carbohydrate, protein, fats, minerals and vitamins, and fibre.'

'Sounds yummy.' Emma winced. 'I guess your poor mum can't do any cooking for you, then?'

'No,' said Lucy. 'No, she can't do that. She does look after me though. She's always giving me good advice.'

'Of course she is,' said Mum, with a warning glare at Emma. 'You don't have to be a good cook to be a loving mum. I'm sure she loves you very much.'

'Yes,' said Lucy quietly.

Jay was just opening his mouth to ask more about Lucy's home life when he remembered their promise to this odd girl. To let her have a few more days before she told them her secrets. He would keep quiet about the strange look on her face just then. It was by no means the oddest thing about her. He could wait.

And then all such thoughts were wiped out of his head. There was a sudden flash of light—intensely green. And then two more—but longer—flickering across the sky beyond the window.

'What the heck was *that*?!' squeaked Mum, peering out. Jay ran to the door and into the back garden. Above them the sky was cloudy—a low, pearly grey which seemed to sag against the tops of the trees. Mum, Emma, and Lucy joined him, all staring up. 'What was it?' said Mum.

'Don't know,' said Jay, turning slowly and scanning the sky in all directions. 'A storm coming, maybe.'

'A *green* storm?' said Mum.

'We saw a green flash a few days ago, too,' said Emma. 'Just before we met you, Lucy.'

Mum looked solemn. 'It's like something out of *The War of the Worlds* . . . you know . . . the green flashes through space, coming from Mars.'

'Mu-um!' Emma nudged her, looking spooked. 'Don't say stuff like that.'

'Well,' said Mum, 'you never know . . . "The chances of anything coming from Mars are a million to one," they said . . .' She grinned. '"But still . . . they come!" Spaceships with little green men from Mars!'

'Not Mars,' muttered Lucy. 'Nothing there. Far more

likely to be a Quorat planet like Ayot. But *they'd* come by cleftonique corridor. They wouldn't mess around with ships.'

'You what, love?' asked Mum, touching Lucy's shoulder again, as if she thought their cold-ridden guest was a little soft in the head. *Which she might well be,* thought Jay. What *was* she on about?

Lucy stared at their mother, looking suddenly shocked and caught out. 'I—I mean . . . it was just something I read in a book once,' she blurted, going scarlet. 'I don't know anything about it.'

'Did you see that?' Suddenly the small garden was even fuller as Nick Dobson arrived.

'Yes! Green flashes! Very odd!' said Mum. 'Sorry if it disturbed you, Mr Dobson.'

The man stopped in his tracks, tilting his head to one side and smiling at her. 'Well, if it did, Mrs Hamlyn, I can hardly hold *you* to blame. And please . . . call me Nick!'

Mum laughed. 'OK . . . Nick. And you'd better call *me* Sue.'

'Could it be the transmitter?' asked Nick. 'Have you seen that kind of thing before?'

Mum shook her head. 'I've never noticed anything odd at all, the only thing is the null. The occasional broadcasting blackout we get in strange atmospheric conditions. We get it because we're so close. You'd think being this close to it, we'd have perfect pictures and sound at all times, but it doesn't work like that.'

Nick peered up at the distant metal finger pointing up into the clouds. 'Maybe someone's messing with it. Perhaps someone's flown a kite against it—or climbed the mast . . .'

'They'd find it hard!' said Jay. 'They'd have to get past a lot of locked fences and barbed wire and then up a sheer vertical climb—and their brains would boil before they were halfway up.'

'Don't be so dramatic,' said Mum. 'They wouldn't. You might feel a bit queasy though. There's a lot of radiation coming off that thing. Oh—nothing dangerous at this distance,' she added hurriedly, and Jay knew she was thinking of her business as one of her best customers stood there beside her. 'It's perfectly safe here! It's only if you're right up against it that you might feel unwell.'

'I know,' said Nick. 'I'm not worried about the transmitter itself. But what if someone was trying to tamper with it? Attach something alien to it? Could they?'

'What—you mean, like terrorists or something?' asked Emma, her eyes wide.

He grinned and shrugged. 'Well . . . I don't know about that, but . . . what's the security like up there?'

'We've never really thought about it,' said Jay. 'It's just a mast, some buildings, some fields, and a lot of bored sheep. But if you tried to get inside it would probably be a different story. There are people there. We see them driving up to it.'

'I think I might take a look,' said Nick.

'Really?' asked Mum. 'You really think you should? Is that what a writer always does . . . check out hunches?' Jay noticed that she suddenly looked rather girlish, staring up at Nick, and he shot Emma a freaked-out look, but Emma seemed delighted. She was even shiftily putting her thumbs up behind Mum's back.

'I shouldn't go there,' said Lucy suddenly (exactly what Jay had been thinking—but not about the mast).

Nick turned around, noticing her for the first time. 'Oh—hello. Sorry, we've not been introduced,' he said. 'I'm Nick—one of Sue's lodge guests.' He held out a hand for her to shake and she stared at it for a few seconds before shaking it.

'Hello . . . I'm Lucy. Jay and Emma's friend.'

'Why do you think I shouldn't go, then, Lucy?' asked Nick, giving her a quizzical look. 'Do you think my brains will boil if I get too close?'

'Um . . . they might,' she said. 'I mean . . . I wouldn't know. But I don't think the green flashing was anything to do with the transmitter. I don't think it was even in that part of the sky. And . . . anyway, it's private property and if you go up there you might get into trouble and—'

'Well, I'm not planning to break in!' he said. 'Just to go and talk to the staff up there. Check that everything's OK.'

'Or we could call the police,' said Mum. 'Perhaps that would be the best thing to do. They could contact the transmitter station staff and check it out and maybe let us know that everything's OK.'

Nick looked around at them all and shook his head. 'You lot,' he said, 'have no sense of adventure. I'm going! If I come back green with my brains dribbling out of my nose, shoot me . . .'

'No way!' said Jay. 'We're coming with you!'

Nick shrugged and chuckled. 'OK. As long as you don't slow me down when the aliens give chase.'

'Or the zombies,' said Jay in a foreboding theatrical voice. 'Seeking juicy mast engineers' brains! You coming, Lucy? Em?'

'Yeah!' said Emma, and Lucy nodded, looking rather ill at ease, Jay noticed. Maybe this talk of invaders from Mars had actually scared her.

'Are you joining us, Sue?' asked Nick. 'Ready for some adventure?!'

'Well, I'd love to go alien spotting with you,' said Mum. 'But I've got new guests arriving in an hour and I have to get their lodge ready. You lot go. And if I see another green flash and smell barbecued human on the breeze, I'll know not to bother with clean towels for you today . . .'

Chapter 11

It took twenty minutes to reach the mast site. Jay led them through a sloping wood, up to the perimeter of the field where the mast towered like a skinny metal colossus over the low, flat-roofed buildings at its base. Skirting the wire fence, they came to a tarmac road leading into the site, past wide iron gates which stood open. A sign warned them off proceeding into the grounds but it didn't threaten attack dogs or electrocution on the spot.

'I don't think they're bothered,' said Jay. 'Nobody comes here. It's not that exciting.'

'Not to you, maybe,' muttered Nick, tipping his head back to take in the very top of the mast, which poked a long, thin white tube into the low cloud. He turned slowly, taking in the scores of metal cables fanning out from the mast across the land around them, pinning it into the ground like tent guy ropes. Except guy ropes didn't need to be attached to immense metal pegs the length of three men, driven into huge concrete footings which probably reached several metres down into the earth.

'Who'd bother to come here?' asked Emma.

'I don't know,' answered Nick. 'Kids messing about, maybe? Or someone with a transmitter fixation. You get some odd types obsessing about these things sometimes.'

'So—not a gang of international activists, then?' said Jay.

Nick laughed but for the first time that prickling sensation he'd felt a couple of days ago took some form. International activists? *Oh come on. You were on active duty a little too long, Dobson,* he told himself. *Should've retired sooner.*

'Probably not, Jay,' he said aloud, striding past the gates. 'But you can never be sure. Someone could come here to make a point . . . get noticed. And knocking out the television, radio, and phone cell signals for most of southern England probably *would* get them noticed.'

'You're not just walking in there, are you?' asked Jay.

'I do seem to be,' said Nick.

'Right . . . well, I'm coming too.' Jay ran to catch up with him, feeling excitement building in his belly. Maybe this guy was on to something. Maybe a gang of international activists was even now holding the small crew of the station at gunpoint while they shot out their controls and got ready to climb the mast and hang some kind of . . . of . . . skull and crossbones type thing . . . his imagination wound up, slightly lamely, even *he* had to admit.

'OK,' said Nick. 'If you must. Just let me do the talking. You two coming with us?' He turned around to peer at Emma and Lucy by the gate.

Lucy shook her head vigorously and Emma shrugged. 'I'll wait here with her. Keep an eye out for more spooky green flares.'

As Jay and this new man, Nick, walked up to the building, Lucy kept her eyes steadily on them. She must *not* look at the mast. She must not even *think* about *Hessandrea.* There was no reason to panic. This was nothing at all to do with her. And even if it was, there was no way anyone here could find out about it. *Hessandrea* was cloaked, completely. She was invisible not only to the naked eye, but also to radar and all other forms of Earth scanning and tracking technology. This could be a problem if some form of aircraft—a helicopter, perhaps—ever attempted to fly close to her and that was just *one* of the reasons why the ship had docked at the mast. No aircraft would ever fly this close to such a structure—it was far too dangerous.

Of course, birds could strike it at any time—except that they wouldn't. Because birds and bats and flying insects could see it. Well, not see it exactly, but sense its presence on a different frequency in a way that humans could not. They flew around it. Otherwise there would be a pile of winged corpses under the mast by now, which certainly *would* attract attention.

Even knowing all this, Lucy felt nervous and exposed. That *Nick* . . . he was different to Emma and Jay and their lovely cake-baking mum. He was . . . professional. There was something in the way he walked. He reminded her of characters she'd seen in action films. Full of confidence and authority. Intelligent and capable. Maybe dangerous. She meant to keep Nick at a distance.

'You're looking very worried,' said Emma. 'You don't really believe what Mum said about aliens, do you?' She grinned and gave Lucy a small nudge.

'What? Aliens?' Lucy laughed. Quite raucously. 'That would be ridiculous.' She gulped and turned away, allowing a breeze which riffled the leaves of the trees on the perimeter to cool her hot face. For a while there was only silence, apart from the regular cawing of a family of rooks, nesting nearby.

'Well, I suppose it's always *possible,*' Emma went on. There was a small, abandoned flatbed truck parked on a stony area near the gate, and she climbed up onto the back of it, walking along its edge, arms aloft, wobbling slightly. 'I mean—it's a huge universe. Stands to reason there must be other planets out there with life forms on them. Somewhere. But if they'd just travelled, like, three million light years or something, I reckon they'd probably find something a bit more exciting to do than hang around *this* backwater.'

'It's very exciting here,' said Lucy, before she could stop herself. 'It's . . . amazing.'

Emma peered over at her, arms still outstretched, eyebrows arched high. 'Lucy—you really haven't been out much for a while, have you?'

Lucy shrugged and blew her nose. 'That's fair to say,' she agreed. 'Although I've travelled a lot.'

Emma fell off the truck. Overbalancing with a whirl of arms she toppled over sideways and hit the stony ground hard. Lucy rushed over to her. 'Emma! Are you OK?'

Emma grunted and got to her feet, dusting herself off and peering at a reddening graze on her elbow. 'One more for the collection,' she muttered.

'It's the dyspraxia, isn't it?' asked Lucy. 'You've not got very good coordination.'

'Well done!' snapped Emma. 'One gold star for paying

attention.' She rubbed her elbow, wincing, and walked back towards the open gate, watching for Nick and Jay.

Lucy picked up a pebble. She chose a smooth round one which fitted neatly into the dip of her palm. 'Here—Emma—catch!'

Emma turned around just in time for the pebble to strike her bad arm and rebound into some tall grass by the gatepost. 'Well, thanks, Lucy!' she said. 'Rub it in, why don't you?'

'Sorry!' Lucy retrieved the pebble. 'But try again.' She chucked the pebble more carefully, with a gentle upswing. This time Emma caught it. 'Well done!' called Lucy, beaming.

Emma gave her a withering look. 'A four year old could've caught *that*!' she said. 'In case you think you're helping—you're not.'

'Chuck it into your other hand,' said Lucy.

'What?'

'Just—do it. Chuck it across. Just a little way.'

Emma looked annoyed but she did it. The pebble flew a short distance and landed in her other palm.

'Now do it again. The other way,' said Lucy.

Emma rolled her eyes, but she threw the pebble and caught it again.

'Keep going. From side to side.'

'What's your point, Lucy?' said Emma, although she continued to throw the stone in tiny arcs from one palm to the other.

'Just . . . see if you can keep doing it until Jay and Nick come back,' said Lucy.

'Why?!'

'Because I'm asking you to.' Lucy smiled at her. 'Please.'

Emma gave her another hard look, but then shrugged and carried on flipping the pebble from one hand to the other.

'What's your school like, then?' asked Lucy, standing beside her and watching the low building expectantly. 'Do you like it?'

'S'OK, I suppose,' said Emma. 'I've got a couple of mates: Tia and Maisy. They're nice. You can meet them some time, if you like. But they're in different sets to me at school because they're clever. I'm rubbish at most things. Especially sports. When they have to pick teams they fight over me.'

'They fight over you?' echoed Lucy. 'Why?'

'Why d'you think? Because they don't *want* me. If I go on anybody's team I slash their odds of winning by at least fifty per cent! I've scored more own goals in hockey and netball than anyone else in the history of my school. *I* wouldn't want me on my team either! But I can never get me *off* my team. Gah! See? I can't even do *this*!' The pebble dropped to her feet and she kicked it away angrily.

Lucy picked it up and gave it back to her. 'Keep going.'

'Are you *trying* to make me feel stupid?' demanded Emma, her eyes glinting angrily as she rounded on Lucy.

'No! Of course not! I'm just encouraging you to lay down some neural pathways!'

'What?!'

'Neural pathways . . . you know . . . new routes through your cerebellum! The part of your brain which isn't working properly. If you keep doing the thing with the pebble . . . and a few other exercises like it . . . you start to train that bit of your brain to get better at coordination.'

Emma stared at her. 'Is that a fact?' Her voice was colder than the pebble in her palm. 'I have *heard* about the cerebellum, you know! *I'm* the one who got stuck with a useless one! I tried this stupid exercise thing years ago and it didn't work.'

'How old were you, last time you tried?'

'I don't know. Eight or nine.'

'Well . . . that may have been a bit too young. Studies show that—'

'Lucy! Just . . . leave it, will you?!' snapped Emma.

Lucy felt confused and troubled. She wanted to help Emma—not make her feel bad. Only last night she had studied some of the latest online scientific papers about dyspraxia and dyslexia and discovered a training system believed to work very well for sufferers. She had memorized it and felt sure she could take Emma through it and help her very quickly. Within days. But . . . here she was again—not behaving like a normal teenager. She was being . . .

'Weird,' said Emma. 'You're weird, you know that?' But there was a glimmer of humour in her face. 'It's OK, Lucy, I know you're trying to help. Just . . .' She pocketed the pebble. 'Maybe later, OK? I've been clumsy and useless for years. I'm used to it.'

'OK, later,' said Lucy. She could programme a whole system to calibrate the level of Emma's problem. She could design a series of exercises and run a 360-degree simulation in the gym or the rec room which would be fun and exciting and would work really fast and . . .

She stopped her fevered plans dead. That was impossible. She could never show Emma her home. Never. She was being an idiot.

Nick and Jay came back, walking together, looking as if nothing much had happened.

'What did they say?' called out Emma. 'Have they had their faces melted by aliens?'

Nick grinned and shook his head as he reached the gate. 'Only one guy there today,' he said. 'Friendly enough, considering we were trespassers. He recognized Jay here as a neighbour so he didn't try to shoot us.' He chuckled. 'Says they noticed a power surge about forty-five minutes ago. Didn't see anything green! Thinks it's just an atmospheric disturbance. There's nothing unusual up there.'

'Did you believe him?' asked Lucy.

Nick regarded her coolly. 'Do you?'

For a moment she didn't know what to say. She was relieved when Jay chimed in.

'I don't think he was keeping anything from us,' he offered. 'And if he was buried inside that place, working, he probably *didn't* see anything up in the sky. There aren't many windows and most of them have the blinds down.'

'So—no big adventure then!' sighed Emma. 'Nothing for you to write about, Nick.'

Nick smiled tightly but said nothing. He flicked another appraising glance at Lucy and then told himself to cut it out. *You're looking for drama where there is none. Haven't you had enough for one life?*

But still, there was the feeling he'd had earlier

that week. A day or so later he'd no longer noticed it, but maybe that was because he was getting used to it. Somewhere inside him a spring was coiled, ready for action. *For what?* he asked himself, as they retraced their steps back through the woods. *You're not in a war zone any more. You're on the Isle of Wight! Get a grip.*

Chapter 12

'Wow. I mean . . . I know Basingstoke's some way from the coast but . . . truly?' Emma stared at Lucy who was gazing across Bembridge Harbour as if she were witnessing one of the Seven Wonders of the World. 'You've really never been to the seaside before?'

'Well, I may have done, when I was little. Before I was four,' said Lucy. 'I don't remember. I've seen it many times on TV, though. Keep rolling, Em!'

Emma sighed, and continued rolling the tin of beans across the warm paving slab she was sitting on cross-legged, less than half a metre from the harbour wall. The tin rolled only about twenty centimetres from hand to hand. It couldn't be much easier. Even so, while she was talking, it sometimes changed direction and she had to break off her conversation and snatch it back before it rolled away.

'Is your Mum allergic to days out too, then?' asked

Emma, rolling the tin back and forth. 'Has she been like this for years?'

'She hasn't been outside for about ten years,' said Lucy, gazing out across the water, her voice soft.

Emma immediately felt stupid and insensitive, realizing it must be really difficult to have nobody to take you anywhere. Lucy hadn't mentioned a dad, so maybe her mum was a single parent too. 'It was nice of her to let you sleep over with me last night,' she said. 'Considering she's never met me or Jay or Mum.'

'She trusts me,' said Lucy. 'She knows I wouldn't make friends with someone unless they were nice. I loved sleeping over. I'm sorry I can't take you back to sleep over at my place.' She bit her lip. She *was* sorry. She hadn't expected this intense need to share her secret life with a friend. And in truth Mumgram wouldn't have approved of her sleepover with Emma at *all.* Which was precisely why she hadn't told her. She hadn't gone back to *Hessandrea* after their expedition up to the mast. She'd just stayed at the cottage, after Emma asked her mum and her mum had said yes, sleeping on a pull-out bed in Emma's room. It had been peculiar to share her sleeping time in a different room with someone else. Peculiar and lovely.

'Keep rolling . . .' said Lucy, glancing back at the tin of beans. 'Faster if you can.'

'I can't believe this is going to make *any difference* to me at all!' Emma huffed. 'You're a loony. And I'm a nutjob for going along with it. If someone from school sees me doing this I'll never hear the last of it.'

Lucy smiled and said nothing. She wondered if Emma realized that she was now able to talk *and* roll the baked beans tin without looking at it all the time. She'd only lost momentum three times in the past five minutes. She was improving; laying down another neural pathway.

Jay arrived with hotdogs from the small café behind them. 'We've got about an hour before we need to be back at the car park,' he told them as Emma gratefully stood her tin up and took her food from him. He placed another bun with its skinny, hot cargo, piped with ketchup, into Lucy's hands. He noted curiously how she *marvelled* at it, before shaking his head and adding: 'Mum says if we don't show up she'll drive home without us and we'll have to catch the bus.'

'Could we? Could we catch the bus?' breathed Lucy.

'Oh no—don't tell me?' laughed Emma. 'You've never been on a bus before!' On the hair cut day, laden down with so much shopping, they had agreed to Lucy paying for a taxi back to Rowridge. She'd been fit to burst about *that*, too.

Lucy blushed. Again. She cursed herself for being

such an idiot. The trouble with Jay and Emma was that they were so nice, so much fun to be around, that she kept forgetting to act out her role. She kept . . . being herself! She was doing hardly *any* lying. How on earth was she ever going to fit in here if she didn't learn to lie? She focused on the hotdog and beamed at them. '*Great!* Mechanically recovered unspecified meat, saturated fat, and corn syrup, formed into a *stick*!'

There was a short silence while Jay and Emma chewed somewhat less enthusiastically. Lucy, though, bit into her hotdog with reverence . . . and then began to wolf it down with great gusto. 'I shall probably be sick later,' she informed them cheerily. 'Isn't it fab?'

'So . . .' said Emma, at length. 'What do you think of the seaside, then, Lucy? Although it's not proper seaside, here. We should take you to Shanklin or Sandown or Ventnor some time. That's *proper* seaside. This is a just a harbour. A working harbour, really—not a touristy one. No penny arcades or ice-cream shops here.' She sighed.

Lucy let her legs swing over the low harbour wall, mirrored in the calm turquoise water below. 'It's beautiful.' She closed her eyes, feeling the warm sun on her face and the light breeze playing with her hair. The smell was intoxicating—rich with salt, minerals, and boat engine oil, hot paint and tar, mixed with the scent of the hotdog stall and the sweet aroma of sun lotion on her skin (which Emma had insisted she buy and put on). The sound of gulls overhead punctuated the ever-present burble of the water and an occasional shout or burst of laughter rang out from the yachts and small fishing boats out on the water. Combined with the company of these most important new people in her life, it gave her a whoosh of blissful contentment. 'It's just . . . better than anything I ever imagined.'

She opened her eyes to find Jay and Emma openly smiling at her.

'I guess we're lucky,' said Jay. 'We've always had it. Because Mum's sister lives here we come over quite often when they want a bit of a gossip. And we've been to every other beach on the island too. Of course, a lot of the time it's throwing it down with rain!'

'We went on holiday to Wales once,' said Emma. 'In the Brecon Beacons—miles from the sea. It was lovely but it was . . . just . . . wrong. I have to be near the sea. It's in my blood!'

'Our dad was a sailor,' explained Jay. 'He loved the sea too. Used to take us out on his boat when we were little . . . before he went . . .'

'Oh. Did he die?' asked Lucy, looking stricken. 'At sea . . . ?'

Jay snorted. 'No! He went to Australia! With a nail technician.'

'Oh! *Oh* . . . you mean . . . he *ran away with another woman*!' breathed Lucy, thinking of *EastEnders* and *Hollyoaks,* where this kind of drama happened nearly every week. 'Was there a *love triangle*?!'

Emma and Jay shrieked with laughter. 'You are SO over the top, Lucy!' gurgled Emma. 'Love triangle! No way. Mum chucked him out as soon as she found out. She said his nails had never looked so good and that's what helped her to work it out. He was getting 'em buffed by his scarlet woman.'

'He's been gone for years,' said Jay. 'He sends Christmas and birthday presents and all that and phones us up sometimes. Keeps saying we should go and visit them in Sydney. We might one day. He's OK, really. Even Mum laughs about it now.'

'Oh—I see.' Lucy screwed up her empty hotdog wrapper and shot it accurately into a nearby bin. 'Well—that's OK then. So your mum can get together with Nick.'

Emma cackled again while Jay looked appalled. 'Mum doesn't have boyfriends!' he exclaimed.

Lucy looked at Emma, who was biting her lip but smiling. 'That could change,' she said.

Jay shuddered and chucked his remaining half of

hotdog into the bin after Lucy's. Emma did the same with the remains of hers, and missed.

'What about *your* dad?' asked Emma.

'I don't really remember him,' said Lucy. 'He was a scientist but he died.'

'Oh . . . sorry,' said Emma.

They walked along the harbour wall, checking out the yachts and motor boats tied up at the pontoons. It was a modest harbour with small craft, many wooden and well used; many clearly moored at the ready for fishing trips rather than for showing off, like the yachts Lucy had seen in films of Monaco and St Tropez.

'Don't walk so close to the edge, Lucy!' warned Emma. 'It's deeper water than it looks!'

Lucy grinned. 'I'm fine,' she reassured her friends. 'I have excellent balance!' To prove it she leapt half a metre up onto the thick, low wooden barrier which separated them from the drop into the harbour. Below, only a metre or two from the limpet-encrusted harbour wall, the wooden pathway of a pontoon floated. Several small boats were secured to it, one or two with their owners aboard, busy with engine maintenance or fishing tackle. 'Watch this!' Lucy felt another rush of bliss as she took three steps and then did a somersault through the air, landing back on the beam with her arms outstretched, like the gymnast she *must remember to pretend to be.*

There were gasps of admiration—not just from Emma and Jay but from people sitting on benches near the hotdog stall, too. Lucy felt delight flood through her. With a glance she measured her position and the length of the wooden barrier, and did a second somersault. Perfectly. More gasps and even a little applause.

'Lucy! Be careful—it's a bit . . .' Jay warned.

But Jay was *always* warning. So was Emma. They should just relax occasionally, thought Lucy.

'Oily,' concluded Jay, as Lucy did another perfect forward flip, landed like an Olympic athlete, slid the sole of one Nike trainer across the sun-warmed slick of pitch on the end of the barrier, did the splits, and fell sideways off the harbour wall.

Emma and Jay stared at each other in horror for a second and then ran to peer over the edge where the *SPLOSH* had sent a fan of water up into a split-second rainbow. 'LUCY!' yelled Jay at their friend's pale form beneath the water. Lucy's face bloomed up through the surface, gasping, her hair floating around her like dark seaweed and her eyes wide with shock.

'JAY!' she gurgled, before going under again, her hands flailing wildly, trying to grab the pontoon. She rose up a second time, long enough to squeak: 'Can't

SWIM!' before sinking under again. Jay jumped in, feet first, hoping he wouldn't brain himself on the edge of the pontoon as he plummeted past.

Emma hung over the edge of the wooden barrier, shouting after them both in panic, her heart racing. She knew that there couldn't really be much danger . . . they were in easy reach of the pontoon. But it was a high tide and the water was deep and full of chains and lines and anchors. What if one of them got caught up?!

A fair-haired man appeared from a nearby boat and ran along the pontoon just as Lucy shot up out of the water again, tearing in great breaths of air, Jay's hands on her arms, pushing her up. The man reached down and grabbed Lucy. 'C'mon—out you come!' he grunted, heaving her out of the water and onto the wooden deck where she collapsed in a shaking, soggy heap, coughing and spluttering, her hair hanging like bladderwrack around her wet pale face.

'You too, mate,' said the man, leaning out to offer an arm to Jay, who was attempting to climb onto the pontoon from the water. It was very hard to pull himself out at such a tight, awkward angle. The man hoisted him up and soon he and Lucy sat, shivering, together. Emma got to her feet and ran the length of the harbour wall until she found the marina gate which led down to the pontoon, and then hurtled along it, the narrow floating deck wallowing under her fast feet.

'It's OK—don't panic,' said the man as Emma arrived. 'They're fine. They're both OK. Although she might have swallowed some Bembridge beer!' He pointed to Lucy who was still coughing, but looking a better colour now. The man had grabbed blankets from his nearby boat and both Lucy and Jay were wrapped in them.

'Should I ring for an ambulance?' called a young woman from the harbourside, waving a mobile phone from within a small, interested crowd of onlookers.

'No—no—we're fine!' called back Jay, waving his thanks. 'Just a bit wet—and stupid!' The passer-by nodded and went on her way, taking the small interested crowd with her.

'Sorry,' muttered Lucy. 'You weren't stupid, Jay. I was. I shouldn't have been doing flips . . .' She gazed up at their rescuer, who was watching the scene with an amused but sympathetic smile. 'It was my own stupid . . . *MARK*!'

'You what?' grunted Jay, between making noises like a cat bringing up a furball as he tried to get some seawater out of his nose.

Emma saw Lucy's face go from waxy white to fuchsia pink in a matter of seconds, her eyes widening until she looked like a six year old meeting Santa. And for Lucy this was fairly close. Emma shook her head in wonder. Could this week get any weirder? Lucy's rescuer was her musical hero. The guy from Level 42.

It was Mark King.

Chapter 13

'Um . . . Coke? That might help . . .' Their rescuer brought out a couple of cans and knelt on the pontoon in pale blue denim cut-offs and a stripy blue T-shirt. Emma had seen him on TV and in the *Isle of Wight County Press* many times, doing charity stuff and promoting concerts and so on. As he handed a can to Jay who thanked him and quickly drank from it, he seemed at once familiar and strange. Like a distant relative suddenly arriving on your doorstep.

Lucy hadn't said a word since she'd recognized her hero. She just continued to stare at him, open-mouthed, her eyes shining. 'Lucy—could you *be* less cool?' asked Jay, nudging her.

Lucy just gave out a kind of squeak as the man handed her a Coke, having opened it for her first. 'I think you may need some sugar,' he said.

'Thanks,' said Emma. 'It's really kind of you. Lucy's . . . well, she's a bit of a fan.'

His pale eyebrows rose. 'Really? That's nice.' He shot a slightly worried look at Jay and Emma.

'Oh no—she hasn't been *stalking* you or anything!' Emma added hurriedly. 'We had no idea this was your boat. She was just being an idiot and showing off her gymnastic stuff on the edge of the harbour and . . . well . . . *splosh*!'

The man grinned at Lucy. 'Well, no fan's ever tried to *drown* themselves to get my attention before.'

'I didn't!' protested Lucy, finding her voice at last and now releasing it in a torrent. 'I NEVER thought I would ever *meet* you, I just LOVE your music, especially "Starchild", because I am one, well not actually but in many ways, yes, because, well, I can't really say why because I said I wouldn't although it's kind of hard, very much harder than I thought it would be, I'm no good at making things up, but you make up music all the time and it travels right across the universe, although you probably don't know that, have you got your bass with you; the Status one with the lights on it . . . ?'

For a few seconds there was nothing but the gentle slap of the water against the harbour wall and the cry of a gull overhead as they all stared at Lucy, who had now shrugged off her blanket and was looking the picture of health and delight. Her hero rubbed his chin, peering at her curiously, and said: 'D'you really think I take a bass guitar with me everywhere I go?' He chuckled. 'Even on my fishing boat?'

'Well . . .' Lucy looked abashed. 'No—I suppose that would be silly.'

He got to his feet and shrugged, blowing out a short breath. 'I've only got the Sigma semi-acoustic. I mean . . . any other kind would need an amp—and that *would* be silly. Come on—you might as well come and have a look.'

'The Sigma!' breathed Lucy, her face awash with awe. She bounced up, heedless of her soaked trainers squelching on the deck, and followed him onto the small boat.

'Seriously—she's *not* a stalker!' added Emma, noting the man's bemused expression. She glanced at her watch. 'We've only got about five minutes, and then we'll miss our lift back home. So . . . just quickly, Lucy—OK. A quick look at the bass . . . and try not to dribble on it!'

They stepped onto the deck and Mark ducked down into a tiny, tapering cabin filled with pale cream padded seating around a small table. There were boxes of angling gear on the table, along with a tall thermos flask, a packet of biscuits, and a pile of magazines. At the far end of the cabin seats, half under a blanket, lay an acoustic bass guitar. The musician turned back to them, holding it at a careful angle above the table with a slightly self-conscious grin. 'I *know*,' he said, glancing at Emma and Jay. 'I am a sad stereotype! But I sometimes get song ideas when I'm out at sea.'

Lucy was staring at the bass as if it were the Holy Grail. 'It's amazing!' she murmured. 'Can you . . . ?'

But he'd already put the instrument across one knee and begun to slap out a distinctive bass line which Jay and Emma both recognized. '"Lessons In Love", yeah?' said Jay. Mum had a couple of Level 42 CDs and played them sometimes in the car.

Mark nodded and then finished with a flourish, patting the golden varnished wood with affection. 'But you need to get home and get dry,' he said.

'Just a little more!' begged Lucy, aghast that this encounter was to be so brief.

He laughed again, shaking his head. 'You can hear some more tomorrow if you like,' he added, smiling at Lucy. 'We're doing a charity gig up at Freshwater.' He reached across to a shelf, plucked an A5 flier off a pile and handed it to her. 'The tickets are sold out but if you want to come I'll ask the guys on the gate to make room for you.'

'Oh yes! Yes, we will!' Lucy literally jumped up and down, making the little boat wallow. 'At Freshwater?' She glanced at Jay and Emma.

'It's not far from our place,' said Jay. 'Is it in the grounds of the big hotel? Freshwater View?' he asked Mark.

Mark nodded. 'Yup—from four p.m. But we'll be sound-checking all afternoon, so if you're passing, drop in and I'll introduce you to the boys—if you can make it. You might have something better to do.'

'I will have *nothing* better to do tomorrow,' declared Lucy. 'Nothing!'

'It'll probably be loud!' he warned. 'Our PA's got sub bass woofers that can rearrange your internal organs!' He winked.

'Can't be too bass-y for me!' said Lucy.

She looked so woebegone as Emma tried to steer her off the boat. 'Come on,' Emma muttered. 'We mustn't outstay our welcome! And don't forget to thank him for saving your life!'

'Oy!' protested Jay. 'I think you'll find *I* was the one doing the saving!'

Lucy turned and clasped her hero's hand. It felt warm and dry and creased—different to Jay's and Emma's. 'Thank you!' she said. 'For pulling Jay and me out of the water and for playing your bass. You've got the best bass lines in this galaxy, you know.'

'Don't worry,' said Emma. 'We're taking her back to the nuthouse now.'

Chapter 14

'Can I drop you off at home, Lucy?' asked Mum, changing gear with a grinding noise. Their old Ford Mondeo really did need some work, thought Jay. But Mum never seemed to get around to taking it to the garage.

'Oh no—really—you don't have to worry,' said Lucy, and even from the back seat Jay could see she was colouring up again. He glanced at Emma, sitting beside him, and knew she was thinking what he was thinking. *What was it* with this girl? 'Please—just stop at your house and I'll walk back from there.'

'It's really no trouble,' insisted Mum. She flicked a glance into the rear-view mirror and made eye contact with Jay. And right away he knew *she* wanted to know more about Lucy too.

'But it's good for me to walk,' went on Lucy. 'I have to keep fit!'

'You certainly *are* fit,' said Mum, 'Doing acrobatics in perilous locations . . . and hopefully you'll stay fit if you don't go nearly drowning yourself again. How come a big strong girl like you hasn't learned to swim?'

'Oh well—I just never got the chance. There wasn't a pool on . . . er . . . anywhere near where I lived. But I will learn now! I will enrol for some classes right away. I really *want* to learn to swim.'

Back at the cottage, Lucy sprang out of the car and thanked Sue profusely for taking her along with Emma and Jay on their outing. 'It was very kind of you,' she said, beaming. 'And I still can't believe that I *really met* Mark King!'

Emma and Jay grinned and rolled their eyes at each other. 'Don't worry, Mum,' said Emma. 'I'm going to make her listen to some stuff on my iPod—see if I can get her to join the twenty-first century.'

'What's wrong with Level 42?' said Mum. 'They're brilliant. You should be proud of them—they're islanders like you!'

'I *am*!' retorted Emma. 'I just don't spend my WHOLE LIFE obsessing about them. I mean—imagine me mooning around after, I dunno, Simon Le Bon out of Duran Duran . . . ? You'd think it was a bit weird!'

Mum smirked. 'No I wouldn't. Simon's *still got it.*'

'For *you* maybe!' Emma shook her head. 'He's old enough to be my *dad*. And so is Mark, Lucy!'

'It's not like that,' said Lucy, quietly. 'It's *the music*. It's the bass. Don't you love bass? Doesn't everyone here?'

'Leave her alone, Em,' said Jay. 'Lucy—you should get home and get into some dry clothes.'

'I'll walk you back,' said Emma, following Lucy up the drive. 'I need some exercise too!' Lucy looked anxious so she added, 'I'll just go *part* of the way with you.' It was high time, Emma was thinking, that she and Lucy had some 'girl time', away from Jay and Mum and random pop stars. Maybe she could get to the bottom of some of Lucy's secrets if it was just the two of them.

They set off along the road but before Emma had a chance to ask Lucy anything she groaned aloud. 'Oh no! Look out, it's Badger!'

'Badger?' Lucy's eyes lit up. 'What . . . out in the day time? I thought they only came out at night.'

'No—not *a* badger . . . *Badger.*' Emma grimaced. 'He's our neighbour. He's always sniffing around our house, trying to get Mum to buy rubbish stuff off him. Probably casing the joint to see if there's anything worth nicking. He's weird . . . and not in a nice way, like you are.'

Badger came sauntering along in the other direction,

a pale, flat-faced pit bull terrier on a piece of thick string at his side. The dog was making growling, choking noises as it strained at its collar and Badger, wearing dirty combat trousers and a stained string vest across his concave, hairy chest, was grunting at it to come to heel. Then he spotted Emma and Lucy and immediately a fake smile wove across his sallow, stubbly face. 'Afternoon!' he called, raising his battered brown trilby hat.

As they drew parallel, the dog lurched at them, snarling, little drips of saliva shaking from its yellowed canines. Emma jumped as Badger grabbed its string collar and yanked it back. 'Don't worry, I won't let Brad bite you! He just wants to play, that's all.'

Lucy hadn't jumped. She was staring with fascination at the dog. And for a moment he stopped and stared right back at her as if equally fascinated. And then he sniffed at her—and went into an even wilder frenzy of barking.

'I dunno what's up with 'im!' shouted Badger over the racket. 'You been cuddlin' foxes or summink?'

Lucy shrugged and shook her head and Emma grabbed her arm to pull her away.

'He's smellin' something strange on you!' accused Badger, as if it were all Lucy's fault that the creature seemed to want to sink its teeth into her.

But Lucy shook Emma off and then she stood her

ground and gazed away into the trees, her hands in her shorts pockets and her posture incredibly relaxed. Very still, as if Badger and the dog weren't even there. Emma had been about to say something sarcastic to Badger, but now she paused and just watched. Lucy was being odd again and it was fascinating. As soon as Emma's attention shifted to her friend something strange happened. After a few seconds the dog stopped straining towards them and just sat down. And yawned.

And at this point Lucy dropped her glance down to the animal and smiled at it. 'Hello, Brad,' she said, in a low, calm voice. And the dog—to Emma's amazement—grinned up at her, its tongue lolling out of one side of its mouth and its tail thumping on the road.

'Well—*that* doesn't happen too often!' said Badger, looking baffled. Even from this distance Emma could smell sour tobacco and old whisky on his breath. 'Brad's never normally friendly. He's not meant to be—I've trained him to be my guard dog. You must have a special way with dogs.' He peered at Lucy, sizing her up with surprise. 'How'd you do that?'

'I watched a TV programme about it,' said Lucy, patting Brad's head. 'You just have to keep your cool and then be really, *really* boring. The dog just loses interest in you and then cheers up as soon as you do.'

'Come on, Dog Whisperer. We've got to go.' Emma grabbed her friend's arm again and steered her away.

'Bye, then. Tell your mum I've got some cheap DVDs she might want to look at,' Badger called after them before slinking off towards his dingy bungalow beyond an overgrown hedge.

Lucy looked as if she was about to say something polite in response, so Emma hissed, 'Ignore him. He's horrible.'

'He's not nice,' agreed Lucy. 'But that's not his dog's fault.'

'So . . .' Emma changed the subject as Lucy led her off the lane and up along one of the narrow tracks across the wooded hillside. 'You'll have to let me know when I'm close enough . . . to your house, I mean. Just say when you want me to go. I know you don't want me to see where you live.'

Lucy was silent for a few seconds and then she took a deep breath and turned to Emma. 'You're right,' she said. 'I don't want you to see where I live. I'm sorry, but it's true.'

Emma shrugged. 'OK—whatever you say. But you don't have to worry, you know . . . if it's a bit run down or an old caravan or something. I don't care about stuff like that. Nor do Jay or Mum. It's all about people—not where they live. Even if where they live is a bit rubbish.'

Lucy laughed out loud, walking on. 'Oh my—no—it's not rubbish! *Hessandrea*'s the most amazing place to live *ever*!'

'Hessandrea?' queried Emma, following her.

'Oh—um—yes. That's what my home is called.'

'Nice name. Sounds like a star sign! Mine's Aquarius. What's yours?'

'Um . . . I'm not sure. I don't believe in star signs.'

'When's your birthday?' asked Emma.

'I . . . think . . . it's the twenty-sixth of November,' Lucy said, batting a springy twig out of her way.

'You *think*?' Emma was startled. 'You don't *know*?'

'Well . . . yes, of course I know. It's November the twenty-sixth! It's just that . . . we don't really worry about birthdays.'

'Oh . . .' Emma paused, wondering for the first time if Lucy's family were super-religious in a cultish sort of way. Some religions forbade celebrations of birthdays and Christmas, didn't they? It was a worrying thought. Maybe *that* was Lucy's secret. Maybe she wasn't even meant to be mixing with ordinary people . . . Maybe . . .

'So that would make me a Sagittarian, I suppose,' Lucy pondered. 'But it's all a load of nonsense, anyway.'

'Yes, it probably is,' agreed Emma. 'Although I *would*

say that, because I'm an Aquarius . . .' She giggled. 'Anyway, how come Hessandrea's this amazing place and you don't want me to see it?'

Lucy paused again as they came to the perimeter where the woodland met the long, thin wire fence designed to keep sheep in the meadow on its other side. 'I do want you to see it,' she said. 'But you just can't. I promised.'

'Your mum?' Emma tilted her head, trying to read all the emotions which seemed to be scudding across Lucy's face like windblown clouds. 'She'd be upset?'

'Kind of,' muttered Lucy.

'Well . . . maybe you'll talk her round one day,' said Emma. 'Maybe she'll be OK with me or Jay coming over. You never know . . .'

'Maybe.' Lucy's smile was doubtful.

'It doesn't matter, anyway. Don't worry about it. OK—shall I turn back now?'

Lucy nodded.

'Want to do something with Jay and me tomorrow? Go to . . . what was it? Some gig at Freshwater?' Emma teased.

'Oh yes!' Lucy's happy face sprang back.

'Well . . . give us a call then. Oh!' Emma glanced at Lucy's damp clothes. 'What happened to your phone?! The seawater probably killed it!'

Lucy scooped her Motokola out of her shorts pocket and peered at it in horror.

Emma took it from her and shook drops of seawater out of it. 'Oh dear,' she said, pressing the ON button and finding nothing but a blank screen. 'You might have to get your mum to buy you a new one.'

'I think Mum will be able to fix it,' said Lucy. 'She's very good with things like that. She—she can't touch it of course, but she can tell me what to do. Anyway . . . I'll phone you from home. I wrote your numbers down . . .'

Emma plucked at Lucy's clumped-up hair. 'OK—go and have a shower before some barnacles decide to settle in your roots!' she advised, and turned back towards home, leaving Lucy to go on alone.

'Keep rolling the tin and catching the pebble!' Lucy called after her.

'I will, you mad muppet!' called back Emma over her shoulder. After thirty seconds she stopped walking. She slid behind a tree and turned to peek around it, watching Lucy walk on across the meadow. There was some land on the other side of the Rowridge transmitter site which had been a temporary pitch for travellers in the past. Perhaps this was where Lucy's family lived. If she was a traveller it would explain quite a lot . . . maybe. Emma felt guilty, spying, but she just *had* to know. She moved cautiously through the woods, careful not to step on any dry twigs which might snap loudly. Lucy was some way across the meadow by now, striding past some little knots of sheep and heading in the direction of the transmitter. Emma crouched by one of the gateposts, watching. She would wait until Lucy got to the far end of the meadow and then she would get over the fence and sprint after her, keeping low and out of sight.

But Lucy suddenly came to a stop and looked around her, as if she suspected she was being followed. Emma ducked down. When she next looked up Lucy was fishing her phone out of her pocket again. From this distance it shouldn't have been possible to see it, but the phone had obviously survived its dip in the marina after all, because suddenly a bright green light shone out of it. Lucy pressed a few of its buttons and then looked around again and walked on. She appeared to consult her watch.

And then she vanished.

Emma blinked and shook her head several times, staring at the meadow where only seconds before her strange new friend had been walking. Now there was nothing there except sheep. What . . . ?! Had there been some kind of landslip? Had Lucy suddenly been sucked into an underground vortex? What?!

Emma climbed over the fence and ran towards the spot where she'd seen Lucy vanish. In absolute confusion she stood on the grass, peering all around her. She even called Lucy's name a few times, startling the sheep, but got no reply. What on *earth* had just happened?

I'm going mad, she thought. *That's it. I must have bashed my head when I fell off Jay's bike . . . that's what all the green lights and stuff is about. I'm just imagining things . . . And maybe I'm even imagining that the others saw it too. Or maybe I'm the only one and they're all just humouring me! And now . . . oooh . . . I'm imagining something else. Lucy vanishing and . . .* She knelt down and looked at the grass. If she *was* going mad it was in a very mathematical way. For she could now see a shape on the grass. A square, about a metre and a half wide, and within it a precise chessboard-like pattern of little squares of grass that were flattened and other squares of grass that stood up to stiff attention.

Emma slid her phone out of her jeans and tried hard to steady her hands so she could take a photo with it. If it came out OK she could show it to Jay and maybe that would prove something. She clicked the phone several times before she managed to get a shot which wasn't blurry. Then she put the phone back in her pocket and turned back to the woods, breaking into a run.

*

High above in *Hessandrea*, Lucy studied a screen showing the camera feed of the land below, her heart racing and her hands across her mouth. *Idiot! Complete and utter idiot!* WHY hadn't she been more careful? Normally she pulled down the cloakshaft around her while she was still at the edge of the woods. Then it would travel with her, keeping her safely invisible and undetected, until she had climbed the mast and got safely back on board *Hessandrea*. But today Emma had been standing right by her so she couldn't do that. She had meant to travel to the far side of the meadow and get the cloakshaft down when she knew she was out of sight of her curious friend . . . but then she'd got the phone going (it wasn't dead at all—*Hessandrea*'s simulator wouldn't make anything too feeble to withstand a bit of water) and immediately a warning signal had beamed out of it from Mumgram. Something urgent—very urgent. And she'd just glanced around, believed she was alone and unseen, and hit the cloakshaft button on her wrist.

As soon as she'd run towards the console to discover the cause of Mumgram's alarm she'd seen the screen view of the meadow below—and Emma, running across it, looking astonished and scared. Staring at the grass, looking scared. Peering closely at the checkerboard residue of the cloakshaft's magnetic field, looking scared. Photographing it, looking scared. Running away . . . scared.

It was the *scared* bit that bothered her most. Human beings on Earth had had *no contact* with the outlying planets (that they were aware of). For centuries the Quorat had waited for the right time to bring Earth up to speed with its distant neighbours . . . but it was always putting that time off. Earth never seemed to be quite ready. Mumgram had told her countless times that to know the truth of her existence would make Earth people SCARED. And scared people were dangerous.

'DAMN!' Lucy kicked the panelling beneath the console. 'DAMN! DAMN! DAMN!' She closed her eyes and felt tears try to ooze out of them. How could she ever explain this to Emma and Jay? She couldn't. The truth was just too enormous for two ordinary Earth teenagers to get their heads around. They would freak. They would either decide she was a liar or they would believe her and be terrified of her and maybe call in the police or the army to imprison her . . . For a while, over the past few days, she had fantasized that maybe she *could* tell them the truth, or at least some of it . . . but now she realized this was insane. Just look at Emma . . . running home, scared witless . . .

'Lucy. ALERT!' Mumgram suddenly appeared at her side in a well of holographic light, reminding her that there was a reason for her folly. An emergency of some kind.

'What is it?' she sniffed, noticing the amber light flickering for the first time.

'There has been an atmostasis breach,' said Mumgram.

'Where?' demanded Lucy.

'On the outer starboard hull. Disturbance first registered forty-one hours, fifteen minutes and twenty-one seconds ago.'

'Well *why* didn't you tell me *then*?!' demanded Lucy, forgetting that she hadn't been here. She rattled her fingers across the keyboard and called up a line of data concerning the ship's outer structure. 'Has something hit us? That's not supposed to happen, is it? The birds and bats and insects all know we're here, don't they?'

'There has been no strike,' said Mumgram, and Lucy could see this on the screen in front of her. The starboard hull, at the coordinates indicated by the sensors, showed no obvious damage. Only a kind of . . . dark shadow registered on the far edge of an image provided by the nearest outer camera.

'What *is* that?' she breathed, peering closely at the

screen, aware of goosebumps sweeping across her arms, neck, and shoulders.

'Preliminary examination is inconclusive,' said Mumgram. 'But there is a ninety-seven point five per cent probability that this is Koth.'

Lucy felt the blood drain from her face. The bridge seemed to slide sideways as if a giant hand had abruptly cuffed *Hessandrea* out of her atmostasis and tipped her over.

'Lucy, you are losing consciousness,' observed Mumgram. 'Please lie on the floor or put your head between your knees.'

Lucy slid to the floor, feeling sick and dizzy. She pressed her cheek to its cool metal surface and tried to breathe. Maybe she had heard wrong. 'Repeat alert,' she mumbled. 'In full.'

'Atmostasis breach on outer starboard hull,' stated Mumgram. 'Disturbance in atmostasis field first detected forty-one hours, sixteen minutes and thirteen seconds ago and amber alert raised. No damage detected. Origin of disturbance uncertain. But there is a ninety-seven point five per cent probability that it is Koth.'

'Koth.' Lucy had not even spoken the word aloud for at least three years. Now it tumbled out of her like a long held exhalation. A death rattle. 'You're telling me . . . that . . . just outside . . . there is . . . Koth.'

There was a pause and then Mumgram stated:

'There is no longer Koth. The entity which has a ninety-seven point five per cent probability of being Koth has now departed.'

Lucy felt her head spin in wide, whooshing turns. She was in a nightmare. This had to be it. Mumgram was just saying this to her in her dream. This vision of her mother, calm and indifferent, as if the Koth had not ended all human life on her home planet—as well as her own—*had* to be a dream. But five minutes later, when the whooshing and spinning finally eased off, Lucy still lay on the floor as if her limbs had turned to lead. She was awake. She was still here, comfortably suspended above her new home planet. Welcomed by Emma and Jay, given hot gingerbread by their mum, sold a bike by a grumpy man, having her hair cut by a talented stylist, rescued and indulged by her favourite musician.

All these wonderful, unique people.

She was going to kill them all.

Chapter 15

'Damn it!'

Nick slapped his laptop shut and stood up, running his hands though his hair. He paced up and down inside the cabin and tried to think. What *was* this? *What* was going on? There had to be something causing this knot of *battle preparation* inside him. He wished, suddenly, that he was back in the RAF, getting ready to fly a mission. Or freelancing again with special operatives. He'd thought he was well out of all of that—but least he would have some intel on what was coming—and would be *doing* something about it.

Here, he had nothing. Not for want of trying, either. This morning he'd finally given in to that feeling and called David, an old special ops friend who was now very high up in British intelligence, and asked him if he knew of anything going down in the South of England . . . or perhaps one of its islands . . . ? David was curious and began to look into it right away. When he called Nick back he was unhelpful, to say the least. 'You're bored, Nick,' he said. 'You took retirement too early! There's nothing happening on the Isle of Wight; you just wish there was.'

'Well—thanks.' He couldn't stop the acid in his voice.

'Seriously, Nick—you might want to consider coming up to Whitehall to see me some time. I could use you. Former fighter pilot, freelance operative, experienced in the field, no ties . . .'

'No—thank you, David,' said Nick, with a shudder. 'I've done my time for my country.'

After the call he'd tried to write. That was what he was here for, after all, wasn't it? To write and forge a new career as a novelist. To experience something *different*. Now, as he paced up and down the cabin, that fantasy seemed laughable. His instincts were screaming at him. Not to tap out a bestseller but to take some kind of action. Against *what*? A green light in the sky? A suddenly improved television and radio reception? A girl who didn't quite seem to fit . . .

He grabbed his keys and phone and left the lodge, walking quickly past the other holiday homes towards the cottage. He would like to go in and talk to Sue . . . but he had no idea what to say to her. Maybe he could ask her questions about this Lucy . . . although that might seem pretty odd.

Emma came running down the drive as he strode on past the cottage. He stopped. 'Emma? Are you OK?'

Emma glanced over at him. Her face was pale and her eyes glittered. She looked shaken and disorientated. 'What's happened?' he asked.

'Nothing!' she squeaked, attempting a smile. 'Everything's fine . . .'

He tilted his head to one side, regarding her. 'Doesn't look that way.'

'Honestly!' she squeaked. 'I'm fine!' And then she was through the cottage doorway and out of sight.

He hesitated. Should he go in after her? Did he count as a friend to this small family yet? Or was he still just a paying guest? He shook his head and walked on. He could think of only one course of action right now—to go back to the transmitter and see if anything had changed. Anything at all.

Jay looked up, startled, as his sister crashed into his bedroom. Pulling off his headphones and pausing his iPod, he was about to have a go at her for not bothering to knock (she'd go nuts if *he* ever went into *her* room without knocking!) when he saw her face.

'What?! What is it?' He sat up jerkily on his bed, knocking a pile of books onto the floor.

Emma stared at him, and now he could see she was shaking, as well as looking porridgy-pale beneath two high spots of colour in her cheeks. 'You won't believe me,' she gasped. She'd obviously been running. From what?

'But you're going to tell me anyway,' prompted Jay. 'What's happened?'

'It's Lucy,' said Emma, leaning on his chest of drawers and wiping the beads of perspiration off her white upper lip. 'I just saw her . . . vanish.'

Jay wrinkled his brow. 'Vanish? How do you mean?'

'I mean . . . *vanish*! Like . . . in a puff of smoke! Only without the smoke. Right in front of my eyes!' Jay raised a sceptical eyebrow. She had known he would. She would do the same if he was telling *her* this story. 'I said you wouldn't believe me!' she snapped. 'But just sit there and shut up and I'll tell it all to you . . . slowly! Listen!'

She shared the events of the past half an hour, looking grave and earnest. Jay wanted to think she was having a joke but he couldn't see any sign that she was winding him up. She looked serious. Worse, she looked scared.

'And here's the pattern on the grass,' she finished, handing over her phone and showing him a strange chessboard-like image in the green meadow. 'This is the place she disappeared from—I'm certain. This is SO weird!'

Jay stared at the image, trying to make sense of it. 'We can call her and ask her!' he said and then cursed as he remembered where *his* phone was. It was lying in a dish of dry, uncooked rice in the kitchen. He was hoping the rice would absorb all the moisture in it and magically bring it back to life. This was a tip he'd heard about.

But Emma's *hadn't* ended up in water that day. She dialled Lucy's number and hit CALL. After a few seconds she blinked and shook her head. 'Voicemail,' she told Jay. 'Lucy? It's Emma . . .' she gulped, trying to sound normal. 'Can you give me a call as soon as you get this? There's . . . something really important I need to ask you.' She ended the call and stared at the phone for a few seconds. 'If . . . if she does phone back . . . what shall I say?'

Jay didn't know. What *did* you say to a girl who could apparently vanish into thin air?

'I mean—we've always known she was . . . strange,' murmured Emma, as much to herself as to Jay. 'I mean . . . the acrobatics and the photographic memory stuff . . . the funny clothes, the Nipe trainers . . . the Motokola phone? All that money she has and no explanation for it; not wanting us to go to her house—and all that stuff about being a *starchild* . . . ? Did you hear that? When she was talking to Mark King? She keeps saying weird things, doesn't she?'

Jay had a sudden memory of Lucy in their kitchen two days ago. Mum had said, *'I'm sure your mum loves you very much,'* or something like that . . . and Emma had said yes and looked so . . . sad. He shared this thought with Emma.

'Maybe she isn't with her mum at all,' said Emma. 'Maybe they had a really bad argument and she's run away or something and that's her secret. She's hiding out somewhere in the woods and . . .' She tailed off. It didn't really matter what Lucy's story was—the HUGE GREAT BIG FRIGHTENING THING was the *point.* Lucy could make herself *disappear.*

'Are you *sure,* Em?' asked Jay. 'I mean . . . could it have been a trick of the light or something?'

'How?' Emma held up her palms. 'You tell me how and I'll believe it. Please! This is freaking me out! I'd *rather* have a logical explanation!'

Jay couldn't think of one. He took Emma's phone and peered at the photo on it again. 'It's some kind of magnetic field,' he said. 'Like a crop circle . . . you know, those geometric patterns that show up in farmers' crops.

Maybe we should show it to Nick . . . he seems to know about this kind of stuff.'

'He's just gone out,' said Emma. She flopped down onto the floor. 'And anyway—I don't think we should tell anyone else. They'll think it's a wind-up.'

'So . . . what *are* we going to do?' asked Jay.

Emma sighed and shrugged. 'Have a cup of tea.'

Lucy's fingers rattled across the console keyboard at lightning speed as she barked at Mumgram, 'I need a trace on the entity. Where is it now?'

'The entity has departed *Hessandrea*'s atmostasis field,' said Mumgram.

'I know that!' snapped Lucy, as an outer image of the hull revolved smoothly on the screen in front of her—shown as it had been eight minutes ago. It was overlaid with its blueprint dimensions; curved lines interrupted by a blurred dark shadow roughly the size and mass of a human child of around three or four, she estimated. But a very different shape. The wingspan, she calculated, would be three metres across when fully extended. With another scattering of fingertips she brought up an image from the databanks on a second screen. 'No,' she said. 'Not flying. Show me roosting.' Immediately the image shrank to a third of its size. 'Calculate mass and match shape to shadow on outer hull,' she commanded and the image slid across to the visual of the hull, orientated thirty-four degrees clockwise and slid into place. It fitted. Almost perfectly.

'It's Koth,' she breathed, closing her eyes and gritting her teeth to stop them chattering. A voice in her head whispered, *'It's over.'* Already a sense of hopelessness was coming to claim her. She *mustn't* give in to that kind of thinking. She exhaled sharply and opened her eyes. 'Mumgram—that trace! It must give off a signature—body heat—smell—vibration.'

'The Koth signature is clearly defined in our records,' confirmed Mumgram.

'So—trace it! It can't have got far in five minutes.'

'The trace will have an error factor of four point eight per cent,' warned Mumgram.

'Just DO IT!'

At once a pale orange ribbon flickered across a third screen—one which showed a map of their immediate area, to a circular radius of ten kilometres. The orange ribbon moved straight, at high altitude, for two thirds of a kilometre north-west. Then it circled.

'3D,' instructed Lucy and the map shifted into a third dimension, offering a 360-degree view of any target area from any trajectory. Manipulating the touchpad with her fingers, Lucy saw the telltale shape of the entity's downward journey. It spiralled. A neat corkscrew of orange drilled down through the air and ended at ground level.

'Motion,' she called, peering at the contracted outline of the Koth on the other screen. Its leathery wings sprang out as it was animated into flight. 'Simulate the Koth landing motion,' she added. The animated creature, its dark brown features a blur of jaws and red eyes amid thick, dusty black fur, began to spiral, dropping a precise increment of height with every tight loop. Lucy tapped the touchpad and the visual swooped to a worm's eye view. Now the Koth could be seen at its most horrific angle. From below. *Descending*. Raptor claws at the ready. With every tight curve the image grew closer, larger, revealing the face; its gaping black mouth cavity ringed with needle-sharp white teeth and inside, the spike of its ovipositor coiled and charged and ready.

The predatory spiral. And there it was, picked out in orange on the map. A horrifying helter-skelter.

'Zoom!' Lucy found her teeth were chattering again as the satellite image bloomed up at her, showing her ever closer detail of the entity's landing place. It was a building she recognized.

Lucy shot out of her seat and went to the armoury.

'An adult Koth is difficult to kill and extremely hard to contain, Lucy,' said Mumgram as Lucy strode back from the armoury, a metre-long frostlaser rifle over her shoulder.

Lucy did not reply. She pulled a steel case of fuel cartridges, on a grey strap, over her other shoulder and opened it to pull out a clip of eight. Breaking the rifle at its load point, she slid the clip in with a metallic stutter, reset and then put her eye to the telescopic site.

'Lucy, you have never wielded a frostlaser rifle,' warned Mumgram. 'You are unlikely to be successful.'

'I *have* wielded a frostlaser rifle!' retorted Lucy. 'Hundreds of times. And my hit rate is ninety-three point six per cent!'

'In a simulation, Lucy,' Mumgram insisted. 'Your hit rate on planet Earth is zero. You are unlikely to be successful.'

'I'm going to kill it,' growled Lucy, and as the orange spiral on the screen reflected in her glassy eyes, her face was a solid mask of intent.

'You are unlikely to be successful,' repeated Mumgram, oh-so-calmly.

'WELL WHAT THE HELL AM I *SUPPOSED* TO DO, THEN?!' screamed Lucy, spinning around to glare at the holographic figure.

'Bring *Hessandrea* out of atmostasis and re-enter space,' said Mumgram. 'Depart Earth and plot a new journey for another suitable planet.'

'What?!' Lucy felt rage surging through her. 'Just LEAVE? Just abandon the Earth to its fate? Oops—sorry—didn't mean to leave a deadly demon behind to destroy all humanity! So long and thanks for the hotdog!' She shook her head, glowering at the hologram. 'You have GOT to be kidding!'

She grabbed her phone, fully recharged and dried, and ported the images on the console across to its small screen. 'I want you to keep a live link with me,' she said. 'If you see any more movement on that trace, you tell me IMMEDIATELY. Do you understand?!'

'Yes, Lucy,' said Mumgram. 'I understand. Please take a life support pack with you. And a viz-visor would be useful.'

Lucy wanted to shout something rude and depart, but she knew this was a good idea. She might not get back to *Hessandrea* soon. She needed to be prepared for that. And the viz-visor was imperative to speed up her search. Dropping her rifle, she grabbed the backpack from the door and shrugged it over her shoulders and then pulled the visor from its side pouch and pulled it on. It looked like a baseball cap . . . from a distance. Nobody was likely to notice the holographic display beneath its peak, relaying the tracer images from *Hessandrea.* She retrieved her weapon and marched for the exit with no further interruption from Mumgram.

She swung out from the platform and onto the top of the mast ladder without a thought for the height or the wind speed. Hidden in the cloakshaft, she was on the ground in less than two minutes. She had to get to the Koth landing point. She just hoped she wasn't too late.

Chapter 16

Before he'd departed, Nick had taken his binoculars from the car, parked back at Woody Bottom. He guessed that popping in to see the staff at the transmitter station would not go down so well a second time. And in any case, whatever was going on, he was pretty sure they were clueless about it. He wanted to get closer to the mast—inspect it. Climb it if possible. The security around it was enough, certainly, to put off any day trippers, but certainly no problem for a man of his resources.

He journeyed through the woods again, keeping quiet, rolling his steps. He didn't even know why. Who would challenge him here? He was going on instinct about this whole thing. Instinct had saved him many times in his military years. It hadn't been enough to save him from a disastrous personal life—one failed marriage, no kids—or some pretty bad nightmares. After leaving the RAF in his early thirties he'd taken some freelance work with British intelligence. Targeting enemies from a jet fighter above a war zone had been coldly clinical. For his country he'd delivered obliteration but never had to *see* it—aside from the occasional bit of grainy video. So, as he ended his twelve years' service, some strange impulse had compelled him to do something *on the ground*—as if to make amends—and his old friend David had found plenty for him to do. Working cheek by jowl with soldiers had taught him a lot and shown him some things he wished he could forget. He wondered, sometimes, if human beings were programmed to self-destruct. What would it *take* to bring them together? Nothing on *this* world . . .

So if activists of some kind were planning something around this remote transmitter, he would be only mildly surprised and not even slightly shocked. And if a pretty fourteen-year-old girl turned out to be in the centre of it, it would be unusual but not unheard of. It was hard to pinpoint what it was about Lucy that made him so suspicious. But there was *something* odd about her. Her language was . . . too perfect. Her manners too . . . studied. He'd seen this before among terror cell recruits. He hoped he was wrong.

Nick paused at the edge of the woodland and put his Steiners to his eyes, training the military binoculars on the mast. The structure was so tall it took several seconds to scan it from the bottom to the top. Today the sky was a high, faultless blue and the tip of the mast with its white cone was picked out perfectly. A pigeon flitted across the bright figure-eight boundary of his view. He pulled back the zoom, adapting to a wider scope which took in the top third of the mast and the sky around it. Rooks from a line of trees on the far side of the meadow suddenly scattered into the air, spooked by something. They rose at least as high as the top of the mast, flapping awkwardly compared to the pigeon, and then several made their way across to the trees which shielded Nick from view. His eyes followed their course instinctively; nothing *else* was happening in the sky.

He let out a gasp and blinked, the sudden shocked flip of his eyelashes reflected and magnified in the glass for a microsecond. *What* is *that?* The rooks . . . they had suddenly changed their path through the sky. *All* of them. One second they were on a straight line towards the trees and the next, they had all turned and followed a wide arc in the sky for several seconds before resuming their original path. Why?

He knew a fair bit about birds. Rooks did not usually fly in formation, like starlings. And even if he was wrong, and they did, it would be at dusk, surely, when they were preparing to alight in the rookery and roost for the night. This was mid-afternoon and there was no wind, either, to affect a small flock of birds simultaneously. It looked simply as if the rooks had suddenly decided to avoid the mast area.

Magnetism, he told himself, lowering the lenses, deep in thought. Some belt of electro-magnetic field from the mast . . . suddenly interfering with the birds' navigation. But this didn't seem to fit. The nagging inside went on; got louder if anything. He pressed the binoculars back to his eyes and watched again. Another pigeon. Flying the same route. Making the same arc in the sky. Then another. Hairs were standing up on the back of his neck now. It was almost as if . . . He shook his head, lowering the bins and laughing at himself. What—a Romulan Warbird from *Star Trek*, up there in the sky, cloaked from view?! He shook his head, laughing at his foolishness.

There was a snap of twigs, some way distant to his left. He froze and then sank slowly among the thicket of brambles and holly, turning his head gradually in the direction of the sound. The goosebumps were back again. The coiled spring inside was singing with anticipation.

As his eyes followed the source of the noise, Nick ordered his breathing silent and remained as still as the ash tree trunk beside him. In a small, clear space, thirty metres from his hiding place, the air shimmied like a heat haze, and Lucy stepped into view.

The viz-visor display laid out the orange trail of the Koth high above the trees. Lucy stared up through the leaves, past the holographic guidance, as if she really *would* see an eerie orange trail hanging in the sky.

'Has it moved further?' she asked.

Mumgram, relayed from *Hessandrea* into her headgear, replied, 'No. It has been still at the point of landing for seven minutes and forty-nine seconds.'

Lucy gritted her teeth. She would track this creature for the rest of her days if she must, but oh . . . if she could just get it *now*. If she could spare Earth from even a taste of the horror. Her heart ramped up in her chest as she strode through the woodland. She had checked that Emma and Jay's mobile signals were well clear—back in their home. Emma's was, now, but of course Jay's phone was dead, so she had no way of knowing where he was. *Inside*, she prayed. *With your doors and windows shut. Please . . .*

For a few awful seconds, back on *Hessandrea*, she had believed the Koth had spiralled directly onto their cottage. But that was wrong. It was close, though. Terribly close. Lucy marched out of the woods and on to the quiet lane, her backpack, viz-visor, and frostlaser rifle doing nothing to describe her as a casual passer-by to anyone she might meet. But she had no time to worry about this. It was a quiet lane. She probably wouldn't meet *anyone.* Well—there was one man she probably couldn't avoid. And one dog.

She reached the dilapidated bungalow in minutes and had to pause at the overgrown wooden gate, taking long slow breaths to calm her racing heart. Her blood seemed to thrum in her ears and there were low, swooping waves of sickness in her belly. She tensed it, clamping down on any movement from that unwise hotdog. There was no time for this. She could be sick later. The orange trail led exactly where she had expected. The tight spiral corkscrewed down into the overgrown back garden, close to the dark overhang of a junk-stuffed garage with no door. Lucy pushed the gate open, snapping some bindweed which had wound itself around the post and sending insects fluttering through the warm air.

Insects were the lucky ones. On Cornelian Eclata insects were now king. Too small for Koth. Had the Koth moved on to birds when all the mammals were dead? Was her home planet now filled with grey-brown drifts of carbon ash which were once living, warm-blooded creatures? Had that ash long since been lost to the circling winds and thrown into the strata clouds? Maybe reptiles and fish had been left untouched, their bodies unsuitable . . .

A sharp volley of barks broke through her unhappy reverie and she clutched the rifle tightly. Brad, the pit bull terrier, suddenly careered around the corner of the house. When he saw Lucy his hostile yips grew less vigorous and his tail began to wag. Lucy stayed still, gazing away as she had done earlier, until Brad trotted up to her, now just breathing heavily and dribbling. She didn't pat his head but gave him a brief nod of acknowledgement. 'Where is it, Brad?' she asked quietly. 'Take me to the scary thing.'

Brad didn't seem to know what she meant. He circled her knees, tail thumping, breathing, dribbling. And then Badger lurched suddenly out of a side door in the house, a thickly-rolled cigarette between his lips, staring at her in surprise.

''Ello, 'ello!' He plucked the roll-up out. 'Come to play with Brad, have you? Lucky you got him to like you. Anyone else, he would've had their arm off by now.'

There was blood on his string vest.

'What's that you got there?' He was peering at the rifle now, and looking slightly uneasy beneath the grin.

'Air gun,' said Lucy. 'I just got it.' She stared around,

seeking the roost. In the dark far corner of the garage was most likely. There were rafters. The orange trail on her viz-visor ended in the garden and then seemed to snake up around this building.

He guffawed and put both hands up, revealing shaggy armpits which sent out a belt of stale sweat. 'I got a gun inside. You want a better one? I'll sell it to you. Or are you gonna shoot me?'

'Only if I have to,' she replied, which he seemed to take as a joke. In the weed-choked garden she could see a large metal container; a canister with a lid, big enough to contain a person. 'What's in there?' she asked.

'Petrol,' he said. 'Just in case . . . you know. Got it last year when there were strikes. You ever need a bit, you come and find me. I'll give you a good deal for cash. So . . . you gonna take out some pigeons or something?'

'Actually, I like to shoot rats,' she said. 'Can I look in your garage? See if there are any?'

He looked a little uneasy. 'Rats? Well . . . plenty of 'em in there . . .'

'Have you got another one of those?' she asked suddenly, eyeing the roll-up between his fingers. 'Could I have one?'

He looked down at it, surprised. 'One of these? You want one of these?'

'Will you get me one?' she asked, smiling at him now. 'I've always wanted to try smoking . . .'

'Are you trying to set me up or something?' He looked around as if she might have organized a police trap.

'Of course not. I'm just bored. I can pay!' She pulled out a wad of notes. At least fifty pounds.

He tugged them out of her fingers immediately but still peered at her through narrowed eyes. 'It's bad for you, you know . . . smokin' . . .'

'What are you, my dad?' she replied, her inflection just like a girl on *EastEnders*.

He grinned and shook his head. 'Wait here—I'll be right back!' He pocketed the cash, turned and lurched back into the house, revealing the circle of red on his shoulder. Lucy sighed and raised the rifle.

As soon as he reached the doorway she shot him. He fell forward across his grimy hallway floor, sprawling face down. His left foot twitched once and then he was still. Brad whined and ran to his master. She shot the dog, too, as soon as it reached the body. The dog collapsed onto the man's back. Good. Both out of view. She checked her watch, did a swift calculation, glancing at the petrol tank, and then entered the garage. In the furthest corner it hung on a rafter, upended, its wings cocooning its hideous face. Lucy realized that right up to this moment she had been trying to believe that maybe it was all a mistake, that something else had triggered *Hessandrea*'s alerts . . . But there was no mistake.

She was staring at the Koth.

'When they are asleep, they're not really asleep. They only rest and affect sleep. Their radar is ALWAYS on. Remember that.'

The words ran through her head as if she were playing the recording from *Hessandrea*'s console. Until she was eleven, she'd played lots of old tapes, memorizing her people's last few years of life; her history; her roots. Sergeant Petrez was one of the more compelling ones. With his fierce black eyes and dark curly hair, the young soldier had recorded and uploaded instructional video and audio diary entries over his last few days, hunting Koth. When everyone else had given up he continued, believing to the last that the Koth could be beaten.

'They NEVER sleep. But they do slow down after they've made a host,' went on Sergeant Petrez, his breathing sharp and rattly inside his protective suit, gasping his thoughts, hopes, and plans into the in-built recorder in the visor. *'Laying the eggs depletes their energy for maybe an hour. They're slower to react in that window of time. Use frostlaser on them first. Hot bullets won't work; even if you hit them it just bounces off that alien skin nine times out of*

ten . . . and even in the slow zone they'll get you before you can kill them. Slow them down just a bit more, though, and you've got a chance. Freeze them. It won't kill them but it'll give you maybe two minutes . . . two minutes to torch them. Never try to torch them when they're at normal speed. They'll get past the blast and get you. And even if you get lucky and score a lame one, it'll blast out eggbarbs in all directions with its last breath and you'll be fighting a dozen more tomorrow—and a dozen times a dozen the day after. You have to freeze it, contain it, and torch it! It's the only way.'

Did Sergeant Petrez ever imagine his instructions would be running through the terrified mind of a fourteen-year-old girl, a decade later on a planet in another galaxy?

High up in the gloom, the Koth swayed gently on its rafter. Its clawed feet clasped the roost securely, each gleaming black talon digging firmly into the old wood. The folded wings were black also but patterned with dark red veins. The creature was bat-like, seen this way, but when it unfurled its wings and revealed its face it was something horrific. No perky ears or squashed snout, like the bats she'd studied on BBC nature programmes. No wide shining black eyes and dainty mouse-like features. The Koth's head was a blunt hood of fur rising from its shoulders, containing only two red wells of eyes and, below, a ring of needle-sharp teeth. You might think it was a voracious carnivore, but you'd be wrong. Koth were vegetarian, feeding on the juice of fruit and vegetation through a retractable proboscis. The teeth were for a different purpose entirely. The teeth secured the host while the ovipositor did its business.

'If you're a host, you're dead.' Sergeant Petrez was back again, his words playing out through the tape in her mind. *'You want to save your friends, your family when you see that red ring on you? Go to the fire pits. You think you'll shoot yourself? No. That's no good. You're still a host, dead or alive. Drown yourself? No way. Baby Koth can swim. Get yourself to the fire pits. Shoot yourself as you jump if you like. But jump. No baby Koth gets out of the fire pits.*

Fire pits were everywhere on Cornelian Eclata. A natural phenomenon all over the planet, they were a vital power source as well as beautiful. Some of the biggest were tourist attractions. If you fell in, though, your life was over in a burst of purple flame. Nothing living ever emerged from a fire pit and in the final dark days of her home planet, that's where most infected people went. Some drunk and singing all the way, others silent and shaking, still others holding hands with loved ones and going in together.

At the age of eleven, when her emotional senses

seemed to heighten, Lucy had stopped looking at the films documenting those final days. It was too much. She had resolutely buried the audio and video files in hard to reach places, so she didn't open them by accident. She chose to focus on the life ahead instead. A world where fire pits were rare and remote and nobody would need to seek oblivion in them. A world without Koth.

If she got infected now, what would she do? How would she stop herself being host to a dozen baby Koth? And then dozens more from each of that dozen? She thought of the canister of petrol and then shook her head and lifted her chin. Yes, she was going to use it. But not for herself.

Above her the Koth eased one wing aside and a dim red pupil in its socket swivelled towards her. Lucy raised the frostlaser and put her eye to the sight. The shaking had left her now. Focus descended. This was it. Save Earth or die trying. She pushed the power gauge up to maximum and squeezed the trigger.

Nick couldn't believe he'd hit the null. The *one place* around the transmitter that day where he could get NO cell coverage at all. On the screen of his mobile an angled blue line through a blue circle informed him of this. His phone was a useless lump of metal and glass.

He was rooted to the spot with indecision. He could run up the hill, chasing a signal—but if he did he would lose his sightline on the bungalow where Lucy had gone. Now that he knew she was a killer, he had no qualms about calling for backup. The way she'd handled that rifle was horrifyingly expert. Why she had killed Badger he had no idea—maybe Badger was an informer for her terror cell who had made some mistake. Maybe he knew too much and had to be dispatched. Nick's mind whirled with other possibilities . . . she had recently befriended Emma and Jay and Sue. Maybe they were caught up in this too. Maybe they were *part* of it . . . ? But no . . . surely not.

Nick put his phone away and returned to the bungalow. The girl was still in the garage. There was no exit from it other than the front and, crouched behind a screen of low scrub on the opposite roadside, he should be able to see her coming back out. But even with his Steiners to hand he couldn't see *through* things and his view was partly blocked by a tangled line of bushes in the bungalow's front garden. He was going to have to get closer.

There must have been a silencer on the rifle—an odd looking thing he did not recognize—because he'd only heard a whoosh and thud before Badger went down; the same again when the dog followed. Seeing Lucy shoot the dog had chilled him the most. It was the coldest part of her operation. So *what* was she after in Badger's garage?

As he edged into the overgrown garden he heard a louder report—more of a crack than a thud and then a crashing sound and a small cry of . . . what? Fear? Triumph? It was hard to tell. He didn't have long to think about it, though, because suddenly Lucy was out of the garage and looking straight at him. Then raising her rifle and aiming.

And that was the last that Nick Dobson knew.

Chapter 17

Damn! Damn! Damn! Lucy stared at the man lying in the stony driveway. The body count was way too high. How was she going to manage all this? How could she explain? No matter. She didn't have time. Lucy turned and bent to pick up the body of the Koth. *Not dead. Stunned. Frozen.*

'Never believe it's dead,' warned Sergeant Petrez, *'until it's ashes.'*

It was heavier than she'd thought—maybe half her own body weight—and slippery with icy frostlaser crystals. Its body and all the moisture inside it had been temporarily frozen. If she'd blasted any human at half this level, they would be dead, but it took very much more than full power to kill a Koth. And the seconds were ticking by so fast—she was already a quarter of the way through her window of opportunity.

Oh but it was ugly. Dragging it to the petrol tank

she found herself staring into its grisly excuse for a face. The eyes were dim but the malevolent red glow was still in them. The gaping circle of sharp teeth was close to her belly as she dragged her foe across the weeds and stones and random lumps of concrete which made up Badger's garden. The barbed black tip on the ovipositor dripped with some nameless yellow goo. It smelt rank, like something rotting. It made her gag. She forced herself to look away and dragged the stunned Koth along faster. She could feel its heartbeat—one thud every ten seconds or so. It was in shut down. Not dead. Shut down . . . but about to wake at any moment.

Heaving it up onto the rim of the petrol tank was the worst. With one hand she slid the heavy lid off the cylinder and let it clang to the ground. The clear liquid glimmered, reflecting the summer-blue sky and sending up a vapour which made her head swim. Picking up the Koth meant bringing its face right up to hers. The redness in the eye sockets seemed to be brighter now. The leathery wings flexed as she hauled it up, her fingers buried in its damp pits. One wing spasmed against her cheek. She bit back a scream and tipped the body into the canister. It went down fast, sending a tidal wave of petrol over the rim, splashing down onto her feet.

'Step back, Lucy,' said a voice in her head—Mumgram's this time. *'Throw the flambit!'*

Already it was bobbing back up again, the fuel defrosting it. Its face cleared the surface and the mouth opened, sending out a fountain of petrol with a squeal. The ovipositor reached out, pulsating, getting ready for a suicidal bid to reproduce. She could see the eggs already moving along the blotchy red tube, like animated peas in a pod. She could see the shuddering which meant it was about to explode and spew eggbarbs out in all directions. She would get hit. So would the spreadeagled body of that man from Jay and Emma's holiday place.

'Now, Lucy! It's got to be NOW!'

Lucy pulled a flambit from her backpack, flicked it alight and pitched the small, fiery sphere across to the canister. For a second it seemed to hover in the wavy air above the vessel, while one dark veined wing rose, flapping soggily, from the fuel and the ovipositor shook faster. A black claw flexed and gripped the rim of the canister. Then there was a tremendous WHOOF! and a blast of flame shot into the air, as high as the bungalow roof. A high, rising squeal could be heard amid the crackles and pops. Lucy stepped back as rivulets of flame sped along the lines of leaked fuel in the grass. The heat of the fire was intense. She could feel it on her eyeballs even with her lids screwed up tight. She stepped back still further, nearly tripping over the body of the man. What was his name? Nick? She knelt down and touched his face; the side of his throat.

'I'm really sorry,' she said. 'I had no choice. There was no time to explain.'

For ten minutes she watched the inferno and then, when the flames had eased down enough, she crept forward and thought she could make out the blackened skeleton inside. She dropped the metal lid back on top, leaving a small gap to allow the air to feed the final simmerings of the last Koth; done to death. The tracer image under the viz-visor blinked out with the life form and she switched the holographic display off.

Then she walked to the bungalow to inspect the casualties. First pushing the dog gently over so that it slid onto the filthy carpet of the hallway and then dragging it through the door to a sitting room by its old leather collar, Lucy checked it over briskly but saw nothing. Then she turned and gingerly tugged at Badger's filthy vest so she could properly inspect his shoulder. The wound was unmistakable—a perfect circle of red puncture wounds and in the centre, like the hub of a bike wheel, a pale blister. The attack must have hurt—but maybe he'd been too drunk to notice.

'You might see only a blister,' the late Sergeant Petrez informed her. *'Some of them do it by stealth. But usually you'll see the ring and there's nothing stealthy about that. You see a ring without a blister . . . maybe there's hope. Maybe. But both . . . or just the blister. That's a no hoper.'*

She shook his uninjured shoulder. He groaned. She shook him harder. He groaned again, and started to turn over. 'Wassitabout?' he murmured. There was dribble on his chin. She shrugged off her backpack and unzipped it, pulling a shotstick out, snapping the lid off and bashing the short needle into his thigh. The adrenalin hit his blood stream instantly and three seconds later he was sitting up, confused but awake. 'What?' he queried, staring at her. 'What?'

'I don't know!' She shrugged. 'You were going to get me a roll-up and then you just keeled over. What is *in* your roll-ups? It's not just tobacco, is it?'

'It's . . . it's all natural stuff. Nothin' wrong with that . . .' he murmured. 'You still want some?'

'Maybe later,' she said. 'But I was hoping you'd come shooting with me. Can't find any rats . . . There's pigeons up by the transmitter, though.'

'I dunno,' he groaned. 'I'm a bit . . .'

She leaned closer and bashed another shotstick into

his other leg. This one delivered a drug which would make Badger more amenable and obedient.

'Ow!' he said. 'What did you do that for?'

'I need you to come with me,' she said, smiling. 'So I can show you my shooting. It's boring on my own. And you've shot things before, haven't you? You can teach me.'

'I mostly shot cats when I was in London,' he said. He grinned lopsidedly and sniggered. 'Kept all the LOST posters too, for a laugh. *Poor Tibbles—MISSING—we love her like family! Do you know where she is?* Yeah! Down the dump, full of lead!' He let out a wheezy laugh and wiped his eyes while Lucy struggled not to look revolted. 'Cats. Stuck up, stinkin' things. Think they're better than you! I'm a dog man, I am.'

He stood up, and she was careful to stand also, blocking his view of Brad's motionless body. 'Come on!' she said, tugging him along through the house by his arm. 'Take me out through the front door!' He did, undoing the latch with trembling hands. As soon as they reached the front step she shouldered her bag and the rifle and said, 'Hey—see if you can keep up with me!'

It was amazing that he didn't look back and notice the funnel of smoke belching up into the air behind the bungalow. He just gave a belch and a whoop and staggered after her, detailing some of the more hilarious cat shootings he'd taken part in with his gang of mates back up in London as they clambered up the wooded slopes. She kept her back to him so he wouldn't see her face. Partly because she was repulsed—and partly because she was deeply sorry for him. Too sorry. It would be easier if she could hate him—and he was doing a good job of making her loathe him. But she had hate only for one thing. And she had just incinerated that.

At last they reached the edge of the meadow and she could call down the cloakshaft. He had no idea what she was doing, of course, and just followed her when she grabbed his wrist and tugged. While they were in contact, he too would be invisible to anyone passing. Getting him up to *Hessandrea* was not simple. She couldn't carry him up and she'd never convince him to climb. He'd have to go via the tractor beam and the loading bay. But that was difficult if he was conscious. She'd have to knock him out again. It might help to lie a little. 'It's not really loaded,' she said to him, raising the rifle with a giggle. 'I'm only pretending.'

'I can get you some ammo,' he said. 'For a price.'

Playfully she pointed the rifle at him, pushing the gauge back down to LOW—still keeping a grip on one of his arms. Playfully he raised his free hand and burbled, 'Don't shoot!' Playfully, she shot him.

As soon as he'd hit the floor she called to Mumgram to transport him to the loading bay. His body, immobilized and encapsulated by the beam, rose steadily, following its own cloakshaft now, and was received into the belly of *Hessandrea.* Five minutes later, she was on board too and down in the loading bay. She found a small, wheeled truck for transporting cargo boxes and hauled him onto it. She pushed him to the lifts which led directly to the containment chambers. In one of these she tipped him onto the floor, wheeled the truck out, and turned to hit the SEAL button. The impenetrable glass slid across and sealed, entombing Badger and the stowaways inside him.

Later she would have to think of how to kill him humanely. The second frostlaser blast should keep him under now for at least a couple of hours . . . and maybe he wouldn't wake up anyway, by then. Either way, she was going to have to end it for him. Sooner or later. She should already have done it . . . somehow, though she couldn't. Not yet. For now she could do only one more thing.

Lucy went back up to the living quarters, got into her bed and cried.

Chapter 18

'There's smoke coming from Badger's place,' called Jay, peering out of his open bedroom window. A dark grey column was rising above the trees.

On the landing Sue paused with a stack of paperwork in her arms; she'd been about to attempt some accounts, a task she always loathed, so she was glad of a distraction. 'Smoke? How much smoke? Bonfire or house burning down?'

Jay shrugged. 'Hard to tell. Quite a lot of it, though.'

Sue sighed. She should probably phone Fire and Rescue but knowing Badger it was just an old tyre in his back garden. She didn't want to drag a load of firefighters out here for no reason. 'I'd better go and check,' she muttered, dropping the papers on a bookcase.

'Not on your own!' said Jay. 'I'm coming!'

'Where are you going?' asked Emma, looking up

from her mug of tea as they trooped down the stairs and into the kitchen.

'Badger's set something alight,' said Jay. 'We're going to find out if it's his trousers.'

Emma was still looking pale and freaked out since relaying her story about Lucy vanishing. The tea obviously wasn't helping that much. 'Wait for me,' she said, bashing the mug down on the side.

The three of them walked up the gravel drive and turned sharp left along the leafy, winding lane. Badger's house was a five minute walk along it. He wasn't exactly a *next door* neighbour, but there was nobody else on this bit of road. Sue often shuddered at the bad luck of Badger moving in. He was the dispossessed grandson of some lord, apparently, who'd spent all his inheritance in London and then 'retired' to the island when he ran out of money and couldn't manage to sell the bungalow or the land around it. Sue was pretty sure he took his dog into Newport regularly, to help him beg. She wished heartily that someone would buy the property from him and send him back to London with the proceeds.

But she didn't wish him destitute with a burned house. Just gone.

'It's not the bungalow,' said Emma. 'It's something in the garden. He's just set fire to some stuff.'

The column of smoke *was* coming from behind the building and they could see it was thinning out now, its source obviously dying down. Emma wrinkled her nose. 'Sheesh. Smells like he's barbecued his dog!'

'Wouldn't put it past him,' muttered her mother. 'If he got hungry enough he'd probably barbecue his gran. Oh dear god!' Sue stopped suddenly as she saw a body lying just inside the gate of Badger's drive. She recognized the tall, lean form and the close-cropped dark hair immediately. She broke into a run and was on her knees beside him in seconds.

'Nick! Nick?' The man was on his back, one arm thrown up over his head and the other outstretched to the side, as if he'd been pushed over backwards with some force. His eyes weren't quite shut and his mouth was slack, the lips puckered and dry. There was blood on his ear. She put her hand to his face, feeling the fine stubble on his chin graze her palm. He was cool. But not cold. She pressed her fingers to the side of his throat and let out a sharp exhalation of relief. There was warmth—and a pulse.

'What's happened? Is he dead?' Emma arrived, breathless, Jay close behind her. 'Shall I call an ambulance?'

Nick stirred, groaned and opened his eyes. Sue leaned

in, touching his face again. 'What happened? Were you attacked?'

He murmured something which sounded like, 'You see . . .' Suddenly he sat up, shaking his head, and then stared across at the open side door to the bungalow.

'Was it Badger—did Badger attack you?' demanded Sue, fury growing in her voice. He shook his head and staggered to his feet. 'Wait—don't get up! You might have a head injury!' Sue warned, rising with Nick and trying to steady him. But he stumbled across to the door regardless and held onto the frame, staring into the bungalow. 'Gone,' he said, at last. 'They're gone.'

'Nick! What happened?!' Sue stood hands on hips, her fair hair blowing in the smoky breeze. He turned to gaze at the woman and her children behind her, three pairs of round, scared eyes, innocent . . . clueless. He felt a sudden and overwhelming need to protect them. But they were already involved. What if Lucy brought others from her terror cell back? To clean up any loose ends?

'Let's go back to the cottage,' he managed. 'I need some water . . . Then I'll explain . . .' Explain what? He did not know what was happening. All he wanted to do was get them all away from this place . . . and away from the whole area if he could. His brain was cold, slow, and fuggy but as he walked he hoped he might be able to work something out; come up with a good reason for them all to get in the car and drive into Newport. Use a public phone to get the cavalry down here. He didn't trust the landline or their mobiles—Lucy had been in the cottage and could easily have bugged them all. Maybe even his own.

He let Sue take his arm and guide him, even though his strength was returning fast. What kind of weapon had Lucy used on him? Some kind of remote taser? There was no wound apart from the bloody dent in his ear where he'd hit a sharp stone. It had felt like he'd been body-slammed and paralysed in that half a second before he'd blacked out. Yes—some kind of taser—and she may have used it on Badger and the dog too. Or not. There were no bodies and, right now, no way to tell.

Jay held back as Mum and Emma took Nick home. He went to look at the burning cylinder. It stunk of petrol and charred old meat. Had Badger *really* tried to cook his dog? The guy was clearly drunk a lot of the time, so who knew? He called out a few times, in case Badger was hiding somewhere, and then did a quick check of the bungalow. It was filthy and smelly and, as far as he could tell, empty. No sign of the dog, either, in the house or the garage. The fire was dying down now, just a thin funnel of fumes rising from the half-moon crack where a heavy lid had been partially placed over the well of metal and flame. The incinerator wasn't near any wood or buildings, so he guessed it would be OK to leave it.

This was probably just a standard bit of meaningless Badger drama, he concluded. Not the first episode and certainly not the last.

As he walked up the drive he spotted something which made him stop dead. It was a piece of thick paper, rolled up. He picked it up and eased it open but he already knew what it was: a flier advertising Level 42 at Freshwater. The same one Mark King had given Lucy. Jay had watched her roll it up and push it reverently into her pocket, just a few hours ago. He suddenly felt cold, despite the heat of the day and the incinerator. There was no doubt about it. Lucy had been here. This afternoon.

'We're going up there,' said Jay. 'Right now. Something really weird is going on and I think it's all to do with Lucy.'

Emma stood on the sun-warmed quarry tiles of their back doorstep, staring again at the chessboard markings in the grass, displayed on her phone. In the kitchen, Mum was plying Nick with tea and cake. They were talking but so far Mum hadn't got much sense out of him. He seemed to be in shock but Emma couldn't imagine Badger hurting him. The man was too much of a coward to stand up to someone like Nick. 'Would you drive me into Newport?' Nick was asking Mum. 'And bring Jay and Emma . . . would you all come with me? Soon . . . in a minute . . .'

Jay heard this too. 'We've got to go *now.* He's trying to get us away from here . . . to stop us finding something out!'

Emma glanced through the doorway at the man at their table. She liked him. And she knew Mum did too. 'Do you think he's . . . you know . . . OK?'

'I don't know,' shrugged Jay. 'But he and Mum will come over all grown-up any second now and we won't have a choice. We'll be going to Newport to report Badger to the police or something.'

'Maybe we should . . .' said Emma. She looked scared.

'But Lucy . . . she was *there*!' hissed Jay, waving the curled flier at her. 'She's caught up in all this, I know it! We need to find out why! She's our *friend*!'

Emma stood up and nodded. 'You're right,' she said. 'Let's go.'

They flitted through the garden as quietly as possible and were soon running along the lane, past the smouldering grey cloud from Badger's place and on up to the steep wooded bank. 'We came this way,' puffed Emma, ten minutes later, as they ran through the trees close to the perimeter. 'Me and Lucy. I walked with her to the edge of the meadow and then pretended to walk back, about . . . here.' She paused and Jay stood still, too, on the edge of the trees, gazing across the grass. It was a very peaceful scene. The mast rose high into the air, its white finger seeming to poke into the velvety blue sky. At its base, the low level station was still; no sign of staff. The only movement came from the sheep, contentedly grazing around the small satellite dishes sited on the ground, and the occasional pigeon or rook flapping overhead.

Emma led him to the spot where Lucy had disappeared. The grass had settled a little but the chessboard pattern was still visible. Jay knelt down and ran his fingers through it. He didn't know what he expected to feel—static or magnetism? He felt nothing.

'Jay—look!' Emma was on her feet, moving away. 'There's another one!' She pointed to a second patch nearby in the grass. It had the same pattern, but the outline was longer—rectangular.

Jay took her phone and pressed the buttons, calling up LUCY from her contacts. 'We might as well try again,' he said.

She had slept, amazingly, for at least an hour. The crying had given way to long, shuddering breaths and, as she cocooned herself in her old, familiar sleep pod blanket, her breathing had settled slowly into the rhythm of sleep. Desperately needed, dreamless sleep. This blissful oblivion might have gone on for much longer if her phone hadn't gone off.

She shot up in her pod and grabbed at it reflexively. Even as she saw EMMA on the caller ID her memories of the past few hours were sliding rapidly into place. Emma spying on her and seeing her vanish into the cloakshaft. Discovering the stowaway Koth. The hunt. Badger. Killing the Koth in a flaming barrel of petrol. Stunning the guy from Emma and Jay's holiday park. Drugging and tricking Badger to follow her back to *Hessandrea* and trapping him in containment to await his terrible end.

Chit-chat with Emma was going to be impossible. She hit the REJECT CALL button and let out a long sigh. The benefit of her sleep wasn't lasting. She should be jubilant that she had saved Emma and Jay—and Earth—from the Koth. But it wasn't over yet, was it? Not until she'd killed all the babies inside Badger. And that couldn't be done without killing Badger too. How long did they have? She checked her watch. According to the files she'd read and the audio records from Sergeant Petrez, incubation lasted between ten and twenty hours. The host normally fell into a coma about four hours before the hatching. That was the only break a host got. You didn't know that much about it in the end . . .

She could take *Hessandrea* back up into space again. She could eject Badger into the void where he would simply expand and blow into atoms, taking all the baby Koth with him. But that hadn't worked before, had it? Not completely. Because one of the Koth had survived deep space on the outside of the ship, hadn't it? The thin atmospheric field around the vessel had somehow protected it for *ten years.* It must have gone into a statis, its heart beating so rarely the ship's monitors had failed to pick it up. It was only after they'd docked and the creature had woken itself that *Hessandrea* had detected its presence. What if the same thing happened again?

But *this* time she would get Mumgram to scan every millimetre of the ship for anything organic . . . even if it had no detectable pulse. She would not be fooled again.

Lucy knew she had been incredibly lucky to kill the Koth. Lucky that it hadn't made it to a more populated area and infected dozens of people. She guessed it had been slow from its long sleep. It had needed to rest, after laying its eggs, for longer than it normally would.

She shuddered again, recalling the terrible proximity of its circle of teeth; the dim, merciless red wells of its eyes; the stink from the greasy fur under its wings. She stood up, ignoring another call from Emma. Maybe it would be best if she *did* fly *Hessandrea* away from here—plotted a new path through Earth's atmosphere and landed somewhere else. She could start over again, couldn't she? After she'd killed Badger and the Koth babies. Find new friends. Her heart clenched inside as she pictured the open, trusting, smiling faces of Jay and Emma. She couldn't bear to think of never seeing them again.

She got up and took a shower. Her face felt like a mask. She had held a grimace on it for so long, it ached. After drying off, she slid into a grey, all-in-one suit—the kind she'd been wearing most of her life—and padded, barefoot, along to the bridge. It was late afternoon—teatime on the world below. She could take the ship up now, dispose of her unlucky passenger together with *his* unlucky passengers—and be back in time for breakfast.

But she wouldn't come back. She had made a total mess of everything. All the careful planning that had gone into her escape from Cornelian Eclata—all those great scientific minds; the effort, the design, the calculation, the inspiration, and the eventual realization of their dreams . . . that even one Eclatan might survive and carry on their line, their story, their legacy. And she had screwed it all up mightily in a matter of days after her arrival. The best thing she could do now was quit. Fly away. Start again on the far side of the planet. Australia would do. She could fit in there. Learn to surf . . .

The phone rang again. Emma. Emma. Emma for the third time. And Lucy felt a lump in her throat. Maybe it wouldn't hurt to have one more chat before she left. To hear that friendly voice again. Maybe Jay, too. She would love to hear Jay's voice one final time.

She hit the ANSWER button. 'Hi, Emma!'

But it was Jay. 'Lucy! Where are you?'

'Um—I'm at home,' she replied, sounding normal despite her heart apparently able to beat somewhere around her tonsils.

'Lucy—we have to see you. It's REALLY important! Look . . . you said you'd tell us, didn't you? You said you'd explain your secret . . . why you've been making things up. Lucy—I think you have to tell us now. There's no more time. Something's happening and we think . . . we think it's about you.'

Lucy stared at the screen over *Hessandrea*'s console. She could see Jay and Emma in the meadow below, standing on the cloakshaft patterns in the grass. They *knew*. Something.

'Lucy—are you there?'

'I'm here, Jay,' she said. 'And I know I said I'd tell you the truth when the time came . . . but I'm not sure the time *will* come now. I have to leave, you see. Me and Mum . . . we're going.'

'What?!' Jay spluttered. 'Just like that? No explanation!'

'Oh Jay, I *wish* I *could*,' Lucy wailed, and tears welled up and dripped over her newly showered face. 'But you'd freak out. And you'd probably call the police or something.'

Down in the field Jay looked at Emma, who had Lucy's voice on speaker. 'Lucy—we know you were down at Badger's place earlier. We found the Level 42 flier. You must have dropped it. Did you—did you do something to Nick? And Badger? Do you know what's happened to him?'

There was a groan through the phone. 'Is Nick OK? I only stunned him . . . he should be fine . . .'

'*Stunned him?!*' Emma's eyes were wide. 'Why, Lucy? Why did you do that?'

'I had no choice,' said Lucy. 'It was the best thing for everyone, please believe me.'

'We want to believe you but nothing makes sense!' cried Emma. 'I saw you disappear today! I spied on you—I'm sorry, but I did—and saw you walk across the field and then vanish into thin air. Lucy—what's going on? Don't you trust us? Aren't we friends?'

'There's someone coming,' said Lucy, suddenly. The screen showed a car heading along the road.

'Who's coming? Where?' asked Jay, staring around, trying to catch sight of Lucy amid the trees or behind the transmitter station.

'Wait a minute,' said Lucy. 'Stay where you are. Stay right there on the grass.' She was in turmoil. Emma and Jay had befriended her, honestly, with open, caring hearts. They deserved more than excuses and lies. Should she show them *Hessandrea*? Tell them about her world? Her heart thrummed harder in her throat and chest. *Could she? Could she do this? Mumgram would have a fit . . . but then, Mumgram could be switched off . . .*

'How do you know we're on the grass?' asked Emma. 'Are you watching us? Where are *you*? Lucy?'

'Um—look—how good are you at climbing?' asked Lucy.

'Er—OK,' said Jay, shrugging at Emma.

'Good. Walk towards the transmitter. You might feel a bit prickly, but don't worry about it. You'll be fine. I'll meet you at the gate . . .'

Emma suddenly felt goosebumps rise across her skin. At exactly the same moment, Jay shivered and started examining his arms where all the fine hairs stood to attention in a chessboard pattern. 'Are we going to vanish?' he asked Emma.

'You already have,' said Lucy, from Emma's phone. 'Keep walking. Don't say anything. They won't be able to see you but they might hear you . . .'

Emma and Jay, now walking, glanced around to see who Lucy meant by 'they' and spotted a car, carrying two of the transmitter station staff, cresting the steep road and heading for the station car park.

'Keep going,' said Lucy, puffing slightly, as if she were walking fast herself. 'Stay quiet. I'm coming to meet you at the gate.'

'They should be able to see us . . .' whispered Jay. Experimentally, he waved a hand at the men in the car. Neither waved back or gave any indication that they could see him, although one casually glanced across the field they stood in, his arm resting in the open window space of the car. 'Are we *really* invisible?' he breathed as they reached the chain link perimeter around the mast.

'Yes,' said Lucy, suddenly in front of them, unlocking the high metal gate, topped with barbed wire. 'You're in *Hessandrea*'s cloakshaft. It hides you from view. But shut up now because sound carries, particularly from above.'

Jay stared at Lucy. She looked different. It wasn't just the odd silvery catsuit thing she had on—there was something about her face, her eyes. She looked older. Authoritative. And alien in some way he couldn't explain.

'So . . .' Lucy smiled at them both, tightly. 'Are you sure you want to know my secrets?' They both nodded, dumbly. 'And you can definitely climb? A hundred and fifty metres?'

They glanced up, then at each other, gulped, then nodded again.

'Come on then—quick is best. Don't look down . . .'

Chapter 19

'Jay—Emma—meet my mum.'

Mumgram registered her new friends. She opened her mouth to welcome them. 'Warning. Intruder alert. Warning. Intruder alert.'

'Now that's no way to say hello to my friends!' protested Lucy. 'They're not intruders; they're guests.'

'Lucy, take your guests to the decontamination chamber immediately,' said Mumgram.

Whoa—she really *has* got issues, thought Jay. But if he'd been honest he would have to admit that Lucy's mum had bigger issues than fear of contamination. For a start, her daughter had just walked *straight through her.* 'They're fine, Mumgram. They don't need decon any more than I do,' Lucy said, motioning Emma and Jay to follow her along the pearly grey corridor. Emma was staring, open-mouthed, at the hologram in its well of light.

‘It is imperative for aliens to have a bioscan and decontamination,’ persisted Mumgram.

‘She’s not real—you’ve worked that out, yes?’ said Lucy, glancing over her shoulder. She had put her gleaming dark hair up into a high ponytail and in her close-fitting silver-grey catsuit she only needed a ray gun to look like a space-girl from some 1950s movie, thought Jay, his heart beating a little faster than before, if that was even possible.

Lucy turned at the end of the corridor and glanced at the woman as she poured instantly into another holographic light well. ‘But she is my mum . . . kind of. This is a holographic depiction of my mum. Her name was Beth. She looked exactly like this when she went.’

‘Where—where did she go?’ asked Emma, her voice sounding high and thin with shock and awe.

‘Out,’ said Lucy. She turned away with a flip of her ponytail and gestured for them to follow. ‘Come on—I’ve got lots to show you and tell you—but not much time.’

She led them into a wide, semicircular room with several rectangular monitors set into its curved walls and beneath these a broad, crescent-shaped console filled with buttons, faders, switches, assorted twinkling lights, and several keyboards. There were four high metal stools, with low backs, sited along the console. Three metres above them stretched a narrow metal catwalk, reached by a metal spiral staircase at either end. In front of the catwalk was a viewing deck. Jay guessed there must be glass or something, but it seemed almost as if nothing was there at all between the catwalk and a curving panorama of the late afternoon sky.

'Wow—mission control!' he marvelled. He turned and gazed at Lucy. 'Just . . . before we carry on . . . can I just check? We are . . . on a spaceship, right?'

'Well, yes,' said Lucy. 'Obviously.'

'And . . . this is where you live?'

'Yes. That's why it was tricky to ask you round.' Lucy smiled sadly. 'And this is a one-off visit. First and last chance to see . . .'

'Why?' demanded Emma. 'Where are you going? Are you running away from something?'

'No—*with* something,' said Lucy. 'Look—I will explain why I'm going before I go. But first . . . let me show you *Hessandrea*. I want you to see my world. And this . . . is it. The only world I've known for ten years, until I came to yours.'

Jay nodded slowly at her. 'So . . . you really are . . . an alien?'

'Yes.' she said. 'Come on—let me show you!'

First she directed them to an image on one of the

screens. The ship was shaped like a kidney bean. Its outer surface, beneath the cloak, was a greenish-silver in colour, like the sea at dawn, smooth and glistening, its flanks and underside studded with jewel-like lights from scores of brilliantly lit windows.

'The green light in the sky . . . it came from here?' queried Emma faintly.

'Erm—yes,' admitted Lucy. 'I think it was something to do with the atmostatis breach . . .'

'What's that?' asked Jay.

'I—I'll come to that,' said Lucy, turning away from them to prod some buttons on the console. Suddenly another hologram opened up in a light well before their startled eyes depicting Lucy's home in 3D. 'Here's the cross section of *Hessandrea*,' said Lucy, brushing the exterior view of the ship with her fingers so that the vessel split down the middle and then opened up like some kind of cosmic doll's house, only about six times the size of their cottage, Jay calculated. 'First the bridge, where we are now,' said Lucy. Three red blips indicated their presence on the bridge. 'Then the living quarters, the kitchens, the medi-bay, and the bioscan pods . . . the simulators and the recreation room. You can see them all! The rec room is the best . . . Come on—I'll give you a tour. Just follow me.'

The living quarters were sleekly designed and reminded Emma of a cruise ship with their space-saving styling. There were rooms with bunks and porthole windows and little stand-up niches under glass hoods which were steam showers, according to Lucy. 'We have water showers too,' she said. 'But steam showers are just as good and conserve water better.' The kitchens looked similar to something you might find in a five-star hotel—lots of shiny metal surfaces and platters, trays, and utensils, neatly stacked and contained behind translucent panels. Its ovens were behind spotless glass doors and there was a row of circular bowls, each with some kind of tap/hose attachment hanging from the ceiling above. It didn't look, or smell, thought Emma, as if much cooking got done here.

'Where are the chefs?' she asked.

'They went out,' said Lucy. 'But the assimilator makes my food. I don't need to cook. I couldn't make anything like your mum does anyway. Your mum's food is amazing. Heaven.'

More pods and beds and an odd medical unit with mysterious gadgetry could be seen on the next stage of the tour, along with a small but impressive gymnasium, its cool blue lighting picking out the purple chrome-like curves and angles of weird workout equipment, similar to the keep-fit machines at their nearest leisure centre . . . and yet somehow very different. Jay wanted to stop and try some out but Lucy was speeding up, taking them somewhere more important. The rec room. 'There's some gym stuff in here too,' she said, waving a door open. 'Kind of.' All the doors slid open at her wave.

It was a large round pod-like room with a blue floor and a gently domed blue ceiling. In the centre was a treadmill and an exercise bike, a rowing machine, and some skiing kind of gadget—a sort of cross trainer—all orientated in the same direction. They were all blue too. At the far end were two red chairs suspended high in circular blue structures without, apparently, any struts or posts or ropes. Just . . . suspended.

Lucy walked to a brightly lit plate on the wall and danced her fingertips across its multicoloured buttons. At once the room was transformed. The walls vanished and they were abruptly swept into the middle of a tropical forest beside a fast-flowing emerald river. Emma gave a startled cry as a bird of prey zoomed past her ear.

'You can run through it or bike through it or even row along the river!' said Lucy, grinning. 'This is my favourite program but there are loads of others. What do you think?'

Jay and Emma glanced at each other and then back

at her. 'I think this is . . . just . . . incredible,' said Jay. 'And I want to play every program in it. Particularly whatever works with those . . .' He pointed to the red chairs suspended in the blue rings. 'But unless I'm getting this all wrong, it feels very much like you're stalling. Distracting us. Like you're not going to tell us the real deal here. Who you are; where you come from; why everybody else has *gone out.*'

Lucy sank down to the floor, beneath the control plate, and sagged against the wall. She wrapped her arms around her knees and rested her forehead on top. Her voice came out small and muffled. 'The sooner I tell you, the sooner it all ends.'

'Why?' asked Emma.

'Because you don't know what I've done. And when you do . . . you'll reject me,' gulped Lucy. 'You'll never want to see me again.'

Chapter 20

'Keep still!' Sue dabbed at Nick's wound, just above his left ear, with antiseptic on a bit of cotton wool. He didn't make any fuss but he kept trying to get up. She still hadn't ruled out calling an ambulance.

'Seriously, Sue—I'm all right,' he insisted. 'The sweet tea helped enormously, but we have to get the kids and get out of here.'

Sue stopped dabbing and regarded her patient, head on one side. He looked flushed; his pale green eyes glittered and his hair was clumped with sweat, as if he'd put gel on it. She raised her hand. 'How many fingers am I holding up?'

He clicked his teeth impatiently. 'Three!'

'Follow my finger,' she said, moving an index finger slowly from left to right. He sighed and let his eyes follow it for about three seconds and then he stood up and grabbed her hand and pulled it against his chest, holding it tight in his fist.

'Sue. Listen to me. We must get Jay and Emma, get in the car, and go into town. Or anywhere with a phone.' His eyes were fixed on her and his tone was firm.

'We've got a phone here,' she protested.

'But we can't use it,' he said. 'It's not safe. Nor are the mobiles. Look—I haven't been a struggling would-be novelist for long. I used to be in the military—a pilot with the RAF—and later a special operative on several missions in Afghanistan and the Gulf. I have a very good instinct for danger. And that instinct has been on amber alert for most of this week. Today it hit red alert. I'm not wrong, Sue. Something is going on around here which you *do not* want to get caught up in. It's something . . .' he sighed and closed his eyes for a moment while she continued to stare at him, incredulously, '. . . it's something to do with this girl, Lucy.'

'Lucy?' Sue frowned and then looked back at him. 'OK . . .'

He let go of her hand, surprised. 'You believe me?'

Sue shrugged. 'Maybe. She's an odd one. Although I wouldn't have described her as dangerous. Just a bit strange.'

'Sue . . . Lucy's the one that knocked me out.'

'What? A teenage girl?!'

Nick nodded. 'Not with her bare hands. She had some

kind of rifle. Nothing I recognize. I think it might have been a type of taser.'

Sue dropped her pack of cotton wool and ran to the kitchen door. 'EMMA! JAY! IN HERE NOW!'

There was no response from the garden. She looked back at Nick, fear beginning to creep across her face. She called again. And then they both heard it. A whimpering sound. 'Oh no!' Sue ran out and Nick followed.

In the garden they heard it louder, coming from the tall hedge by the side gate. A high-pitched whimpering. 'JAY! EMMA!' *Oh lord—what if Lucy really was some kind of nutcase and had tasered her children?!* Sue darted forward, dropping to her knees, her jeans skidding across the damp grass. But beneath the thick privet hedge she found neither her son nor her daughter.

Nick was close behind her. 'Who is it? Emma? Jay?'

Sue looked around, blinking. 'Neither. It's Brad Pitt.'

For a second, Nick did wonder whether the day could get any odder. Then Sue carefully tugged a pale, four-legged figure out of the leaves. It was a pit bull terrier. The one owned—and entertainingly named—by Badger. The dog was shaking, its tail tucked tightly between its legs. 'Brad.' Sue held him cautiously. 'What's up? Where's Badger?' She glanced at Nick, puzzled. 'He's normally quite ferocious. He's bitten me twice.'

'Doesn't look too good, does he?' said Nick. He gnawed on his lip, wondering whether to tell Sue the rest. The dog whimpered again. It didn't look injured—just shocked and weak. Maybe Lucy *had* only tasered Badger and the dog. It would explain why there were no bodies in the cottage. Maybe Badger had just come to and staggered off, forgetting Brad. Or maybe he'd been dragged away. Nick couldn't imagine Lucy being fit enough to drag a grown man any distance—although she was undoubtedly strong and Badger was fairly skinny.

'Sue—there's something I haven't told you,' he said, deciding to be blunt. 'Lucy also shot the dog. And Badger.'

Now she *did* look disbelieving. 'But . . . *why*?'

'I don't know,' said Nick. 'But I'm sure it's got something to do with that.' He pointed up to the distant mast. 'Something is going on up there—the change in reception, the weird green flashes . . . the birds.'

Sue got up and Brad snuffled around her legs, seeking comfort. 'Nick—listen to yourself! You sound . . . a bit . . . nuts.' She held up both hands. 'I'm not saying you *are* nuts, but . . . TV and radio reception changes all the time. The engineers probably just tweaked some sticky-outy bit on one of the aerials! And the flashes . . . well . . . weather phenomenon! And . . . what *about* the birds?'

'They appear to be flying around something by the top of the mast. Something big. Something I can't see.' Even as he said it he realized how certifiable he sounded. She was probably going to run back into the cottage and barricade the door any second now, taking the dog with her for defence.

She was looking at him very hard. Trying to work him out. After a few seconds, the dog whimpered again and she glanced down at it. 'OK,' she said. 'Suppose I decide you're *not* having some kind of psychotic episode . . . and suppose I put this pathetic mutt in the kitchen with a bowl of water and then you take me up there and show me what you mean . . . ? We can shout for Jay and Emma on the way.'

'Yes—good! Please, let's go.' It wasn't ideal; he would far rather get her well away from here. But she clearly wasn't going anywhere without her children and nor was he. Privately he planned to persuade them all back here and into the car and away as soon as they caught up with Emma and Jay.

Sue put Brad in the kitchen with some water in a bowl and a blanket to lie on and came out, locking the door behind her. She insisted on using her mobile phone as she followed Nick onto the lane. 'Jay's phone's dead,' she said. 'He dropped it in Bembridge Harbour this morning. Well—he dropped *himself* in Bembridge Harbour. But Emma should have hers.' She dialled her daughter's number but it went straight to voicemail. She left a message: 'Call me IMMEDIATELY, Emma! It's an emergency!'

It didn't take long to reach the edge of the woodland. Nick held Sue back from view of anyone beyond the trees, trained his binoculars on the sky beside the mast and watched intently until a number of rooks took to the air. Then he handed the bins to Sue who put them to her eyes and watched. After a few seconds she brought them away from her face and turned to look at him. 'You're right. They *are* flying around something.' He nodded. 'But . . . couldn't that be some kind of magnetic field, from the mast, sort of pushing them away . . . messing with their navigation?'

'It could,' he said. 'But it doesn't look like that. I can't really explain why—I'm no bird expert—but the movement is too precise, every time . . . different kinds of birds, too, all making the same shape whenever they get close to the mast.'

Sue shivered. 'Come on—let's get back. Emma and Jay aren't here. They might be home by now. Probably wondering what on earth Badger's mangy mutt is doing in the kitchen.'

But at the cottage there was still no sign of Jay and Emma. Nick looked at the shivering dog on Sue's kitchen floor and felt a cold knot of dread begin to build in his belly. Something about the miserable creature filled him with a very bad feeling.

'Sue—is there any chance I can persuade you to get in the car and go now? I'll find Emma and Jay and drive them after you—meet you in Newport . . . ?'

'No chance at all,' said Sue, crouching down beside Brad and patting his slightly damp fur. 'Not without Emma and Jay. I'll buy into your conspiracy theory a *bit*, Nick—but not that much! Eeeuw.' She wrinkled her nose. 'He smells really weird.'

'Like what?'

'I don't know . . . musty . . .'

Nick dropped down to Brad, sniffing for a suspect almondy smell and tentatively running his hands along the dog's back and shoulders, seeking an injury under the fur. He found nothing to suggest the stitched incision he'd been dreading. He'd seen dogs used as walking explosives in the Middle East. Usually the bombs were strapped to them but it was not unheard of for a dog to be carrying a device inside, after some grim surgery by a hardened vet.

He relaxed. No—the creature smelt musty, true.

Like something from a damp cellar, but this dog was no canine time bomb.

'OK—I'm going to find Jay and Emma,' he said, standing. 'And I want you to be ready to go as soon as we get back. Promise me! And get a few essentials together in case you need to stay away for a while.'

Sue raised an eyebrow. 'Nick . . . are you really sure about this? It seems so . . . farfetched. Why don't I just call the police about Badger and report him missing, maybe hurt, and let them get on with it?'

'DON'T make any calls from the landline!' he insisted. He took her hands and guided her to her feet, locking eyes. 'Sue—look at me. Do you trust me? Do you?'

'I hardly know you,' she murmured, shaking her head. And then her face softened. 'But I do trust you. I just can't sit here, though! I want to help you search.'

'But what if they come back here?' asked Nick. 'It makes better sense for you to stay here and wait for them while I search. Keep calling them and stay in touch with me.'

Sue shook her head again. 'I will wait here for half an hour! No more. Nick . . . please get my kids and get back here fast!'

'I will,' he promised, releasing her hands and striding to the door. 'Be ready.'

Chapter 21

'Bethany Rumier, Science Officer, aboard the *Hessandrea* deep space voyager, twenty-three, fifteen, fifty-two.'

The woman's face was the same as the hologram, Emma realized. And although it was only 2D on the flat screen monitor, it was more *real* than the holographic version—more animated. Beth Rumier looked tired but focused as she punched a few buttons on the console and stared into the camera of whatever device had recorded this log entry so many years ago.

'Nine-fifteen Earth time,' she continued. 'Yes. We're on Earth time now. It makes sense to start getting used to it.' She gave a wry smile and glanced sideways as if someone else was nearby, watching. 'Even though we've got more than seven Eclatan years—and ten Earth years—to spend getting used to it.' She dropped her eyes for a few moments, considering, and then raised them to the camera again, a tight smile lifting her features just slightly. She had nut brown hair and hazel eyes and a wide, humorous mouth. The same elfin pointed chin as Lucy and the same well-marked eyebrows, thought Emma, glancing round at their space-girl friend as she leaned on the back of the high stools, between Emma and Jay, watching with them.

'If I'm honest,' said Beth with a nervous laugh, 'I never really thought this would happen—that we would ever launch out into space and leave Cornelian Eclata behind . . . for ever. But the home planet we knew is totally infected. Its human era is over. We managed to leave warning beacons at the inter-stellar comms centre, to keep explorers away. I really hope they take heed. We've also managed to inform the Quorat and they know of our plans. They wish they could help . . . but they're too far away. A handful of our people escaped through cleftonique corridors to Stradarus before they were shut, but . . . well, we number thirty-one, and we're the biggest—and only—group of survivors as far as we can tell.'

She then reeled off a list of names—everyone on board—concluding with, 'Lucy Hessa Rumier. Aged two and a bit in Eclatan years—but nearly *four* in Earth years!' A warm smile wove across her face and she ducked away from view for a few seconds before returning with a little girl in her arms. The child had wide blue-green eyes beneath a floppy dark fringe and a soft, dimpled face as she beamed into the camera. Beth squashed her daughter's pink cheek against her own. 'Say hello, Lucy,' she instructed, and Lucy lifted a chubby hand and said, 'Hello.'

Jay glanced from the child on the screen to the girl next to him and felt oddly moved. 'Why did you leave your planet? What was it that infected your people? Some kind of plague?'

'Some kind . . .' agreed Lucy, pausing the film and replacing it with another. This time a young soldier in military fatigues identified himself as Sergeant Petrez. He seemed to be underground, half his narrow face lit by a pale yellow glow from somewhere below. 'You have to be smarter than Koth,' he said. 'You have to think like the Koth to know it . . . and then learn how to kill it before it gets you. I know everyone's giving up but there's NO WAY a soldier can do that. Not against Koth. Not ever. I've got a suit—a better suit than the first ones—and I'm going to use it and get out there and start fighting back. One of those ugly schteckers made a host of my little brother. Turned him into an incubator for its monsters.' The man's features darkened and the camera he was holding in his outstretched palm shuddered, making his grimly set face shake on the screen. 'I'll tell you what I've learned about how to kill them in my next feed. And don't you believe that they can't be killed. They *can.* You just have to know how . . .'

The film vanished into a black dot and Jay turned to stare again at Lucy. 'What the hell . . .' he said, '. . . is the Koth?'

Lucy went to press another key but Jay grabbed her hand and shook his head. 'No! Enough with the public information films!'

Emma nodded. 'Lucy—just tell us. Tell us in your own words.'

Lucy glanced from one to the other and then sighed. 'I'll try. But you have to remember, I was only little.' She moved away, rubbing her face, and then sat down, cross-legged, on the floor. Emma and Jay slid off the high stools and went to join her, sitting close by. 'The Koth came in on a freighter, they say. This big cargo ship.'

'Sea-going or space-going?' asked Emma, like it was the most natural thing in the world, thought Jay. They'd had less than an hour to accept the fact of an alien spacecraft in their world but she seemed to be rolling with it . . .

'Sea-going,' said Lucy. 'But our seas also had space portals. The oceo-space centres combined their technology, you see, for craft which could journey beyond our atmosphere in both directions—into the cold vacuum of space or into the cold depths of the oceans. The technology for both types of craft is very similar. So probably the Koth came from outside our atmosphere . . . from space. But the first we knew about them was when the freighter came in from a four-month voyage across the Great Sea. Everybody on it was dead. Everybody except one guy, who'd locked himself in a box in the hold and was pretty much insane. They couldn't really get any sense out of him. The dead people looked as if they'd . . . composted.'

'Composted?' echoed Jay. 'What—like the stuff down the end of the garden?'

'Yes—like that. Like heaps of mulchy, musty organic matter,' said Lucy. 'They were still roughly the shape of human beings but they hadn't decayed like any dead body you've ever seen. The people who found them were baffled. For about a week. By the end of the week it was abundantly clear what had happened to the men on the freighter. Because it had happened to everyone who'd gone on board the ship. The ship was held in a closed, covered dock, while it was under investigation. Someone said it looked like bats had moved in and were roosting high in the rafters. They weren't bats. For a start, the size was wrong. Some were as tiny as moths. And some were as big as dogs with wings. They hung upside down like bats, though. And their faces . . .' She gulped. 'Their faces were like something from hell. I can't describe them. I can show you pictures—of all of this. It's all in *Hessandrea*'s archives.'

'What happened?' prompted Emma, noticing that Lucy's hands were shaking.

'They attacked. One by one they spiralled down and attacked the staff in the port. Very fast. Some of them very stealthily, so people didn't always know, but most of them fiercely—hungrily.'

'They were predators . . . of humans?' asked Jay.

'Not in the way you think,' said Lucy. 'They don't eat meat. They eat vegetation. Not that anyone knew that then. They had teeth and they left wounds but the attacks weren't deadly. The staff escaped the dock building and sealed it and got the wounds treated. They seemed quite minor. They had no idea . . .' She tailed off, staring at something, somewhere, that Emma and Jay couldn't fathom.

'Koth breed,' she resumed, a few seconds later. 'Fast. They're asexual—they don't mate with each other. They just reproduce through egg laying but they have a very specific way of doing that. The eggs must be inserted into warm, living flesh. Human flesh is just fine.'

Emma gulped and glanced at Jay who was looking as horrified as she was.

'What happened next?' asked Jay.

'The port staff—nine men and three women—were all in a coma ten hours later, hospitalized,' said Lucy. 'And shortly after that the baby Koth started to hatch through their skin. The skin went yellow and tight and . . . woody, almost . . . like it was degrading back to carbon. And then these peaks would suddenly rise up across it, like small volcanoes . . . and from each a baby Koth would erupt and fly away. Twelve, from every host. Sometimes less—never more. The hosts were all dead by the time the Koth emerged. We think. We hope.'

Her friends were silent, trying to imagine such a horrific scene. 'Then . . . then what?' whispered Emma.

'Twelve times twelve times twelve times twelve . . .' said Lucy. 'That's twenty thousand, seven hundred and thirty-six Koth in three days. Two hundred and forty-eight thousand, eight hundred and thirty-two in four days. Nearly three million by day five. They spread so fast and grew so fast. The baby Koth matured and could lay eggs themselves within hours. By the time the scientists had even half worked out what was going on, most of the port town was infected. Twenty-three thousand people—none of them quarantined. Whole streets were nothing but human compost in less than a week. Livestock and pets too—but mostly humans. There was panic. Terror. The authorities could only say "stay indoors" but indoors wasn't safe. The baby Koth were the size of moths when they hatched—the size of an Earth sparrow inside an hour. If they could get to food they doubled in size every hour. And they were searching for food within seconds of hatching—flying through gaps in houses, shops, schools—lodging in trees and bushes. Small, brown, virtually invisible in amongst leaves. Undetectable on aircraft. They hitched rides all over the planet. We had no chance.'

'Didn't you fight back?' asked Jay.

'Of course!' said Lucy. 'The military suited up and went nuts, trying every weapon they could lay their hands on. But short of setting the whole planet alight, there was nothing they could do. They tried gas and biological weapons, airborne insecticides, poisoned crops, nuclear blasts. Eclata's scientists were all locked away in bunkers trying to work out what the Koth's weak point was. They never found it. The only solution was to abandon the planet.'

'So—that's what you did,' breathed Emma. 'You escaped.'

Lucy nodded. 'There was a bunch of scientists—about thirty of them. They were out in a base in the middle of a desert where they'd been working on a mission to explore deep space for years and were building a ship—*Hessandrea.* In the last two weeks, once they realized the Eclatans were going to be wiped out, they started loading supplies and making plans to evacuate from the planet. The Eclatan leaders were due to come with us, with their families. But they never made it. If they had we would have numbered more than one hundred. But they didn't. They all died on the journey across the desert to the *Hessandrea* launch station. So that left just the scientists, the engineers, and the pilots and their families. When they realized the others weren't coming, they launched. We threw ourselves up through the atmosphere and onto the mercy of deep space.' Lucy smiled, glancing up at the view of the early evening sky—streaks of pink cloud against the blue—as if she was thanking deep space for taking her into its embrace for so long.

'We plotted a journey to a planet that could sustain us,' she went on. 'There were several planets in our galaxy which were closer but we couldn't go there. Some were at war and would never even allow us past their moons. Some had barely any water and only primitive life forms.

Ayot and Tarbalis sent advice and condolences but we couldn't go there. We all look much the same but we breathe different gases. We wouldn't have survived a day on either planet; not without a permanent protective suit and that's no way to live. A handful made it to Stradarus through cleftonique corridors—sort of temporary planet-to-planet wormholes, I guess you'd call them. But those were closed as soon as the Stradarans realized no quarantine was safe enough. We knew Earth was the best option even though it was such a long journey.'

'So the Koth took your world,' concluded Jay. 'And you came here for refuge.'

Emma took Lucy's hand. 'Why would you think we would reject you? Of *course* we don't! We're just . . . amazed. I mean—wow—our new best friend is a space-girl! An alien!'

'So . . . the crew,' said Jay. 'Where are they all?'

'They went out,' said Lucy.

'Wow—you mean they've already spread across the island? Across the country?' marvelled Jay. 'Aliens all over the UK! Wow!' Jay shook his head. 'It explains a lot!' said Jay, grinning. 'The Nipe trainers for one thing.' But Lucy didn't smile. Lucy's lovely laugh remained locked away. She stared at her feet and her face seemed to turn solid, mask-like.

'You don't know,' she said.

'What?' asked Jay. 'What don't we know?'

'What I've done.'

Chapter 22

Nick rummaged through the large waxed canvas holdall under his bed and gave a grunt of satisfaction as he pulled out a bright red tube. He had several off-shore rocket flares—all still well in date. He grabbed three and shoved them into his backpack along with some other useful things. He wished he'd brought his service pistol with him. Of course, when he'd arrived on the island and sought refuge in this charming cedar-wood cabin, the last thing he'd expected to need was any kind of weaponry. He'd only packed the flares with some romantic notion that he might go out boating at some point.

Wearing army boots, khaki cargo pants, and a dark green sweater, all he now needed was a balaclava for the full guerrilla look. But he settled for a grey peaked cap to stop the light glancing off his face.

Back through the woods he moved as he'd been

trained. Silently. Rolling his steps, pushing on faster when the wind gave him cover by rustling the leaves. He couldn't be sure how many were involved in Lucy's cell. There could be just a tiny group—only two or three—ready to take desperate measures like tasering people or even kidnapping them. Or there could be a dozen spread out across the island, checking in by mobile phone or radio, using the mast area as a communication hub as they planned some major assault.

He'd thought about contacting David again—but until he had something concrete to offer up there was no point. The flares in his bag—and the camcorder—might be able to give him something concrete.

At the edge of the woodland he scanned the meadow and the low building housing the mast station control room and its staff. From here he couldn't be sure, but it didn't look like anyone was at the site. Of course, he would have been relieved to find Emma and Jay here—or anywhere along his route. But he was also relieved to *not* find them just yet. Ideally they'd show up *after* his experiment, in time to run back to the cottage and get away. There were no cars parked outside the building now; the engineers had probably clocked off for the day. In any case, he was going to have to leave the cover of the woodland. Back here the angle was all wrong and it was just too far away. The flares had a height range of up to three hundred and fifty metres—around twice the height of the mast. That was important. They needed to be travelling at speed when they reached their target. If there *was* a target and he wasn't just cooking up a load of nonsense because of some deeply buried desire to see action again.

But no. Lucy really *had* shot him. And Badger and the dog. *That* was nothing he'd cooked up. And Sue had also seen what he meant about the birds. And they'd *all* seen the weird green light in the sky. Whatever was happening, it was slowly taking shape. Revealing itself. And Nick was about to speed that revelation up a bit.

He ran across the grass, his movements low, level, and economical, towards the abandoned flatbed truck trailer on the gravel turning area beyond the gate. This was the perfect launch pad.

It took him a few minutes to set up the camcorder with the tripod on the flatbed. He positioned it to focus on the area to the side of the mast; the patch of sky that no bird flew through any more. Then he took out his first flare and prepared to use it, pressing the red REC button on the camcorder.

'My name is Nick Dobson, former Flight Lieutenant Dobson of the RAF, currently retired . . .' he began, wondering how to continue. 'What you're seeing here is the Rowridge transmitter on the Isle of Wight. The date and time you can see on your screen. It's my belief that there is some unidentified object or . . . field of some kind . . . I want to say force field but then you'll all have me down as some kind of *Star Trek* geek who should really get out more . . . so let's just say a magnetic field. Several people—myself included—have witnessed some odd green lightning in the clouds around this space. And I've observed that no birds fly through this area, although they do skirt around it in a defined arc. But that's hard to prove on camera so I've brought something which should make it all clear. Either that I'm on to something or that . . . well, I should just give up, go with the flow, get some stick on pointy ears, and learn Klingon.'

He grasped the first red flare and held it aloft. 'Well . . . here goes nothing!' And he pounded the bottom end hard against the flatbed. The flare ejected at once, with a firework *whoosh.* It shot high into the air and then did something very odd. It seemed to strike an invisible surface, its powdery red smoke suddenly fanning out like a parasol and highlighting a shallow dome-like curve for a few seconds before drifting Earthward again.

Nick sat back on his heels, gaping in shock. He had pictured exactly this in his mind—but until now he had not been able to truly believe such a fantastic idea; that something big and dense and unmoving was *really* floating there in the sky at the top of the mast. Now there was no arguing with it. He gulped and scrambled back to the camera with his second flare. 'Did you see that?' he croaked. 'There's something up there!' The hairs were standing up along his arms, neck, and shoulders and his heart was thundering in his chest. He did not know whether he was terrified or thrilled. He set off a second flare, changing the angle slightly. The same. A blast into the air and then the impact star of red as it struck the invisible object above.

Shaking, he picked up the camera and raced across to the far end of the field, turning back to fire the flare again. He'd need many more to fully gauge the size of this thing. His brain was whirring with calculations and wild fantasy. It could be the size of a football stadium or just a house . . . it could be a Russian or Chinese spy airship with camouflage technology well beyond any Western power's current reach—or it could be the lowered proboscis of some vast intergalactic space insect . . .

Whatever it was, his mind couldn't do any more backflips. This day simply could not get any freakier.

And then a rectangle of light appeared four metres

to his right—a silver-blue door in the middle of an empty field. And Lucy stepped out of it.

The alarm had gone off with theatrical timing. Lucy had just opened her mouth to confess what she'd done to Badger when Mumgram appeared in every light well in the ship, a siren sounding behind her warning: 'Lucy! ALERT! *Hessandrea* is under attack. Lucy! ALERT! *Hessandrea* is under attack!'

She had fled to the console, Emma and Jay just behind her, and discovered two hits on the defence shields. Insignificant hits which caused no problem to the ship at all. Except that for someone to shoot a missile at *Hessandrea*—twice—they would have to know she was *there.*

'Look! It's Nick!' yelled Jay, above the sirens.

'What's he doing?' Emma stared in fascination. Nick was on the truck thing she had stood on a couple of days ago—and he seemed to have a camera with him. Red smoke was floating about in the air.

'Why is he here?' asked Jay and then he remembered, with a thud of shock, and turned to Lucy. 'He must have seen you before you knocked him out. He's come after you!'

Lucy slumped against the console and put her face in

her hands. 'I only stunned him . . .' When she looked up, Jay had an expression on his face which sent spirals of cold dread through her chest. Like he didn't know her *at all.*

'You *stunned* Nick . . . and you still haven't told us why. All this stuff . . .' He waved his hands around him. 'And your story about the Koth—it's been amazing. But you've still not explained—somehow—why you attacked Nick!'

Lucy gulped. 'Look—all of this . . . I had no choice!'

They all gazed back at the monitor and saw Nick get down off the truck bed and start running across the field, taking the camera with him.

'Oh no! Oh no—I can't let this happen! I can't let him go!' moaned Lucy, looking stricken. 'He needs to understand!'

'What are you going to do?' asked Jay, and there was ice in his voice. '*Stun* him again?' He couldn't believe that all the amazing stuff he'd seen and heard had made him forget what this girl had done.

Lucy turned and ran out of the bridge. 'Not if I don't have to! Please—just wait for me. I'm bringing Nick on board. There's something I have to tell you all—and he has to know too now . . .' She shouldered the frostlaser rifle and ran for the exit dock. 'Mumgram—

be ready to cloak me and follow—and uncloak when I give the word!'

As soon as she reached the ground she saw what Nick was preparing to do. He was about to fire off another rocket. What on earth did he think he was doing? But then she saw the camera and it was obvious—he was getting proof of *Hessandrea*'s existence. If that was all it was it might not matter—she and *Hessandrea* would be gone in an hour or less. But the red flares would attract all kinds of attention. Suppose the emergency services came to check it out? Suppose they sent helicopters or spotter planes? With small craft in the air she couldn't possibly launch *Hessandrea.*

But she MUST launch *Hessandrea* before the baby Koth hatched. She must destroy them all in space to be sure they were gone for ever. And then she must leave. Find a new home on the other side of the world. Make new friends . . .

'Cloakshaft off,' she called into her wrist communicator. At once her invisibility lifted and she stepped into full view.

'Nick,' she said. 'We need to talk.'

The man put down his camcorder, slowly, carefully. In his other hand he held a red stick which she recognized as a rocket flare.

'I'd feel happier about talking,' he said, 'if you'd drop your weapon on the grass.'

'Can't do that,' said Lucy. 'But I'm not pointing it at you, am I? I'm sorry about earlier. I had no choice. It was for your own safety, believe me.'

He stood, still holding the rocket flare. There was a concrete fence post right behind him. He could easily whack the flare against it and send it right at her. This was a stand-off.

'All right,' said Lucy. 'I'll drop the frostlaser if you drop the rocket flare. Count of three . . . OK?' She held out the rifle in one hand. He did the same with the rocket flare. 'Three, two, one—DROP!'

They both looked at each other in surprise as the weapons hit the grass with two dull thuds.

Even as she blinked he ran at her and flipped her over. She had three seconds to judge that he was good—martial-arts trained and fit. Fortunately, so was she. She twisted in his grip and sent a sharp kick into his ribs before she hit the ground, sending him staggering backwards for a few vital seconds. In that time she rolled and leaped back onto her feet, hands raised, ready to block and deflect. He dived, feet first, swept both boots at her ankles and had her in a scissor grip and toppling over.

As her face slapped into the cool turf he was upon her

in a second, but she sent an elbow back and reconnected hard with his ribs before wriggling away and springing upright once more. A heavy thud to her middle told her she had missed a beat and given him time to chop his right hand into her sternum. She doubled up, winded, and rolled across the grass again, where she flung her hand behind her head and grasped the frostlaser.

He kicked it away before she could fire. At least . . . that's what had been his plan. But the kick was angled wrong and the impact of his boot triggered a blast which hit him broadside. In a second he was down, sucking in air, unable to move but still conscious. Lucy sat up, panting, laid the rifle down and went to bend over him. 'Nick—please! This is all pointless! I'm going to tell you everything anyway.'

He stared at her, fury in his eyes, paralysis in his limbs. 'You'll be fine in just a few minutes,' she explained. 'I *was* going to ask you, if I'd had the chance, to climb up with me. But you won't be able to stand up for another ten minutes, let alone scale a one-hundred-and-forty-metre mast and climb on board!'

His eyes widened and swivelled skywards.

'Yes—you're right. There *is* something up there,' she admitted. 'It's *Hessandrea* . . . my spaceship. Now—if you just close your eyes and relax I'll get you on board with the tractor beam. It only works on passive objects so, if you should get any energy back mid-journey, please don't move! It could go a bit wrong if you do.' She clicked something which glowed green on her wrist and gave it some instructions. 'And I'll go up the mast and meet you in the cargo dock,' she told him. 'See you in about five minutes . . .'

Nick didn't speak. He couldn't. He watched the girl stand, collect her weapon, along with his backpack, camera, tripod, and flare, and vanish again. And at that moment his skin tingled with pins and needles and, still lying flat, he began to rise, steadily and slowly, as if he were on an open-air lift. A gentle downdraft across his face made his eyes water. And slowly, slowly, he saw the sky above him ripple and reveal a curved flank of dark silvery metal with a green sheen. A blue-white circle of light opened in it. He rose into the light and lost consciousness.

Chapter 23

He came to with three pairs of anxious eyes upon him. Lucy—and Emma and Jay.

'Where the hell am I?' he burbled.

'You're safe,' said Emma. 'It's OK—Lucy's not dangerous . . . I *think*.'

She and Jay exchanged glances and shrugs. If they were honest they had no idea whether Lucy was dangerous. What they'd experienced on board *Hessandrea* had blown their minds and, frankly, Emma wasn't sure of *anything* any more. She and Jay had watched Lucy and Nick fighting on the monitors and it was like some surreal computer game—they had both stood there, open-mouthed, while two people fought each other like martial arts champions on the grass below. Two people who, only that morning, had seemed like perfectly harmless, affable friends, living in the ordinary world.

When Nick disappeared into the cloakshaft a few

seconds after Lucy, Emma had turned to her brother and said, 'Jay—will you kick my leg?'

He turned wide and distracted eyes on her. 'What?'

'Kick me!' she ordered. He shrugged and did so.

'*Ow!*' She rubbed her shin and looked at him balefully.

'You did ask . . .' he said.

'I know. I just wanted to be sure this wasn't a dream,' she muttered. 'And I'm still not . . . I could have just dreamed the pain of you kicking me . . .'

Then Lucy had arrived and taken them down to a large, brilliantly lit cargo dock area. It was filled with hundreds of storage boxes, made of some pearly white material, with lettering on them which Emma and Jay couldn't read. On the hexagon-patterned blue floor lay Nick with his eyes closed. When he woke up, Emma was flooded with relief. Although what he was going to make of *Hessandrea* and Lucy the space-girl, she could only guess.

'Emma—Jay . . .' he croaked, unsteadily raising his hands as if they were very heavy and rubbing his face. 'Are you OK? You're not hurt?'

'No—we're fine,' Emma assured him. 'Just a little bit freaked out, that's all. I mean, it's not often you find out your friend is an alien and lives on a spaceship, invisibly hovering in the air quite near to your house . . .'

'Who else is here?' he asked and then, looking at Lucy, 'Who's running this ship? You'd better take me to them.'

Lucy smiled thinly. 'I'm running it,' she said.

'*You're* running it?' He sat up now, running his hands through his hair and screwing up his face, working away the stiffness. 'Just you? You're telling me you're not part of a cell?'

'A cell?' Lucy shook her head. 'Well . . . I suppose you could say I *was* part of a cell, kind of, to start with. But not now.'

'OK—so what happened to everyone else?' he asked. His voice was hostile and Jay couldn't blame him; he'd been shot at twice by Lucy now, as well as given a pretty hard time in a fight. That had to dent any bloke's ego a bit.

'Oh, Nick—there's so much to tell you,' said Emma. 'And we don't even know the half of it yet. But Lucy's OK! She's still the same girl she was yesterday! She's still our friend.' In the corner of her eye, Emma saw Lucy stare at her in amazement.

Lucy stood up and offered Nick a hand to help him to his feet. 'Nick—I do have a lot to tell you, but I really don't have much time. Please come up to the bridge and I'll let Mumgram give you the history of Cornelian

Eclata and why we had to leave and come here . . . she'll be much quicker and better than me. You can have something to eat and drink, too . . . it'll help you recover.'

He grunted at her, still glowering about the shooting and the fight, but followed on keenly enough as they returned to the bridge. Throughout the journey, via a high-speed lift which seemed to be made of white crystal, and along past the sleep pods to the bridge, he stared around in awe, drinking in the reality of *Hessandrea* much as Emma and Jay had, earlier that day.

Lucy seated Nick at the console and offered him some sleek silver earphones. 'It'll help you concentrate and get the story quicker. I'll run the films in succession . . . then you'll understand.'

They left him watching and went to collect hot drinks and sweet biscuits. Emma and Jay found they were suddenly—amazingly—hungry, so Lucy, with a quick dance of her fingers against the control panel in what she called 'the sim room', ordered the same for all three of them. One wall of the sim room was covered in hatches of different sizes, made of a dark red metal of some kind. The food sim hatches were on one side of the room and clearly used often by Lucy. 'Here you go,' she said, handing them each a round, deep cup of hot chocolate (or something like it) and what she called 'carbisks'. The drink was definitely chocolatey but had a very nutty flavour and the carbisks reminded Jay of rusks—the big, sweet, floury biscuits he'd had when he was little.

They took the same back to Nick a few minutes later, to find the films had ended and the earphones were off and he was examining the console in great fascination. As Lucy, Emma, and Jay came back he turned and regarded Lucy with a whole new expression of astonished awe . . . and only a hint of wariness.

'I don't know what to say to you,' he murmured, eventually.

Lucy shrugged and put the hot drink into his hand. 'Go on,' she said. 'You'll feel better.'

Nick took a sip—and then several gulps. Then he put the cup down and got back to marvelling at Lucy and *Hessandrea.* 'OK—I've got my head around why you're here now. And . . . I'm . . . well . . . staggered. I've always believed other civilizations are out there in the universe—somewhere. Seemed logical to me . . . but . . .'

'I know—it's bound to be a shock,' said Lucy. 'But Nick—and Emma and Jay—there's much more you need to know before I go.'

'Your world . . . your ship . . . the whole Koth taking your planet thing . . . phew!' Nick blew out his cheeks and blinked several times. 'But what I want to know now,' he said, 'is what happened to the rest of your crew.'

Lucy sat on the floor again, her back against a wall and her arms hugging her knees. Emma and Jay joined her. After a few seconds Nick sat down with them too.

'They went out,' said Lucy, 'into space . . .'

Chapter 24

'Something about space must have slowed it down, because it didn't attack for a week,' she said. Her face was pale and, for the first time, Jay noticed how tired she looked. There were blueish shadows under her eyes and her mouth was . . . crumpled.

'A Koth came with us. Nobody ever worked out how. Maybe it came in on some of the supplies—the fresh fruit and vegetables. We didn't know anything about it until one of the crew—a pilot called Hansen Jolath—fell into a coma in his sleep pod. He was probably attacked while he slept, because it was only when he didn't arrive on the bridge for his next shift that they went to look for him and found him . . . unwakeable. He was taken into the medical room and they found a little blister on his back. No teeth marks; just the blister. He smelt funny, apparently. Some of them said he must be ejected—straight away—into space. But others argued for his life—that he should be quarantined, in case he *wasn't* infected. It could still be something else . . .' She hugged her knees in tighter and stared at nothing for a few moments before she continued.

'So they put him in containment and watched. And his body went rigid and his skin yellowed. And as soon as the baby Koth started to erupt out of him they blew him out into space.' She took a long slow breath. 'I didn't see any of this at the time,' she went on. 'I was too young. Mum shielded me from it. But it was all recorded. It's there in the film archive if you want to see it. And it wasn't over, of course. The original Koth was still on board and at this point the systems weren't properly up and running and finding it through the sensors wasn't possible. They'd launched in such a rush, *Hessandrea* wasn't fully operational, you see. Another crew member was attacked. Kastin Robuth—a doctor. This time there was no doubt. There were teeth marks and he felt the pain and saw the Koth. It was about the size of a large bird, he said. He tried to hunt it down with the hours he had left, but couldn't find it. He asked them to blow him out into space as soon as he lost consciousness—not to wait and see. He couldn't stand the thought of being a host . . .'

Emma shuddered and Jay gave her shoulder a squeeze. He could imagine it too.

'So—after that, it worked its way through everyone on the crew. They tried everything they could think of. They suited up—some of them—and went hunting for it. But there were only ten deep-space suits on board. They were designed to allow the maintenance crew outside to make any repairs. Very lightweight—but you could pierce them if you really tried. And they'd all been hung up in the cargo dock—the place the first Koth attack happened. So nobody could be sure whether a tiny Koth—moth-sized—hadn't already got inside.'

She closed her eyes briefly and then carried on. 'One of the crew got infected but didn't tell anyone. She was terrified of going to containment—it was like walking into your own grave. So she hid. They found her in a coma—in the loading dock, and they had to smother her in plastic because the Koth were just about to hatch. One got out while they took her body away. They hunted it down and froze it and vented it within two hours. They got the big one, too, the next day.'

'But then there was another . . .' guessed Jay, his face grim.

She sighed. 'It took eleven days—earth time—before there were just two of us left. Beth and Lucy Rumier. And Mum nearly won. My mum nearly did it. She killed the last Koth when it attacked her in the sim room. She cornered it and blasted it with the frostlaser to immobilize it and then vented it into space. *Hessandrea*'s sensors were properly working by this time and confirmed that there were only two living entities left on board. Mum and me. We were finally safe. Then she saw the teeth marks and the puncture wound on her back. So she spent four hours programming herself into the ship's holographic system and connecting her voice to the computers. She created a new mum. A mum that could not be killed by Koth. Then she cuddled me for a little while, read me a story, put me to bed . . . squeezed my hand. And went out.'

Emma felt tears well up in her eyes and gulped several times.

'She went out through the cargo dock,' added Lucy in a soft monotone. 'Because in containment, someone else had to press the button. And the only someone else was me. And she couldn't have that. She had to do it herself. When I woke up my mum was still there . . . in a way. But even then, I knew she wasn't real. She didn't smell of anything. And I couldn't touch her. But . . . she wasn't a bad substitute. She got me here.'

There was silence for several seconds as Jay, Emma, and Nick absorbed Lucy's story and tried to imagine being four and having only a hologram to love for ten years. Having nobody to pick you up when you fell over; nobody to stick a plaster on a wound or touch your forehead to know you were unwell. Nobody to brush your hair and give you a hug. Just an untouchable, ever-present source of guidance to help you do all of this for yourself.

Lucy looked up at them and then got to her feet. 'But she didn't just get *me* here,' she said and grimness settled into her voice. 'She also got the Koth here.'

Nick was on his feet in an instant. 'Here? On Earth? Are you sure?'

Lucy closed her eyes. 'Yes. One of the Koth—only one—was *outside*, clinging to *Hessandrea*'s hull for *ten years*. It must have put itself into some kind of stasis and somehow it survived, hiding in the thin layer of gravity around the ship. There was no sign of it through the scanning systems, I promise you. I *promise*! I would *never* had landed if I had known. It must have woken up once it reached the warm atmosphere of Earth. I only found out today.'

Nick and Emma and Jay looked pale and horrified.

'But—it's OK! I've killed it!' Lucy nodded vigorously at them. 'The Koth is dead. I tracked it through *Hessandrea*'s tracer system. It hadn't got far. It was at Badger's place—in his garage. I went after it with the frostlaser, immobilized it and then dropped it into a tank of petrol and set light to it. It's dead. Totally, totally dead and gone. Nothing left. No danger.'

Nick shook his head. 'So *that* was what you were doing! And you shot me because I showed up at the wrong time . . . ?'

She nodded. 'You only get about ninety seconds to despatch a Koth once it's been frostlasered. No time to even start to explain anything to you.'

Nick nodded, slowly. 'And Badger . . . did he get caught up in the crossfire too?'

'Not exactly,' said Lucy. She studied her feet for a few seconds before looking up. 'Come and see.'

She led them through the ship to the containment chamber, where Badger lay on his front on the blue panelled floor of a small grey room, his head turned towards them and his eyes filmy grey slits in his face.

'Oh no,' whimpered Emma and Jay groaned in horror.

'Look,' said Lucy. 'On his shoulder.'

A circle of red teeth marks patterned the skin of Badger's bony shoulder, some hidden by the grubby string vest. In the centre was a distinctive pale pink blister. Emma felt sick as she noticed that Badger's skin was looking taut and yellow. Was he already 'composting'?

'He's infected . . .' breathed Nick, resting his palms on the glass and staring through in horror.

'Yes,' said Lucy. 'I saw the marks on him almost as soon as he showed up. Then I had to think of a way to get him here so I could contain it. The only other way would have been to get him into the fuel tank after the Koth and set fire to him too . . . but I . . . I couldn't do it.'

'So you blasted him unconscious to get him out of the way until you'd killed the Koth,' went on Nick. 'And then you had to blast me too.'

'Yes. Sorry,' said Lucy.

He nodded. 'Apology accepted. I'd have done the same.'

'How did you get Badger here?' asked Jay. 'You didn't drag him all through the woods, did you?'

'No,' said Lucy, with a little humourless laugh. 'I woke him up and used a shotstick to drug him slightly. Enough to persuade him to take a walk with me. Then I blasted him unconscious again and got him on board the same way as I did with Nick.'

Jay stared at the sprawled, motionless form behind the glass. 'Well . . . it couldn't happen to a nicer bloke,' he muttered, grimly. 'But I still wouldn't wish it on him.'

'What are we going to do with him now?' asked Emma.

'You're not going to do anything—I am,' said Lucy. 'I've got to launch *Hessandrea* again—take her up beyond Earth's atmosphere. Further than that . . . and then I'll eject him into space. I have to go soon—before the baby Koth hatch. I must be sure they're all blown out and none of them can hitch a ride back to Earth on *Hessandrea.* If I'm not completely sure about that, I won't be coming back.' She turned to face them all. 'And maybe that's best. Why would you want me? I nearly brought annihilation to your world.'

'Take me with you,' said Nick, suddenly. 'Please. I can help. I'm a former RAF pilot.'

'I know,' said Lucy. 'I looked you up. You've got medals.'

Jay and Emma regarded their cabin guest with awe. 'Really?' said Jay. 'An RAF pilot! Wow! That's so cool! Why didn't you tell me?'

Nick shrugged elaborately. 'Erm . . . space-girl here has slightly eclipsed my gig, don't you think?!'

Jay beamed at Lucy. 'Yeah,' he said. 'She has.'

Emma was not smiling. 'You've got to come back, Lucy! You can't go off into space on your own again. You've had less than a *week* here. It's not fair.'

'If I can be sure . . .' said Lucy. 'Totally sure . . .'

Mumgram suddenly poured out of a light well

beside her and said: 'LUCY—ALERT! Airborne vessel detected on a flight path for *Hessandrea*.'

'Damn! It's my flares!' cursed Nick as they stared at the screen again—this time viewing a red blob on an aerial view map, travelling at speed across the stretch of water between Southampton on the mainland and the island.

'How do we know it's coming here?' asked Jay.

'*Hessandrea* will have intercepted its comms,' explained Lucy. 'Mumgram—how long have we got?'

'Six minutes and thirty-five seconds,' said Mumgram.

'Sit down in the seats—all of you!' barked Lucy. Suddenly she was all movement, her fingers racing across the buttons, switches, and keyboards of the console.

'What's happening?' squeaked Emma, as Jay and Nick climbed onto two of the four high stools.

'Get in your seat!' yelled Lucy. 'I've got no time to get you down now! I have to launch before that helicopter gets here. You'll all have to come with me!'

'But—but . . .' Emma's squeak got higher. A strong hand fell upon her shoulder and shoved her across to her seat.

'Get in—now!' commanded Nick. Emma did and as soon as all three were in place Lucy threw a lever and the stools suddenly dropped down towards the floor, some thick padded restraints curving up from the backs, over their shoulders and across their chests, pinning them firmly in place as if they were about to take a rollercoaster ride.

There was a clunk and hiss and Jay felt something smooth and leathery rise up behind his head. Beside him the same was happening to Nick and Emma. Head restraints were now growing out of the chair and cupping their skulls from cranium to forehead.

'Don't panic!' yelled Lucy as she raced up and down the console, throwing more switches and scanning an assortment of screens which were filled with swiftly scrolling data—figures, letters, star-chart images of Earth and its place in the galaxy, a real-time visual of the land below them and the airspace around them, weather patterns overlaid across it, symbols that Jay couldn't understand, flipping over and over in steady rhythm. He didn't need to understand the symbols. He knew what it was. A countdown.

'Luceeeee!' he called as a vibration began to build under him—all around him—all around them all. 'Are you really taking us to space?!'

'Yes!' yelled back Lucy, peering into a multi-dimensional holographic star map of the Earth in relation to the Moon and Mars while smashing her fist against an obdurate button on the console. 'Just try to relax!'

Chapter 25

Sue put down her mug of coffee and went to peer at the dog. Brad Pitt didn't look well. He lay under the table on the blanket, shivering. He could just be pining for Badger, she supposed.

And Badger would probably show up at any moment, anyway, asking if she'd seen the dog. It wouldn't be the first time Badger had disappeared for a few days and then wandered back, hungover and wrecked. He had a habit of popping in to visit at these times, usually hoping for a free hand-out from her larder. Usually she gave him something just to get rid of him.

Yes—any time at all their loathsome neighbour would show up to reclaim his unlovely dog. But for now, Brad appeared to be her responsibility. She patted his head and he felt warm and clammy, and gave off that odd musty odour again. He opened his eyes and looked at her briefly before closing them again. Probably he'd eaten something disgusting from Badger's garden and was about to throw it up all over her floor.

She got up, washed her hands thoroughly, and left the kitchen to take up the sofa in the sitting room while she waited for Nick and Emma and Jay to come back. Or maybe Lucy would show up and shoot *her* too. But she just couldn't believe that. Lucy was odd but not bad. Sue eyed the phone and thought about calling the police and reporting Badger missing—but they would never take her seriously. The man had only been 'missing' for a few hours and he was a grown adult (allegedly) who could have gone anywhere at any time. She *might* get the RSPCA worked up about dog neglect but even that was doubtful.

It was more than half an hour since Nick had left. She was torn. She wanted to race out and start looking for Emma and Jay herself, but she knew that he had a good point. If one searched and one stayed put it made better sense. Didn't make it any easier, though. She went to the window, hoping to see her children wandering back down the drive in the evening shade. She didn't see that.

She did see another green flash in the sky and scores of birds suddenly taking off, rising up from above the trees around the mast and fleeing through the air in a widening circle.

'What the hell is going on up there?' she murmured against the glass.

Chapter 26

For the first five minutes, Emma thought she *might* live.

She was absolutely petrified, clamped against her chair, as her very bones shook and her brain turned cartwheels inside her head, but she thought she had a chance of surviving.

But after what must have been five or six minutes of the brutal shaking, her consciousness began swooping about like a wounded bird, and blood trickled out of her nose and splayed out across her cheeks in a scarlet moustache. She could see it reflected in one of the glassy monitors close by. She tried to lift her hand from the armrest of the chair—tried to reach for Jay or Nick—anyone. But it was impossible to move it.

This can't be happening, this can't be happening, this can't be happening, her brain chanted over and over. But there had never been a dream—or a nightmare—like this. She could feel it, smell it, taste it . . .

'NOT MUCH LONGER! YOU'LL BE OK!' came a voice, through all the crashing and the screaming and vibrating of the huge powerful engines to which they were all flimsily bound, powering up and up and up through the atmosphere. It was Nick's voice, she realized. 'HANG IN THERE!' he yelled again. 'IT'LL BE FINE!'

His voice was comforting. He was an RAF pilot, wasn't he? He knew about this stuff. G-force . . . or something. And that was as much as her brain could really manage. She clung on, the scent of flowing blood sharp and metallic in her nostrils. An image of Lucy that first day, standing in the field, blood on her upper lip, flashed through Emma's mind. Of course. That was why she'd had a nose bleed . . . she'd just arrived and maybe the descent through Earth's atmosphere was just as bad as blasting up through it. Emma longed to reach space. Once they were in space it would all be OK, wouldn't it? Everything would go quiet . . .

And perhaps she passed out then because the next thing she knew, she was right. Everything had gone quiet. And above the catwalk, through the wide, curved window, a dark blue, star-pricked sky drifted slowly by.

Or maybe she'd just died and that was a view of heaven.

Something cold and damp slopped across her face. 'There you go,' said Lucy. She was mopping her friend's upper lip with a flannel, looking stricken. 'I'm sorry, Emma. The nose bleeding is really grim.'

Emma sat up, dazed and trembling, and realized all the restraints had disappeared into the seat. Her clothes stuck to her sweat-drenched body. Beside her, Jay was mopping his own face and looking pale and shocked. Nick, though, was out of his seat, face already cleaned up, frenziedly examining the bridge console and monitors and periodically gazing out into space in awe.

'How far out are we?' he asked Lucy and she rattled off a series of numbers and coordinates which meant nothing to Emma but seemed to make sense to Nick.

'We need to get out a bit further before I'll risk ejecting Badger and the Koth nest,' said Lucy. 'We should be about right in ten minutes. So just take it easy for a bit before we have to . . . you know.'

'C-can we g-get back?' Emma hardly knew where to find her voice but it came out somehow.

'Yes! Yes, of course!' said Lucy, taking her hand. 'I will take you home! Don't worry.'

Emma nodded, her teeth beginning to chatter. The shock was pounding through her now but it was an odd relief to let it shake out through her limbs. After about five minutes of this, during which Jay also began to talk, she started to feel a little better. Lucy delivered another cup to each of them, filled with more of the nutty cocoa-y stuff which she and Jay drank gratefully, although Nick was too busy studying the ship to stop and drink.

'This is amazing,' he kept saying. 'So like our technology—but light years ahead!'

'There are tutorials you can see, if you like,' said Lucy. 'To teach you more about *Hessandrea*—how she was built; how she flies. And the simulation room is loaded up with programmes too—so you can practise flying her and the scouts.'

'Take me there!' Nick had a light in his eyes that Jay and Emma hadn't seen before.

'I will,' said Lucy. 'Afterwards.'

His face became more sombre as he remembered the point of their journey. He rested a hand on Lucy's shoulder. 'You really are a remarkable young woman, Lucy, you know that? And even if the rest of our planet will never know it, I'm thanking you on their behalf.'

'Don't thank me yet,' said Lucy.

She tried to put them off. 'You don't have to see this,' she said. 'It'll probably give you nightmares.'

And Jay didn't want to see it. Nor did Emma, he could tell. But there was no way they were letting Lucy go through this on her own.

'The containment chambers are designed to vent directly into space,' she explained as they all walked along the corridor to the containment bay. 'Just in case anyone brought a disease on board—a bad one. You can't know how these things will work in deep space, while the atmosphere is slowly changing. A normally harmless virus can mutate.'

'Why would the atmosphere be changing?' asked Nick. 'Surely it's consistent? Sealed in with you all when you left the planet?'

'Consistently *changing*,' said Lucy. 'Earth atmosphere is different to Cornelian—the gases are very similar but the mix is different. So the atmosphere on board *Hessandrea* was programmed to change, very, very slowly, over our ten year journey, so we could acclimatize and barely notice it. The ship can travel many times faster than that, but if we'd arrived on Earth in just a few weeks we would have been very sick. We'd probably have died. It's a bit like the way you have to climb your mountains very slowly if you don't want to get altitude sickness. You need to acclimatize.'

'Of course,' said Nick. 'I should have thought of that.'

'We're here,' said Lucy and Jay felt everyone's mood drop to somewhere colder and greyer than he'd ever been before.

They stood before the wall of opaque glass and Lucy slid back a metal panel to reveal a keypad and a series of lit buttons. One of these—under its own deep hood—had the word VENT written on it. Lucy hit another button which switched the glass to transparent. At once the white light of the containment chamber shafted through to the corridor.

Jay heard Emma draw a shocked breath at the state of the man now. His skin was a deep ochre yellow and he lay exactly as they had last seen him, looking almost fossilized. The tips of his fingers were blackened. His eyes, though, were still slightly open, and occasionally rolling behind the half-closed lids. Lumps had risen across his back—each about the size of a large marble. Jay counted them. Twelve. Just like Lucy said.

'There's not much time. They're about to hatch,' said Lucy. 'Please say your goodbyes . . . prayers or whatever you want to do. Quickly. I have to eject him now.'

'Will he feel it?' asked Jay, gulping. 'He is still alive, isn't he? Can he feel . . .' he pointed at the lumps, '. . . them?'

'I don't know,' said Lucy. 'Nobody's ever lived to

tell us. And there wasn't time for proper study before it was all over. There's not that much information at all in *Hessandrea*'s logs. You have to remember, it only took two weeks on the planet. Two weeks and it was all over. Then another eleven days on *Hessandrea*.'

'Do you want to say anything?' said Nick, glancing at Jay and Emma.

Jay couldn't think of anything. What *did* you say when a man you deeply disliked was about to be ejected into space with twelve deadly parasites riding his body—while he was still alive? He didn't think there was a prayer book in existence which covered *this*.

Emma might have said something but as she opened her mouth to speak it became a gasp and her eyes went round and fixed, staring through the glass. Jay looked too and put his arm around her as Badger's yellowed skin began to bubble.

Lucy's hand flew towards the VENT button but it was caught in mid-air. Nick held her wrist in a firm grip. 'Wait!' he said. 'Wait! I need to see.'

They were all horribly entranced as several baby Koth emerged, fast, erupting through the brittle skin and turning in a circle on top of the wound they'd just created. They stretched out glistening brown wings, flicking them free in one shivery movement, and then flew up against the pale mesh metal walls and clung to them. They looked like large, leathery moths.

'We have to vent them NOW!' shrieked Lucy and she twisted away from Nick and hit the VENT button. At once the outer wall of the chamber slid apart in four triangles, revealing the dark void beyond. Badger's stiff, spreadeagled body flipped up and over. He looked like he had suddenly decided to perform a circus act. Then he spun out of the chamber into space. He was beyond view almost instantly. The baby Koth, smaller and lighter, seemed to take longer. Three or four of them shot out with Badger—they had still been emerging from his skin and just travelled with him. But the others clung onto the cream mesh walls for longer. Jay counted five of them and knew there had to be more. One flew past and out and then another. And another. Jay counted three left, high in the far corner of the room, their tiny talons clinging desperately to the mesh and their wings fluttering like flags.

'Lucy—can't we just keep these three for a little while—to study them?' urged Nick, trying to reach past her to the vent OFF switch.

Lucy stood in front of the control panel, her face like rock. 'Didn't you ever watch *Alien*?!' she hissed. 'Can't you see what a BAD idea that would be?!'

Nick stepped back, nodding and holding up his hands. 'OK. OK . . . but if those things ever arrive on Earth again, I'd like to know how to defeat them—wouldn't you?'

'This has all been filmed,' said Lucy as the last three baby Koth finally gave up their grip, one cartwheeling right past the glass with a silent scream from its hideous face, and were sucked into space. 'You can study the film,' she said. 'And all the data Mumgram can give you.'

The triangular panels slid back into place and the containment room was still and empty. Emma rested her forehead against it and drew her first breath in over a minute. 'Are they all gone. Really? For ever?'

'Mumgram—is there a Koth life form on board *Hessandrea*?' asked Lucy. Mumgram appeared just behind Jay, making him jump and gasp. His nerves had been shredded enough by the last few minutes. He felt exhausted.

'There is no Koth life form on board *Hessandrea*,' stated Mumgram.

'Please trace any Koth or human life form within charting distance beyond the ship,' said Lucy.

At once a 3D map hologram of their part of the galaxy appeared in place of Mumgram. It showed fading ribbons—one red and twelve orange—spiralling into nothingness through the void. 'There are traces of human and Koth matter atomizing across four-hundred thousand kilometres, within the—'

'No life force?' cut in Lucy.

'No life force,' confirmed Mumgram.

'Nothing clinging to the hull, dead or alive?'

'The hull is clean, Lucy.'

Lucy sank to the floor. 'I think I need a cup of tea,' she said.

Chapter 27

'Tell me more about your home planet, Lucy,' said Nick, handing her a cup of Tetley. He and Jay and Emma had been amazed to find real teabags and fresh milk in one of the vast refrigerators in the kitchen—Lucy had bought them in Newport. 'Tell me how it's different from Earth,' he went on. 'And how it's the same.'

'It's a lot like Earth,' began Lucy, sitting in one of the low soft chairs along the gallery above the bridge. Her Earth guests had taken the other three and were each cradling a mug of hot tea, like any family from *EastEnders* dealing with a bit of a shock. 'It's about the same size. The mix of species was a lot like those on Earth. We had mammals, birds, reptiles, fish, insects . . . The landscape is very similar too. Mountains and valleys and seas, and rivers and forests. It's more volcanic, though—but not dangerously. The fire pits are so abundant all around the planet, they seem to self-regulate and keep the pressure of the molten mantle inside nice and steady—no big eruptions for many centuries. We used the fire pits as a power source. There weren't many wars. We'd learned, mostly, to live in peace and we had such amazing plans . . . That's what makes it so sad. My people . . .' She gazed away through the glass at the gently unfolding universe. 'All the plans. All the dreams . . .'

As Lucy and Nick talked, Jay could feel himself getting sleepy. Maybe it was just the shock, he thought, because he was fascinated by everything Lucy said. Then he checked his watch and sat up straight.

'Whoa! It's really late!' he said. 'Mum'll be going nuts!'

Nick and Emma also looked stricken.

'I'm sorry, Jay. I can't take us back down right away,' said Lucy. 'We're locked into a slow orbit in preparation for landing and I can't speed *Hessandrea* up just yet. We won't be over the island again for . . .' she consulted her watch, '. . . another eighteen hours and six minutes.'

They gaped at her. 'Mum will be freaking out!' exclaimed Jay. 'She'll think we've been kidnapped! Which . . . we, kind of, have . . .' He shrugged at Lucy. 'Well . . . we didn't get much choice, did we?'

Lucy's blue-green eyes glimmered a little as she bit her lip. 'I know. And you've been such good friends to me too. I'm so sorry . . .'

He grinned at her, in spite of the crisis. 'Don't worry. I wouldn't have missed this for anything. But poor Mum . . .'

'You could always phone her,' said Lucy. 'Tell her . . . you're having a sleepover!'

'What—phone Mum from space?' Jay screwed up his face. This was all so weird.

'Well, yes. The signal's really good from here,' she said. 'And if Emma's phone isn't working, you can always use mine.'

Emma flicked it open and saw all five bars shining. 'It's fine,' she said. 'Well . . . here goes. Although how I'm going to convince her everything's normal, I don't know.'

'Don't try,' said Nick. 'She's not an idiot and she knows about Lucy shooting me. Just make sure she knows you're safe and coming back. That's the main thing.'

Sue shot up on the sofa when the phone rang, confused and disorientated. It was dark. How late was it? She was aghast when she realized it was past ten. She seized the phone. 'Yes?'

'Mum, it's me!'

'Oh, thank god!'

'I'm really sorry to worry you,' said Emma.

'Where *are* you? And Jay? Is Jay with you?'

'Yes—and we're both fine! Nick's with us and so is Lucy.'

'Lucy? Is she . . . OK? She hasn't tried to shoot you or anything?'

A laugh. A normal, comforting sound. 'No! She's fine. Look, Mum, we're all OK but we can't get back to you until tomorrow—lunchtime-ish. We're sleeping over at Lucy's.'

'Where? Where is Lucy's?'

'Mum—you won't believe me when I tell you! It's out of this world!'

'Emma, I really want you and Jay to come home right away,' said Sue. 'I mean . . . you haven't even got toothbrushes!'

'I know, Mum . . .' Emma's voice was calm—*carefully* calm. 'Please. Trust me. We are OK. And we *will* be back tomorrow. Just . . . get some sleep. We've got amazing things to tell you when we're back.'

'Tell me now!' demanded Sue.

'Oh, Mum—it's really hard to explain. We'll need to show you!'

'Right—Emma—put Nick on! I want to speak to him NOW.'

'OK—here he is.'

'Hello, Sue,' said Nick. He, too, sounded calm. But she

knew he couldn't possibly be. 'I don't have much time to talk, but you're fine to stay at home now. I was wrong about what was going on with Lucy. She's fine and you are quite safe. Just hang on until we get back tomorrow and we'll explain it all to you.'

'Can't you tell me now?' Sue demanded. 'I'm going nuts here! I'm just about to call the police!'

'Sue, please, just trust me—trust us all, until we get back to you tomorrow. What we've got to tell you . . . it's *incredible.* Really incredible.'

'It's OK, Mum,' Jay yelled in the background. 'It's *brilliant*!'

'See you tomorrow, Sue,' said Nick. 'Just hang in there.'

And then he cut off. She stared at the receiver and shook her head. For all she knew he might be a kidnapper, collecting teenagers for an evil plan. But he wasn't. She knew that. She did trust him and even though she was full of confusion she felt better for hearing Emma and Jay, sounding so obviously excited and happy. Whatever it was, she guessed she'd have to wait to find out. Tomorrow. Everything would be OK tomorrow. She just needed to sleep the time away.

She checked in on the dog before she went to bed. He looked much the same and smelt worse. At least he hadn't thrown up or pooed all over the kitchen. Tomorrow she'd take him to the RSPCA shelter if Badger didn't show up.

'Don't worry, Brad,' she muttered. 'Your master's just spaced out somewhere.'

Chapter 28

Emma turned over on the bunk in the sleep pod. It was squishy but firm at the same time. Cosy. The pod was small and curved at its corners and gently lit by some pale golden orbs at the head and foot of the bunk. The walls were a soft green and there was a golden-coloured carpet. She was tired out but it was hard to relax. She shuddered again as she thought of poor Badger, being blasted into space, infested with tiny flesh-eating aliens. How on earth was she going to *sleep* after that?

But Lucy had insisted she try. 'Emma, you're exhausted. You too, Jay. You've been through incredible g-force . . . and shock after shock. You need sleep. There's so much more I want to show you while you're here—but I won't. Not until you've both slept for at least five hours!'

Nick had grinned at this and stood back, folding his arms and raising his eyebrows at Emma and Jay. And then Lucy had turned to him. 'You too, Nick! I know you're more used to this kind of thing than they are . . . but you're twenty-five years older! The bioscan shows you've been pretty stressed too. Sleep, please!'

Emma pulled the white quilt up over her shoulder. Her heart kept doing little leaps and rattles inside her, as she relived the astounding and terrifying events of the day. Eventually though, it began to calm down. The air inside the pod was cool and sweet, like a summer meadow. Emma imagined that's where she was . . . in a summer meadow with a breeze riffling through her hair and the lulling sound of bees and distant birdsong. The day had been amazing. Possibly most amazing of all, was that she fell asleep.

Jay slept too and even Nick, although he was so wired with excitement that this was, later, a surprise to him. What none of them knew was that Lucy, back on the bridge, had adjusted the oxygen mix in their sleep pods to enable their brains to finally cool and slip into slumber. She took three hours herself, too, after shaking her hair free of its ponytail and laying down on her bunk in her sleep pod. She hadn't altered her own oxygen level—she didn't dare. She needed to be alert in case of emergency. A Koth showing up on the hull after all . . . Lucy *knew* it wouldn't—but some primeval part of her might take years to believe Mumgram when she said all trace of the entity was gone. Really gone.

Even so, after the incredible day she'd been through, she did sleep a little. Dreamlessly. As she woke she shivered at the memory of the last twenty-four hours. And then she felt ripples of happiness. She was *not alone.* Her friends were here with her and they hadn't rejected her for the danger she'd put them all in. They were on her side even though she didn't deserve it. But as she got up and headed for the cleansing booth Lucy felt the happiness subside. She owed it to them to get them home and then leave their lives—leave them as safe as she'd found them.

Breakfast was curious. Lucy served up a weird combination of carbisks and sweet fruit and nut protein shakes—and eggs on toast. She had bought the eggs, butter, and bread in Newport too, and taught herself how to use a small corner of the lonely, shiny kitchen.

'This isn't bad,' said Jay, waving a forkful of buttered toast and poached egg. 'Mum might give you a job doing breakfast for guests!'

Lucy smiled and looked down at her plate.

'You *are* coming back, Lucy,' said Emma, guessing her thoughts. 'We're not going to let you disappear into space on your own. Not after everything we've been through. Earth is *your* planet too now. You have to stay.'

Lucy changed the subject. 'I've got so much to show you before landing—mostly in the rec room! Are you ready?'

Nick, who had folded his eggs and toast into a one-hand sandwich, was still checking out the console on the bridge and consulting some kind of tutorial on one of the monitors with little nods and grunts of approval.

'You know,' he told Lucy, smiling dreamily, as she dragged him away. 'I always wanted to be an astronaut. That's why I joined the RAF—to get as close to space as I could. I hoped I'd be able to get onto the NASA space programme one day. But it was never to be. HA! What do I need with NASA now, eh?'

'Nick . . .' began Lucy, dropping his arm and turning to him. 'You understand, don't you, that you can't really tell anyone about this. About *Hessandrea.* It's got to stay a secret . . .'

Nick nodded. 'Of course. Probably.'

'Probably?' Lucy said, sharply.

Nick looked at her, levelly. 'Lucy, I promise I will not give this away to anyone without your permission.'

'I'm sensing a "but",' said Lucy.

'There'll always be a "but",' he said, grinning. 'But I still promise.'

'Come on! The rec room!' Jay was bouncing on his feet, remembering the incredible rainforest simulation from yesterday.

The rec room was a revelation for Nick. He took to it in seconds, marvelling over the amazing holographic imagery, the surround sound, and the air jet impact technology which mimicked wind pressure and physical contact and made the programmes feel so incredibly real. They all ran, rowed, and cycled through the rainforest, ducking away from flitting parrots and leaping monkeys and then rested awhile in a wheat field under a cornflower-blue sky, before leaping up to do battle with comical fluffy creatures called Spogs (a kind of guinea pig once living on Cornelian Eclata according to Lucy). But what they really wanted was to try the seats suspended in the red circles.

'Those are for scout training simulations,' said Lucy. 'They're brilliant fun. We can all have a go.'

'Scout training?' echoed Emma, pulling a face. 'What—like pitching tents and making campfires?'

'No—scout *ship* training. Look—I'll show you . . .'

Lucy strapped Emma and Jay in first. The chairs were suspended by some kind of magnetic force and after Lucy shouted a command they both juddered and seemed to rev up, as if there were a big, throaty engine beneath the seats. Emma found a control stick lowered down in front of her and as soon as she grasped it a holographic bubble surrounded her.

She was slowly adjusting to this weird hyper-reality. The rainforest had taken her breath away—and she'd fallen off the bike she'd been 'riding' twice. But she'd got back on right away even so. Had she not, a few days ago, decided never to get on a saddle again . . . ?

Now she was in a small spaceship, with a set of winking lights in front of her and a wide, curved screen before her eyes, offering a view of starlit space . . . and incoming enemy craft. 'It's an alien attack game!' she laughed and began to play, quickly working out the commands and the actions of each button and sending laser fire out towards the incoming craft. She had to pilot the scout ship too, which felt about as big as a small truck or van and was scythe shaped, with a circular space for the cockpit, big enough for two, maybe three people.

She heard whooping beside her and saw, through a holographic window, Jay swooping about in his chair, firing madly at aliens too, surrounded by a semi-transparent holographic bubble of his own. She pulled the controls towards her and felt her own chair tilt and swoop, mimicking a deep-space ride with such force that she could feel the motion and the velocity juddering through her.

'Point your finger out on the joystick,' advised Lucy, outside the hologram but still clear in her ear. 'Towards the target as you fire. I don't know why but it helps with targeting. Try missiles too—the orange button on the left. You need to allow about three seconds for the missile to strike when your target is at this distance. Aim for where you think it *will* be . . .'

'Oooh—it's too confusing!' wailed Emma as her first missile missed by miles and the enemy craft, a hexagonal thing which glowed a dark purple and spat red laser beams back at her, easily flew past the strike point. 'I'll never get it!' She felt the seat judder sharply as enemy laser beams impacted. 'I'm rubbish at this. Let Nick have a go.'

'You're not rubbish. You're *learning*,' corrected Lucy. 'Try again and aim slightly closer in this time.'

Emma sighed but tried again, and this time her missile clipped the alien craft and sent it spinning. She followed it up fast and her third missile converted the craft to an exploding star of glittering shrapnel. 'Yessss!' she yelled out.

'I told you,' said Lucy. 'Your balance and coordination are getting better. You've been laying down new neural pathways!'

Emma grinned. 'I don't think rolling tins of

beans about has suddenly qualified me for the space programme!' she laughed.

Nick took his turn after Jay and flew the scout like . . . well, like an RAF pilot, while Lucy climbed in after Emma and impressively matched him with her own piloting skill. It was mesmerizing to watch them both swooping and swivelling in the chairs while delivering blast after blast against enemy craft, simultaneously dodging spinning meteors and space debris. Nick, too, was whooping with delight within minutes. He looked as excited as Jay had.

Eventually, though, Lucy called a halt. Like the rest of them she was puffing and bathed with sweat from all the exertion and adrenalin. Her face, thought Jay, seemed to be illuminated from within, giving her eyes an almost unearthly, alien light.

Well, she is an alien, he told himself. *And you need to remember it.* And maybe she'd be gone, for ever out of their lives, this time tomorrow. A little late to realize he was very probably very slightly in love . . .

Lucy called, 'End all games,' to the rec room computer and everything went still and silent, leaving them all breathing heavily and beaming at each other on the soft blue floor.

'I don't think I've ever . . . in all my life . . .' gasped

Lucy, '. . . had so much fun.' She shook her head. 'Having friends makes it ten times better.'

'Can we just have another spaceship fight?' asked Emma, glancing at the floating red chair. 'I was getting really good!'

Lucy shook her head, although she smiled inwardly. Emma *had* been improving at a phenomenal pace. The rec room had a way of helping you do that. Over the past couple of hours neural pathways had been thrown down inside the girl's head at a far greater speed than they ever could be on Earth.

'Sorry, Emma,' said Lucy. 'It's time to take you all home.'

'Will going back be like . . . you know . . . coming out here?' asked Emma, biting on a fingernail.

'Yes,' said Lucy. 'It's a bit bumpy. But you know what to expect this time and you know you'll be fine.' She saw Nick flick her a glance and didn't add that entry into any planet's atmosphere was the single most dangerous part of any space journey. Nick didn't mention it either.

In the event it was every bit as 'bumpy' as the last one. Lucy, strapped in alongside her friends, felt it possibly even more than the first time. Just a week ago she had done all this on her own and she had been terrified, shaken physically and emotionally, until she had believed she couldn't possibly survive. This time was different. She was fairly sure she *would* survive, but now she was terrified that Jay or Emma—or even Nick—might not. Jay and Emma were not physically or emotionally trained for this. Nick possibly was—but he'd been retired from active service for at least a year and had to have lost some of that fitness. What if one of them had a heart attack or a stroke or something? How would she ever forgive herself?

'You have arrived,' said Mumgram. And the silence that followed these words seemed to push right into their ears, like a thick duvet. *Hessandrea*'s engines had ceased thundering while they were still above the jet stream and she had then travelled down to her docking point above the transmitter on a steady magnetic trajectory. Inside, the docking machinery had buzzed and beeped and thrummed through the vessel, but outside, had anyone been watching or listening, it was silent and invisible.

'Welcome back to Earth,' said Lucy as their restraints unlocked and slid back into the chairs, releasing their rattled heads and limbs. Her voice was shaky. Jay staggered out of his chair and gave her an unsteady hug.

'I can't believe you did all that!' He had been amazed at the way she had taken charge of the descent, shouting commands to the ship's console and then responding, lightning fast, to the commands that Mumgram barked back at *her*. She had been the last one into her seat, the restraints in place barely seconds before the thunderous ride began. Lucy felt warm and damp in his arms and he could feel her heartbeat—every bit as rapid as his own. And, for the first time, she allowed herself to *be* hugged, for just a few seconds.

Emma came and made it a three-way hug and then Nick stepped up and patted them all on the shoulders.

And then Emma's phone rang.

'It's Mum,' she said, staring at the display, her voice full of emotion. She answered. 'Hi, Mum—we're nearly home!'

Sue's voice came back tinny, via a hands-free kit. She was clearly driving. 'Oh thank goodness! I've been worrying all night! I called you about fifteen times this morning.'

'Sorry—we've been a bit distracted,' said Emma, grinning at them all.

'Well, I can't wait to see you all and find out why!' Sue yelled, above the car engine noise. 'But I'm not at home now and probably won't be for a couple of hours.'

'Why? Where are you?' asked Emma.

'I'm taking this blasted dog to the vets!' called back Sue. Her voice was cutting in and out. 'I don't really know why I'm doing it . . . but he's pretty sick. He's got some kind of liver failure or something, I think . . . His gums and his eyeballs are all yellow. And he stinks like an old cellar.'

Nick grabbed the phone off Emma. 'Sue! Sue—it's Nick! Can you hear me?'

There was some response through the crackling reception but they could only just hear it. The island's hilly roads were notorious for their patchy cell coverage.

'Sue—I want you to stop the car!' yelled Nick. 'Get out of the car and leave the dog inside it. And shut all the windows and lock the doors . . . and don't go back in. Not until we get to you . . . where are you?'

Lucy's face had gone grey.

Emma and Jay looked at each other with dawning horror. There was only hissing from the phone. They couldn't hear their mum at all now.

Chapter 29

Sue glanced at the dog in the back seat as she gave up on the mobile. She didn't think Brad Pitt would survive whatever it was he had. He looked pretty rough and smelt worse. She'd found him that morning in much the same position as she'd left him the night before, slumped on the blanket under the kitchen table, very still.

She'd thought, for a few seconds, that he was dead, but then gingerly touched his close-cropped white coat and felt warmth—almost feverish heat, in fact. The dog was breathing shallowly. His eyes were half-closed and an unhealthy, filmy yellow. Carefully lifting his muzzle she'd seen that the yellowy shade was all along his gum line too.

Taking him to the vets was as much about her own needs as the dog's. Or what she didn't need. She really didn't, with all her other worries, need a dead dog to bury. He was a heavy beast and she'd have to dig quite a hole in Badger's back garden to bury him. It would be a grim task on a hot day—and that smell wasn't going to improve post-mortem. She'd far rather get the vet to give him a merciful end and let the practice take care of the body. Of course, if he could be treated and saved . . . and she could afford the treatment . . . she probably would.

'Damn you, Badger!' she muttered. 'You're a pain in the neck even when you're not around. Why couldn't you deal with your own dying dog?' She would really let him have it when she saw him next.

But at least she knew that Emma and Jay would be there, in one piece, when she got back. She hadn't heard much of what Emma had said, except they were nearly home. She hoped she'd got across where she was going. As long as they'd heard her, Emma and Jay would know the vet practice she would be going to, in Freshwater. They used to have a dog until a couple of years ago, and always took her to the same place, Chris Fothergill's practice, in Bedbury Lane. Poor Beanie, their black Labrador, had been treated there for her various old-age problems before she'd died. Sue had got to know Vanessa, Chris's veterinary surgeon partner, quite well and they still had the occasional friendly chat if they bumped into each other.

'Sheeesh!' Sue waved a hand across her face and then

opened the window. The musty smell from the dog was definitely getting worse. She was profoundly relieved when she finally reached the surgery and pulled up onto its forecourt. She'd rung ahead and managed to book some of Vanessa's time.

Vanessa came out when she saw the car pull up. In a pale green tunic, her red hair pulled into a ponytail, she opened the door to the back seat and winced at the smell. She and Sue hefted the dog inside, hammocked between them in the thick, dark blanket Sue had brought.

Inside her consulting room, Vanessa examined the dog on her high, disinfected table. 'He's pretty far gone, whatever's caused this,' she said, pulling up his muzzle and clocking the yellow gums. 'I wouldn't get your hopes up, Sue.'

'He's not my dog,' said Sue. 'Poor mutt belongs to my neighbour, who seems to have conveniently vanished off the face of the Earth! The poor creature's been in my house all night, smelling like that. What do you think it is?'

'Some kind of hepatitis most likely,' said Vanessa. 'But what caused it? Could be a number of things.' She rang her fingers through the dog's coat, parting the fine hairs. 'Yellow skin too—he's jaundiced.'

She went to say something else but was drowned out by a sudden thumping bass line, shattering the afternoon peace and making the windows rattle. 'Sorry!' she said, raising her voice and stepping across to shut the window. 'There's some kind of big charity concert going on over at the hotel. They've been sound-checking all morning. It's quite funky . . . but the patients aren't so keen!'

'Oh—that must be the Level 42 gig,' said Sue.

Vanessa raised her eyebrows, impressed, as she prodded the skin behind Brad's shoulders. '*You're* well informed!'

'Well, my kids' friend Lucy is a big fan,' explained Sue. 'She met the lead singer yesterday and got an invitation to see them. I'm probably going to have to drive them all back here in a couple of hours.'

'This is odd,' said Vanessa, peering more closely at Brad's fur. 'Some kind of lumpiness along the spine . . .'

There was a sudden chime and Sue jumped. 'Oh—sorry—my phone. I'll just take it outside.' Vanessa nodded, absorbed in the weird bumps on her patient's body.

Sue stepped out into the corridor. It was Emma again, she saw. 'Hi, Em—you back home now?' she said.

But it wasn't Emma on the phone. It was Nick.

'Sue—where are you?' he demanded.

'What's up?' She felt fear lurch in her throat. 'Where's Emma? Where's Jay?'

'We're all together and they're fine—SUE! Listen! Where are you? Are you still with the dog?'

'I'm at the vet's. She's looking at Brad now. Why?'

'You have to get everyone away from the dog. Right away. Make sure he's locked in the room—shut the windows first and then get out.'

'Why?' Sue glanced through the glass panel in the door and saw Vanessa, still peering closely at the comatose canine, wrinkling her nose and palpating his skin.

'He's got a very infectious disease—and it can be passed on to humans,' said Nick. 'Please, Sue—trust me—you have to do what I say—NOW!'

'Mum—just DO it!' That was Jay, shouting in the background. He sounded terrified.

With a sudden thudding in her chest, Sue opened the door and grabbed Vanessa's arm. 'OUT!' she commanded. 'I've just heard this is something really bad. We have to get out of the room and seal the dog in.'

Vanessa looked surprised and seemed about to argue until she caught sight of Sue's face and then she followed her outside and shut the door behind her. 'What's all this about?' she asked.

Sue still held the phone to her ear. 'We're out—and the dog's inside. The windows are shut. What's going on, Nick?'

'Pass me to the vet,' he said. Sue handed the phone over.

'Who is this?' asked Vanessa.

'My name is Nick Dobson and I'm with the Ministry of Defence,' he replied. (It was *close* to the truth and he didn't have time to go into detail.) 'The dog you have in your surgery has a seriously contagious disease, fatal to him and possibly to human beings. Who am I talking to?'

Vanessa straightened her back and replied, 'Vanessa Hansen, veterinary surgeon. What disease is it, exactly? I need to notify—'

'Vanessa, can you see the dog from where you are?' cut in the man. There was definitely an authority in his voice. It gave her chills.

'Yes—and I've examined him fairly thoroughly. He has jaundice, a high temperature, rapid heartbeat—he's unconscious, probably dying. He smells odd too. Nothing I can identify without further tests.'

'Did you find a wound on him? Something circular? Or just a puncture wound?'

She turned back to the glass panel. 'Just a small puncture wound—at the top of a line of lumps along his spine—hidden under his collar. I was just examining the lumps when you called. Oh—wow! That's nasty!'

Back on *Hessandrea*, Nick stared at the three terrified

young faces around him, listening to the conversation playing out through the speaker. Emma had her hand over her mouth, her eyes wide and glistening with tears. Jay was rooted to the spot, his jaw clenched. Lucy's eyes were closed and she was leaning against the wall.

'What—what are you seeing, Vanessa?'

'The lumps are *moving*,' came back the reply. 'This must be some kind of parasite, yes? I need to know what the protocol is, Mr Dobson. And I need to know it now.'

Nick ran his free hands through his hair. Protocol. What the hell *was* the protocol?!

'I will be sending a team to seal and contain the area,' he said, sounding calm despite his mounting horror. 'I need you to get everyone out of the building and—'

There was a small shriek. 'Oh! Oh my word!' gasped the vet. 'There's something erupting out of his skin . . . what the hell *is* this?'

'Tell me the door is sealed!' said Nick. 'And the windows are shut!'

'The door is closed,' said Vanessa and now they could hear panic in her voice. 'And the windows are too.'

'Get tape,' said Nick. 'Thick gaffer tape if you have it. Tape all around the door.'

'He wants tape around the door!' said Vanessa, touching Sue's arm. Sue was gaping at the scene unfolding beyond the glass panel. 'Get some from reception. Tell them to give you gaffer tape.'

Sue got the tape from a baffled receptionist. As she reached the door Vanessa was still on the phone. 'Hang on,' said the vet and then took off her shoe and smashed the heel into a nearby fire alarm on the wall which immediately launched into shrill beeping. 'Everyone OUT!' she bellowed through the small building. 'This is NOT A DRILL!'

Sue quickly taped around the door and then got the phone back off Vanessa. 'Nick—we've sealed the door with tape. Please tell me what's happening. Is this anything to do with you and my kids and Lucy?'

'Yes,' he said, and there was fear in his voice, under the calm tone. 'We thought it was all over. We thought we'd killed them all.'

'Oh—oh—what the hell . . . ?! Look at them!' Vanessa was stuck to the glass panel, her face a grimace of revulsion and fear. Inside the consulting room the dog's body had been ripped open along the spine in a series of ruptured peaks and insect-like things were emerging and flapping their wings.

'MUM! GET OUT OF THERE!' screamed Emma. 'RUN!'

But Sue was rooted to the spot, staring at the horrific

scene through the glass. Now the insect-like things were flying up, in spirals, gaining height and getting steadier on their newborn wings. Some landed on a weeping fig plant on the windowsill and began eating the leaves voraciously. It seemed to her that they were growing in size before her very eyes.

'It's OK, Emma,' Sue breathed. 'They're sealed in. They can't get to us. Do you know what they are?'

'They're called KOTH, Mum,' sobbed Emma. 'And you have to RUN!'

'Sue—I need you to keep this call open,' said Nick. 'We're tracking you through the signal.'

'I'm at the vet's in Bedbury Lane,' murmured Sue, trying to keep her panic under as she stared, in disbelief, at more parasites flying out of Brad Pitt. 'Right by Freshwater View Hotel—you can't miss it—it's where Lucy's Level 42 gig is happening today.'

As if to add to the dream-like quality of this insane scenario, there was a sudden blast of noise which shook the glass. The band soundcheck from the hotel grounds suddenly pounded through the air again as she and the vet continued to watch the horrifying show beyond the viewing panel.

'It's just another hell town story,' sang Lucy's hero.

'Another blaze of hopeless glory.'

'We should get out of here,' gulped Vanessa, but neither of them moved.

'And you don't have to end it for me.

It's gonna end. All by itself.'

The music stopped abruptly and, above the insistent beeping of the fire alarm, began again; an aggressive, pulsing bass line.

'We should go!' added Vanessa.

'Wait,' said Sue. 'What's that?'

'What is it, Sue?' asked Nick, from the phone. 'What are they doing?'

In the room the Koth were no longer spiralling upwards. Two of them were on the window, crawling around the wooden frame, three were on the plant, feasting, and seven were flying around the room at head height, in a steady level circle.

But every few seconds, with the deepest pulses of the bass from the soundcheck, the creatures in flight seem to stall a little. They sagged and dropped in the air . . . and then seemed to pull themselves back upwards with some extra-hard flaps of their small leathery wings.

'I—I think it's the music,' she said. 'They don't like it much.'

'How—how are they reacting?' asked Nick.

'It seems to be messing with their flying a bit, that's

all,' said Sue. 'The ones that are flying are a bit shaky whenever the loudest bass line bits happen—oh—there they go again!'

On *Hessandrea* Nick was staring into the middle distance, his brain working overtime. 'Lucy—tell me again about the atmosphere on Cornelian Eclata!' he demanded.

Lucy opened her eyes and blinked a couple of times. 'It's like here—close to Earth atmosphere but kind of . . . thinner. I can find out the exact gas mix from Mumgram.'

'Wait! Tell me about the sound! What does it sound like on Cornelian Eclata?' he cut in.

'Oh—well—it's like Earth—but . . . thinner. Higher,' she said.

'What about music?! What's your home planet music like?'

'Well—we didn't have much,' she said, trying to focus on what he wanted to know, when she just wanted to bury her head in her hands, she was so scared. 'We—um—we didn't really do music like you do. Just some . . . well I suppose you'd call it classical. Orchestral. Wind instruments and strings, mostly. No pop or rock. You don't get bass line and drums in Cornelian music.'

'No bass line!'

'No—that's why I love your music,' muttered Lucy. 'But now isn't really the time, Nick. We need to—'

Nick cut her off with a command. 'Mumgram—show me a holographic display of Koth brain structure!'

Mumgram seemed to have no issue with Nick making a demand of her. The holographic display arrived instantly. It showed a small brain in the Koth's skull, patterned like a human brain but much less complex.

'Mumgram,' said Nick. 'Can you determine whether there is a crystalline structure within the Koth brain?'

'I can,' said Mumgram.

'Well—is there?' he yelled.

'There is a crystalline structure towards the frontal lobe of the Koth brain,' replied Mumgram. 'It appears to be connected to the Koth's auditory, balance, and navigational cortex.'

Nick grinned and shook his head. 'No bass in space,' he said. 'No bass on your planet—and what there is you can't hear too well in that thin atmosphere . . . SUE! What are they doing now?!'

'They're eating a plant and getting bigger. How is that even possible, Nick? Where the hell have they come from?'

'Another planet,' he said.

'They're still flying about . . . but . . . they're looking

quite wonky!' yelled Sue, over the shrill fire alarm. 'Another *planet*? Nick—are you winding me up? I'm freaked out enough!'

Nick turned to Lucy. 'We've got to get there with your frostlaser rifles! Right away!'

Lucy nodded. 'I've got plenty. I'll show you how to use one.'

Then there was a shriek from the phone. 'Oh *no*! No no no no *no*!'

'What? WHAT, MUM?' yelled Jay.

'Oh god!' moaned Sue. 'We didn't think of the skylight!'

There was a skylight in the ceiling of Vanessa's consulting room. It was open.

'I don't know what to do,' wailed Sue. 'They're flying up through it, Nick! What can I do?'

Chapter 30

For some time Lucy floated. Everything around her went grey and mist-like while a hot red pain began to burn behind her solar plexus, where she had always imagined her soul might live.

She had failed. She had not checked the dog properly. She had not seen the single tiny blister hidden under the dog's collar. She hadn't looked hard enough. She had disregarded the chance that the Koth might strike twice in quick succession—and that one of those strikes might be a stealth strike, requiring only a quick hit with its barbed ovipositor. Probably Brad had been sleeping in the sun. There had been no need to attack—merely to inject.

And now her worst nightmare had come true. She alone was responsible for killing everyone on Earth. The death toll would rise into billions . . . and an unending torrent of blood would be on her hands.

She sank against the wall, dimly aware that they were talking to her—shouting at her.

'I didn't mean to, I didn't, I didn't . . .' she whispered.

'NOW!' Nick was suddenly right in front of her, pulling her up by her shoulders. 'Lucy! We have to get out of here and get to my car and get to Freshwater. We need frostlaser rifles. And we need YOU! NOW! Don't freak out on us! PLEASE!'

It was the sight of Jay and Emma behind him, looking at her imploringly, that snapped her mind back into play. 'We don't need your car, we can be there in about two minutes,' she said. 'We'll take the scouts.'

'The scouts? But they're just a *game*, Lucy!' Emma wailed, clearly thinking Lucy had lost her mind.

'No—they're a simulation of the real thing,' said Lucy. 'There are two scouts on board *Hessandrea.* I'll take Emma in mine—Nick, you take Jay in yours. Follow me!'

They ran to the scouts via the weaponry vault, and she gave each of them a frostlaser rifle, heavy and cold in their hot, shaking hands. 'I'll tell you how to use it when we get there!' she yelled, running into the scout dock. 'No time now!'

The scouts were suspended in the dock, side by side, like twin crescent moons. Exact replicas of the spacecraft in the simulation, they were silvery and beautiful. Nick and Jay boarded theirs through an oval hatch while Lucy led Emma onto the other craft. 'I'll pilot—you be ready to shoot,' she said. 'The scouts have frostlaser cannons. You used them in the game, remember? And we can track the Koth from here, too, routing through Mumgram on *Hessandrea.* MUMGRAM! Patch me through to scout B—open comm! Nick, Jay—can you hear me?'

'Yes,' came back Nick and Jay in unison.

'I'm sending you the map image and a tracer on each of the Koth,' said Lucy. 'There will be twelve. Mumgram is picking up their signature now . . . see!'

On scout B Nick and Jay, strapping into their pilot and co-pilot seats, saw a multidimensional map image bloom to one side of the console, charting the roads, the sea, and the rolling terrain. It zoomed in to a semi-rural residential area. There were red dots on it, moving in wide lazy loops above an area with yellow dots—some scattered, some clustered—below. One of the yellow dots was flashing.

'What are the yellow dots?' asked Nick, grasping the control stick and determinedly calling back all that he'd learned in the gameplay from earlier.

'That's people,' said Lucy. 'And the flashing yellow dot is Sue—or anyone who has Sue's phone.'

Nick said nothing. The flashing dot was static. He

hoped Sue and Vanessa had done as he'd begged and locked themselves in another room, using the gaffer tape to seal all the windows and the door and any air bricks. The Koth, around sparrow size now according to Sue's last report, looked too big for narrow cracks and vents, but they might be capable of squeezing in. He had no idea.

There was a sharp noise—air abruptly rushing past the scouts as a section of the hull slid back and daylight poured in. 'NICK!' yelled Lucy. 'CLOAK your scout before you launch. We mustn't be seen! Use voice command—Mumgram has imprinted to *you* for scout B! She won't take orders from me now, on your scout.'

'Mumgram—cloak us!' called Nick and there was a silvery flicker in the air and the confirmation:

'Scout B—cloaked.'

'Strap in, Emma,' said Lucy. 'And take the starboard frostlaser cannon. I'm going to need you back me up. OK—time to go! Prepare yourself!'

Later Emma would reflect that nothing ever *could* prepare you for suddenly being in a small spacecraft, travelling invisibly across the sky, your sweaty hands grasping the sight and trigger of an alien weapon, preparing to blast some killer mothbats from another galaxy into solid iceballs and thereby save your entire race from annihilation.

Nothing. Except, perhaps, the past twenty-four hours in Lucy's company.

Now, though, wasn't the time for reflection. 'We're going to shoot them out of the sky—turn them into lumps of ice, is that it?' she yelled as the island's lush summer landscape flew past, two hundred metres below in a green blur.

'YES!' yelled Lucy. 'That's it!'

'Can't we just shoot them dead in the air?'

'No—it's not certain enough. Their skin is incredibly tough and deflects the ordinary laser unless it's at point blank range. And if you're that close, you're already dead. The frostlaser freezes them, though, and gives us a chance of catching them and killing them.'

'Then what? How will we find them after that? And what will we do?'

'Good question!' yelled Jay, across the open comms from scout B. 'We can't vent them into deep space from here! What do we do with them?'

'I incinerated the last one,' yelled Lucy. 'But we won't have time for that. We'll have to land and collect the frozen bodies. The scout cannons are stronger than the rifles—freezing should last about five minutes on small Koth. We should have time to get them and contain them.'

'That's if we can get them *all*,' muttered Emma. 'What if we miss one? Just *one*?! And what if they're already laying eggs in people?'

'They won't be yet,' said Lucy. 'They're not big enough . . . I think they need to be at least an hour old.'

'You *think*?' said Nick, deftly piloting alongside Lucy's craft. Although they were cloaked, his computer system was tracking scout A and showing it clearly.

'Well—that's what I know about Koth behaviour on Cornelian Eclata—it could be different here on Earth,' admitted Lucy. 'It took the Koth much longer to incubate inside the dog, for a start. It's obviously different in dogs. Sorry . . . I'm not an expert. I didn't know anything about the bass music affecting their flying either . . . because we didn't have any of that at home . . .'

'It still is, too,' murmured Nick, watching the red dots as they grew closer and the real world view before him began to correlate with the computer's multidimensional image. There was a certain pulse to the way they were moving. A rhythm . . .

'MUMGRAM!' he called. 'Can you get us an audio feed from our target area? Can we hear what's out there?'

At once the music rushed into them. Loud—pulsing—rhythmic and funky. It was surreal as they prepared to do battle.

And now they could see it. In the grounds next to the hotel, two trucks and a canopy across a stage. Lighting rigs on scaffold towers. Seating set out for two thousand people or more. Banks of square black speakers on either side of the stage. People dotted around—musicians on the stage—a couple of guys offstage, behind the seats, on a sound and lighting desk.

And swarming above them, unnoticed, the Koth. 'Now the world is just one step away,' whispered Lucy, shuddering.

'We're close enough!' she shouted, suddenly fuelled by a burst of angry adrenalin. 'TARGET! FIRE! FREEZE THEM!'

In scout B, Jay seized the control stick and sight for his frostlaser cannon. The small visual display in front of him overlaid the real view outside, the red dots moving swiftly and in all directions. His own blue sight dot swung around, desperately seeking a target. He fired and a burst of blue laser shot out on the visual and also in reality beyond the transparent curve of the screen onto the outside world. *Damn!* The Koth dodged easily.

Nick tried next and seemed to get close but again his blue laser fire missed. He realized the music had stopped. And below them one or two people were looking up.

'Lucy—how much noise are we making out there?'

he yelled as scout A zoomed above him and arced around.

'A bit!' yelled back Lucy. 'Can't help it! It's the laws of physics! They might see laser fire too—but they can't see the scouts!'

Emma was determined not to be sick. The sudden swooping movements were making her head swim. *All you have to do is find them and fire!* she told herself. *There's no time to panic!*

'This isn't looking good, Lucy!' Nick called. 'They're spreading out. The music's stopped. Another two minutes and they'll be all over Freshwater!'

'I know!' wailed Lucy, missing another Koth by a millimetre and crying out in frustration and despair.

'We have to contain them!' went on Nick. 'Have to stop them or at least slow them down! Lucy—I have a plan. You may not like it . . . but I think it's the only way.'

'Whatever you've got—tell me!' yelled back Lucy. 'I'll do it!'

Thirty seconds later scout A landed.

On stage the musicians were taking a break. There was a feedback issue—some odd swooping noises—and the sound crew were looking into it with some puzzlement. Most of them had sloped off to the small marquee for some cold beers but Mark had brought a bottle of Peroni with him earlier, and now opened it up on the stage, his Status Graphite still slung around his neck. He hoped the day wasn't going to get too much hotter. He could do without people fainting. He took a swig and suddenly wondered if that odd girl who'd nearly drowned by his boat yesterday would show up.

And then that odd girl who nearly drowned by his boat yesterday showed up.

She appeared to have landed in a ghost-like silver spacecraft of modest dimensions and sprung out of it, hair flying. He wondered if somebody had slipped something into his bottle—but he didn't have time to wonder for long. The spacecraft had vanished, but the girl was real enough—running across the field towards him, full pelt, her face a mask of steely determination. 'MARK!' she bawled. 'MARK! PLAY BASS! PLAY IT LOUD! PLAY IT REALLY—*REALLY*—LOUD!!!'

Mark glanced around for security, uneasy. He'd saved a nutter, it was obvious. Then he felt a stab of genuine fear when he saw the rifle she was carrying.

In a second she was on the stage, leaping up like an athlete, and he was backing away, holding up his hands. 'Lucy! Hey—c'mon! There's no need for this, love! Put the gun down.'

'It's not for *you*!' she cried, spinning around and aiming

the rifle into the air at some sparrows or something. 'It's for *them*! But I'm not good enough—not fast enough! We need bass—really loud, heavy bass! It seems to slow them down—PLEASE! Switch everything on—turn it right up as far as it goes!'

Her eyes were shining. She seemed to be wearing some kind of shiny space-girl outfit. Maybe this was a TV set up—he was being pranked for Channel 4 or something. Down on the field people were running towards him now and making urgent shouts and calls into their radios and mobiles.

'LUCY!' came a stressed male voice, apparently from her watch. 'They're going into a descending spiral pattern. Just above you! They must be old enough to breed! You have to make him play NOW!'

She glanced up and blanched. And then . . . 'Mark—I'm sorry—I don't want to do it this way, but we've only got SECONDS!' And she pointed her rifle directly at his head. 'PLAY! *NOW!* LOUDER THAN YOU'VE EVER PLAYED BEFORE!' she screamed. Then she grabbed a spare microphone and bellowed at the road crew running towards the stage: 'YOU! JACK UP THE VOLUME OR THE BASS PLAYER GETS IT!'

It wasn't his most impressive solo. His thumb and fingers were slick with sweat but he still gave it his best. The bass notes poured out in a non-stop torrent and someone on the sound desk whacked the volume up so high it was distorting hideously through the bass cabs. His ears were ringing with it and his heart was clattering in his chest. He glanced at his hijacker and saw that, although her rifle was still steadily aimed at his head, her eyes were on the sky and a slow smile was spreading over her face.

Something fell onto the stage a couple of metres away from them and spun in a tight circle, twitching. In an instant the girl blasted it with her rifle and then trained the gun right back on him with a shout of delight.

'You're doing it! It's working! They're not just slowing! They're DROPPING!' she screamed, ecstatic and obviously utterly insane. 'Keep playing! Keep playing! You're helping me kill them!'

'Great,' he murmured as he stared at his unhinged fan. 'Kill the sparrows with a solo, Mark. Why not . . . ?'

Chapter 31

'Emma—warning!'

On board scout A, Emma jumped in her seat.

'Mumgram? Are you talking to *me*?'

'Yes, Emma. Warning. A Koth entity is now travelling beyond the defined perimeter of frostlaser reach. Observe the flashing red dot on your monitor.'

Emma did so. The flashing red dot showed one Koth heading north-west, towards the coast. She wailed aloud. 'Now what? What can *I* do? Nick! Jay! There's one getting away!'

'We're chasing down three over here!' came back Nick's voice through the open comm. 'You need to chase yours, Emma!'

'But . . . I'm grounded! On my own! Lucy's holding Level 42 at gunpoint!' squeaked Emma, aware dimly of how barmy that sounded, even here and now.

'You can DO it, Emma!' yelled back Jay. 'You were

brilliant in the simulator! You *have* to do it again! NOW!'

Emma gave a little sob as she unstrapped herself from the co-pilot's chair and got into the main seat which Lucy had vacated three minutes ago. She knew it was now or never. A lethal alien life form was heading for mainland Britain and all that stood between it and the annihilation of thousands, if not millions of people, was one thirteen-year-old girl with dodgy coordination and bad spelling.

'No pressure,' Emma whimpered to herself, hitting the LAUNCH button. Three seconds later she was thirty metres up.

'Emma, would you like to engage autochase on your target?' asked Mumgram.

'YES!' shrieked Emma and felt her skull whack into the head restraint as scout A suddenly shot across the sky in hot pursuit of the rogue Koth. On the screen she could see that it was still affected by the bass noise a little, but as it moved further away from the concert ground it was flying more steadily. It must have been further out than the others when the bass solo struck.

'Emma, you are close enough to fire,' advised Mumgram, and Emma swivelled round in the chair, pointing the frostlaser sight at the alien on the screen and beyond the screen, out into the real world.

BLAST!

Missed! And the Koth skittered sideways above the trees and dropped several metres. NO! She mustn't lose it in the trees!

BLAST!

That one was even more wide. *STUPID!* She was panicking now. 'I can't DO this!' she wailed. 'I can't even ride a BIKE!'

'You have been calibrated, Emma,' responded Mumgram, calmly. 'And results indicate that you are capable of this procedure, with a prospective success rate of seventy-six per cent.'

'REALLY?' Emma was amazed.

BLAST!

The Koth spun, this time clearly affected by the near miss, and scout A, locked to the movement of its target, spun with it, making Emma lurch violently left against her restraints. And now she saw something which filled her heart with icy dread. There was a clearing below them now. And in it were people. A campsite. Families, having a picnic by a winding stream. Oblivious to what was happening in the sky above them.

And the Koth had begun to spiral.

'NO!' screamed Emma. For she knew what the spiral meant. Lucy had told them all. The spiral came before the egg-laying attack. If this Koth knew it was in danger, its prime directive now was to lay its eggs to ensure the next Koth generation. And it had just spotted hosts. Dozens of them. Fit, healthy, living hosts. And if it didn't think it could get there in time it would explode itself and send out eggbarbs to shower on those people below . . .

'Mumgram! Predict the spiral!' she bawled, suddenly remembering the sim game the night before—how she had needed to *predict* the place the enemy *would* be by the time the laser hit.

At once the spiral was shown to her on the monitor, a glowing ribbon of orange, ending on a yellow dot. The yellow dot was a human being. The red dot of the Koth was now travelling down the spiral as if it were on a helter-skelter. Lucy had said this was a precise, mathematical manoeuvre which never varied. Never.

Emma set up her sight and aimed halfway down the predicted spiral on her screen, watching the Koth move down towards it. She was shaking so much she could barely keep her grip. This was all going to go wrong.

'EMMA!' she told herself, in a cold, cold voice. 'STOP SHAKING! *NOW!*'

And Emma stopped shaking. She felt as if a cold veil had descended on her and switched all the tremors off. Now all her focus—every fibre of her body and mind—was on the intersection point of the Koth and her frostlaser sight.

And as the Koth made one more turn, centimetres from her target point, Emma lifted her eyes to the real view, five metres away, pointed her finger and squeezed the trigger.

Frozen solid, the Koth fell like a rock.

'Target achieved,' said Mumgram, and Emma screamed with delight.

'I did it! I did it! I did it!'

'Well done, Emma!' yelled Jay, through the comm. And she realized he and Nick must have been listening in, in spite of their own battle. 'Now you have to collect the body! Fast, before someone else does.'

Emma landed the craft behind a toilet block on the campsite, still cloaked and invisible, and then ran to the Koth's body. It lay in a clump of grass next to a paddling pool, only a metre from the little girl it had probably been aiming for. Emma knelt down to stare at it. It was the size of a crow. How had it grown so fast? It looked like it was in a chrysalis—a chrysalis of ice. She shuddered as she slid her palm under it and hoicked it into a plastic bag she'd found near a bin close by.

'Eeugh,' said the little girl, standing up from the shallow water in a pink swimsuit, ice cream all over her face. 'Nasty.'

Emma glanced up and her and nodded. 'Yeah. Nasty,' she agreed, and ran back to scout A with the frozen alien.

Back at the concert site she landed scout A next to where Nick and Jay had landed scout B—in the field area behind the seating and the sound crew. Nick was outside the craft, Jay just behind him. Both were carrying frostlaser rifles. The music had stopped now but all the people were still fixated on the stage—they didn't look back at what was happening behind them. 'I shot three! Three of 'em!' Jay called joyfully to her, as she stepped outside.

'That's three, plus my six—and Emma . . . did you collect it?' Nick looked at her, searchingly.

She held up the carrier bag and squeaked: 'Yup! Koth kebab, anyone?'

'There's a sealed refrigerated container in scout B,' he said, taking it from her. 'Jay, put this one in too—and blast them all again with your frostlaser, the way I showed you, OK? Emma, get back on board scout A. The worst is over, but I still have to collect one from the seating area and the one on the stage. And I have to rescue Lucy too . . .'

'Um . . . any chance you could stop pointing that at me now?' Mark stopped playing. He looked flushed and his blue-grey eyes were bright. 'I mean . . . you're not really going to, um—'

Lucy suddenly blasted the rifle—at the thing on the stage—for the third time. Then she trained the weapon back on him. The whole manoeuvre had taken three seconds.

'Come on. You don't want to blast me . . .'

Lucy smiled at him so winningly he realized there was absolutely no doubt that she belonged in a secure unit with several armed guards. 'I'm not going to blast you, Mark. But the moment I stop pointing this at you, one of those guys,' she tilted her head at the bunch of musicians and support crew and security guards gradually creeping towards her below the stage, 'is going to leap up here and get me in an armlock. At least, he *thinks* he is . . .'

'I thought you were a fan, not a nutjob,' sighed her hero.

'Oh I *am*!' she insisted. 'A fan, that is. Even more so now. But there was no other way. You and I—and my friends in the scout ships—have just saved the planet from a swarm of deadly intergalactic space parasites. Sadly, I don't think you're ever going to believe that. Look—there's one.'

She indicated the thing on the stage. He had to admit that it did look pretty freaky. Under the ice he could make out a circle of razor-sharp teeth and some dimly glowing red eyes.

'What I really need now,' she said, 'is to collect this one . . . and all the others . . . and eject them into deep space so they can explode safely and never get back to Earth. Does that make sense, Mark?'

'Oh. Yes. Absolutely,' he replied. 'Explode them. Explode them in space. I would.'

'So, I'm going to have to be scary for just a minute or so longer,' she added. Behind the knot of security, musicians, and crew, she could see Nick quietly collecting the other frozen Koth, blasting it again, and giving her first a thumbs up and then one finger, indicating that her Koth, here on the stage, was the last.

Lucy eased the setting on her frostlaser rifle down to the mildest stun level. 'Before I do this, I just wanted to say,' she said, 'first . . . they won't be hurt at all—they'll just be out of my way for about fifty seconds. And second . . . I'm really sorry I'll miss your gig. I hope it goes brilliantly well.'

'Lucy—don't—don't do that!' Mark urged as she turned the frostlaser rifle on the advancing people.

'Relax!' she said. 'Take care of yourself.'

Then she blasted them all, in a wide arc. They toppled over instantly and she grabbed the frozen Koth in her bare hand, leapt from the stage, and ran to Nick, who was holding out a plastic bag. 'Dump it!' he yelled, and she did, gratefully, the numbness in her fingers not enough to stop her shuddering at the touch of the alien.

They ran to the scouts, which, although still cloaked, shimmered into view just briefly as the hatches opened and they each boarded one. At the top of the ramp Lucy turned to look back. Mark was standing on the stage, bass in hand, staring after her.

'The world will never be able to thank you enough!' yelled Lucy. 'Byeee.'

Chapter 32

'Mumgram—run a trace over a fifty-kilometre radius,' said Lucy, back on the bridge of *Hessandrea.* 'Is there any Koth signature?'

'There is no Koth signature within a fifty-kilometre radius,' replied Mumgram. 'There is no Koth signature on Earth.'

Lucy slumped into the seat by the console, exhaustion slamming into her with the relief.

'Mumgram,' said Nick, placing a comforting hand on her shoulder. 'The twelve Koth in containment. Can you detect eggs inside them?'

'There are twelve mature eggs in each Koth,' confirmed Mumgram. 'And an indefinite number of immature eggs.'

'So . . . none laid,' said Nick. 'Time to get these ones vented, yes?'

'Yes,' said Lucy. 'But you don't have to come with

me this time. There's no reason to put yourself through launch and re-entry all over again. It'll do you all in.'

Emma and Jay looked at each other, relieved. 'Agreed,' said Nick. 'You two go home now and call your mum and get her back safely. Tell the vet to incinerate the dog, too.'

'What about you?' asked Emma. 'Lucy told us all to get off.'

'She did, didn't she?' he grinned. 'But I'm not going to.'

Lucy sat up and gave him a hard look. 'I could *make* you get off, you know!' she warned.

'I don't doubt it,' he replied. 'But you don't really want to do that, do you? Come on—you're shattered. Let me help you do this last thing and we'll both know it's done and all is well. Then we can all go back to Sue's place for tea. What do you say?'

Lucy felt overwhelmed. She wanted help. Mumgram would always be there for her . . . but to have Nick there too . . . an actual physical presence. She really did want that. She nodded.

Lucy took Jay and Emma down the mast. It was utterly terrifying, climbing down it. Far more scary than climbing up, Emma thought. But on the meter of terrifying over the past twenty-four hours, it hardly even twitched the needle.

At the bottom, using some kind of magnetic beam from her wristwatch communicator, Lucy undid the electronic lock on the metal gate, checked they were alone, and let them out. But Jay turned back and pulled her into a hug. 'You are coming back, aren't you?' he demanded. 'You ARE!'

'It's over,' she said. 'Or it will be soon. So . . . maybe. I don't know. I have things to decide.'

'Don't you dare just leave!' he said and felt his lower lip shake and his eyes get wet. And didn't even care. 'Don't you *dare.* Promise me!'

She smiled that Lucy smile and dropped a kiss on his cheek. But she didn't promise.

Emma hugged her too. 'You won't go, I know it,' she murmured. 'You love Mum's cooking too much!'

And then Lucy stepped back onto the ladder and vanished into the cloakshaft, leaving Emma and Jay alone on the far side of the gate.

They walked back across the field wordlessly. At the trees Emma flipped open her phone and called Mum. 'It's OK, Mum,' she said. 'We got them all. You're safe now. Tell the vet to incinerate the dog and come on home.'

*

'We're almost there, Lucy,' said Nick as he strapped himself in and prepared for his second launch in *Hessandrea.* 'Your mum would be incredibly proud of you.'

Lucy said nothing. She felt wrung out. Only one thing pulsed urgently in her mind now. *Vent the last twelve Koth.* She and Nick had carried the airtight container from scout B and counted all the frozen creatures into the containment bay, sealing them into the same room that their siblings had been blasted from hours earlier.

Just an hour later, deep in space, Nick nodded at her. She pressed VENT and the life forms, still dozy from the effects of the bass on their brains and the frostlaser on their bodies, gave no resistance to the void of space. They were gone in seconds, in a cloud of atoms. No trace left on *Hessandrea.*

'Back home for tea and medals, then?' asked Nick, grinning, but looking as exhausted as she felt.

'We can't go back straight away,' said Lucy as they returned to the bridge. 'We have to line up and wait for the world to turn.'

Nick nodded. 'Breakfast, then?' He raised one eyebrow and smiled.

'For you, maybe,' she said.

'Sleep, Lucy,' he told her. 'We'll talk when you're up again.'

Sleep was full of alien chases and the faces of her friends and an ache in her heart which was still there when Nick came in seven hours later and woke her with a cup of Earth tea and some Cornelian recipe carbisks.

'You coming home, then, Lucy?' he asked, sitting against her sleep-pod wall with his own mug.

She looked at him steadily. 'How can I? I've given away far too much about *Hessandrea* . . . about the scouts . . . about me.'

'Nobody else knows about *Hessandrea*,' he said. 'And if they even saw the scouts they probably didn't believe their eyes. And you . . . *well* . . .'

'It wasn't as easy as I thought, fitting in,' she said, gazing ruefully into her tea. 'I think I might always stand out.'

'Cheers to that,' he said, raising his mug.

'Honestly, Nick, I don't deserve it,' she said. 'I just skipped down into your world, thinking everything was there for *me*. I only ever thought of what *I* was going to get out of it. I didn't ever consider what I might *do* to your world. I don't belong there. I'm an alien. I should move on.'

'You really do like to beat yourself up, don't you?' he said.

'I'm just being practical!' she insisted. 'I mean,

suppose one of those people at the concert ground sees me again—or even Mark. It's a small island! He might! After all, I did hold him at gunpoint! I'll be arrested and then they'll find out I have no family and they'll want to know where I live and where I've come from and where my mum is or my dad is and—'

'Would you like to be my daughter?' said Nick.

She gaped at him.

'I realize I may not be as cool as Mark King . . .'

'What?! What do you mean?' she demanded. 'How can I be your . . . I mean . . . it's not that I don't want to. You'd be . . . a lovely dad . . . but how can we do that?'

'*We* can't,' he admitted. 'But I know a man who can. Someone I have worked with, very high up in the government. I . . . contacted him yesterday, while we were going into battle with the Koth. I told him to send a team to the island to contain a possible outbreak.'

'You did *what*?!'

'He did as I asked and it's all—already—contained. I've been online on your ship's console. There's a cover story in the *Isle of Wight County Press* about it today. A freak swarm of bats out in the daytime, brought about by global warming . . .'

'But . . . what about me and the frostlaser and the scouts and . . . and . . .'

'I spoke to my contact on my mobile an hour ago. Turns out the only person who saw the scouts was Mark,' said Nick. 'And he's agreed to not speak of it any further. He was the only one who saw what the frostlaser rifle did, too. He's staying schtum about the whole thing.'

'He *is*?' Lucy's eyes were round, like blue-green marbles, in her amazed face.

'If there's one thing my old friend Chambers is good at,' said Nick, grinning, 'It's convincing people that extraordinary things happen . . . and it's best we just go on as normal. He's done aliens before. He doesn't have any problem with them. And, more importantly, he's good at sorting out no-questions-asked adoptions,' he added. 'If . . . if you think you could be happy as my daughter. I know I'd be proud to be your dad.'

'Nick . . . I've shot you twice!'

He shrugged. 'Teenagers! What're you gonna do?'

Lucy closed her eyes and leaned back on her pillows. 'I need to think,' she whispered.

'Great. Think. You've got ten minutes,' he said. 'And then I think you'll find it's re-entry time.'

Chapter 33

'Is she still up there?' asked Jay. 'Can you be sure? She hasn't just gone . . . ?'

Nick settled down on the tartan rug and eyed the picnic basket. 'She promised she wouldn't just go,' he said. 'If she decides to leave she'll come and see us one more time.'

'She won't decide to leave, though, will she?' said Emma, throwing her apple from hand to hand in high perfect arcs and barely noticing. 'Sorry, Mum . . . it's lovely but I'm just too nervous to eat.'

Sue nodded. The picnic lay largely undented. 'I could, though,' said Nick, and scooped up a corned beef and pickle sandwich.

'How come *you're* so relaxed?' asked Sue, prodding his shoulder.

He turned and gave her a lazy smile through his munching. 'She'll stay,' he said.

'And then what?' asked Sue. 'Are you sure you can trust this Chambers guy and his government people not to be all over her like ants? Studying her? Taking her away somewhere and doing tests? I mean . . . you hear things, don't you?' Her mouth hardened and there was a flinty spark in her eyes as she added, 'I won't LET that happen to Lucy!'

He smiled even more at her then. 'I don't believe you would, either,' he said, reaching out and touching her face.

Jay and Emma raised eyebrows at each other and Emma raised her thumbs too, making Jay groan and look away.

'Anyway, you won't need to go into action-woman protect mode,' said Nick. 'None of us will. I trust Chambers absolutely and he trusts me. If she stays, Lucy will live with me here on the island and I will give her a normal Earth family life. Well . . . kind of. I might . . . need your help, of course.'

Emma saw he was looking directly at her mother as he spoke and she couldn't stop grinning, even though, after a while, Mum gave her a 'Stop it—you're embarrassing me!' look and then started fiddling about with the picnic, trying to hide her pink face.

'She's going to come down to us,' said Jay, his eyes fixed on the top of the mast. 'I know it. I know it.'

Lucy stood in the exit bay, the top of the mast just a step down from the platform. Far below she saw a wood pigeon fly past.

'Mumgram,' she said. 'Am I doing the right thing?'

Her holographic mother smiled at her from a well of light.

'A dad,' went on Lucy, before Mumgram could speak. 'And best friends. A life. Down there. Up here . . . I'll always be safe and I'll know I did no more harm. Down there . . . I might do harm. But . . .'

'Lucy,' said Mumgram. 'You have arrived.'

Ali Sparkes was a journalist and BBC broadcaster until she chucked in the safe job to go dangerously freelance and try her hand at writing comedy scripts. Her first venture was as a comedy columnist on *Woman's Hour* and later on *Home Truths.* Not long after, she discovered her real love was writing children's fiction.

Ali grew up adoring adventure stories about kids who mess about in the woods and still likes to mess about in the woods herself whenever possible. She lives with her husband and two sons in Southampton, England. Check out www.alisparkes.com for the latest news on Ali's forthcoming books.

AUTHOR'S NOTE

The exercises that Emma performs in *Destination Earth* are inspired by exercises which really do seem to help people with the alternative brain wiring of dyslexia and dyspraxia. Of course, Emma got a fair bit of alien fast-tracking to speed up the laying down of those neural pathways which help with coordination and word recognition—among other useful things. Without interplanetary help it will probably take a *bit* longer. There's no neat 'cure' for dyslexia and dyspraxia and many of us don't see it as something to be cured in any case. Most of us know a person whose alternative cerebellum leads them also to be imaginative, lateral-thinking, quirky, creative, and brilliantly unique—and we wouldn't have them any other way. But if you're frustrated with balance issues or struggling to read or tie your shoelaces you might want to look into the exercises. You can find more information on this and other resources at www.dyslexiaaction.org.uk and www.dore.co.uk—and from many other similar organizations around the planet. Try rolling a tin of beans from hand to hand while you're at it . . .

EXCITING ADVENTURES BY

Ali Sparkes

READ THEM ALL NOW!